TRIP SWITCH

ALLISON SPEKA

Speka Press

For Zak, my favorite travel partner.

Trip Switch

ONE

Lila

ONE OF THE HAPPIEST MOMENTS OF MY BEST FRIEND'S LIFE WAS about to take place right behind that door and here I was, stalling on the sidewalk out front. I had a meticulously wrapped gift in hand and was wearing a black and lilac floral dress I had only worn one other time—on a first date that had ended up being a complete dud.

That was the worst; when you saved an outfit for a special occasion, only for that occasion to fall miles short of any of your expectations. At least no one at Charlie and Nathan's engagement party would have seen me in it yet. It was like I was giving it a second chance. Although, judging from the bizarre, nauseated feeling brewing deep in my gut, I wasn't sure this dress's second outing was going to be any better than its first.

Shut up.

I mentally scolded myself for the negative thoughts. My best friend was getting *married*, for crying out loud. Her engagement party was going to be *fun*. Charlie and I had fantasized about this day since we were just twenty-two, fresh out of college, with a blossoming friendship and still naïve to all the dating atrocities in our near future.

Nathan might be a bit, um. . . stoic, but it was obvious to anyone with eyes that he loved Charlie. There wasn't anything he wouldn't do for her. I was so over the moon thrilled for them that I had burst into happy tears the moment she'd told me.

The only thing causing my mixed emotions was that I had hung on to the stupid thought that, when Charlie did turn up at my house one random Sunday morning, eager to show me a new piece of jewelry on her left hand, my own life wouldn't be quite so far behind.

My rust-colored hair was gathered in a loose bun at the nape of my neck. I had been going for elegant, but now it just irritated the delicate skin there, begging me to throw it up in a high ponytail.

"Are you planning on going in, or were you going to watch the party from here?" A deep, cheerful voice interrupted my thoughts.

Oliver, Nathan's brother, strode up to where I stood rooted in place. His light blue button-down shirt could have used one more pass with an iron, and his hair was still damp from the shower he'd likely just taken after climbing, or mountain biking, or whatever it was he'd gotten up to today. But all he had to do was flash his megawatt smile and he looked perfectly adorable. What must it be like to have endless boyish charm?

"I just got here," I lied, letting him scoop me into his arms for a quick hug.

As Charlie and Nathan had become more and more inseparable, so had Oliver and I. We shared a near-endless amount of optimism, always eager to jump into something headfirst. Like that time we'd discovered there was an amusement park on top of a mountain, only a few hours away from Denver. We couldn't get anyone else to go with us, but we'd made the drive the next morning because we were too excited about the prospect of riding a mountain-side roller coaster. And it had been worth it, despite the six extra hours we'd sat in traffic on the way home.

"We had to circle the block to find parking, and you've been standing here the entire time." Another deep voice said from directly behind me, this one without even an ounce of cheer. I spun around and came face to face with *him*.

Harrison, Oliver's best friend, smirked down at me, and I wished—for the millionth time in the year since meeting the man—that his smug expression and uncouth comments had no effect on me.

His tattooed biceps bulged out of the black, short-sleeved button-up he wore. It aggravated me to no end that he towered over me, even though most men did. But God had done too much when he was crafting Harrison. Sure, He'd given him a crappy personality, but there was still no reason for Harrison to have both that sharp of a jawline *and* that perfect of a body. Maybe he had a terrible smile, and that was where the universe had decided to balance him out. I wouldn't know, because he'd never graced me with one.

"Harrison. Good to see you." I smiled sweetly, but neither of us made a move to hug. Hugging was not the level we were at. I doubted anyone—except maybe Oliver—was on hugging terms with Harrison. And even then, I couldn't picture it.

"Nervous to go inside alone?" he guessed. While the comment itself wasn't obnoxious, and actually half-true, something about Harrison's delivery made the tiny hairs on my arm stand at attention.

"Not at all."

"So, you're just practicing your stalking skills, and seeing how far away you can stand and still see into the window?"

I sighed with exasperation.

Oliver chuckled. "You two kill me."

The twinkle in Harrison's dark eyes revealed he found the whole thing amusing, but his amusement never felt like it was in a good-natured way. And this was definitely not Harrison's way of flirting, no matter how hard Charlie had tried to convince me it was.

Even though a small part of me kind of wished it were true.

Harrison was so not my usual type, yet I couldn't seem to get my primal responses to register that information. I would never call what I felt toward him a *crush*, at least not out loud, but my stomach did do strange flippy things whenever we were in the same room together.

I would never admit that to anyone. As far as anyone else was concerned, we didn't care for each other. And to be fair, in my mind, I completely and totally didn't. My body just never got the memo.

"I was just feeling a little light-headed and wanted to collect myself before heading in," I said. There, that was at least a little closer to the truth.

A palm was on my forehead before I had a chance to react. "No fever. You feel a bit cold, if anything," Oliver said confidently as I jerked away from his hot palm.

"I'm not sick. I must just be dehydrated or something."

"Or something." I hated the way Harrison eyed me up and down, like he somehow had any idea about the complex thoughts spinning around in my head surrounding today and the engagement. He didn't know me at all. We were essentially strangers. He'd made sure of that every time he turned down any attempt I'd made to try to get to know him. Now we were just unwilling acquaintances, forced together by mutual friends.

Oliver sauntered up the driveway and I was left with no choice but to follow, Harrison trailing closely behind me.

"They said no gifts." Harrison pointed to the pink and white striped present clutched to my chest.

"Oh, um. It's for Charlie."

"Nathan can just buy her anything she wants. What's the point?" he asked, tactlessly pointing out that Nathan had more money than the rest of us could even fathom. Being a tech genius and starting a successful dating app in your twenties was apparently a fantastic way to never have to want for anything ever again. Harrison reached out to touch the ribbon I'd carefully tied into an ornate bow, but I jerked the package away before he could make contact.

"Money can't buy everything." I didn't bother to keep my tone polite.

"Let me guess. A collage? Or a painting of the two of you, perhaps?"

"No," I said, quickening my pace to reach the door and get into the house where I could hopefully avoid Harrison's negative attitude for the rest of the evening. The most irritating part was that, once again, he wasn't far off.

Like the cheesy person I was, I'd made Charlie a scrapbook full of our memories together, one that told our whole story. It held the first picture we'd ever taken together, at an office happy hour when we'd started working at the same company. It also held the picture we'd taken a few months ago in our new, modest office, where we ran our successful meetup app, ConnectHer, designed to connect like-minded women. I thought it'd be a sweet way to commemorate that phase of her life as she catapulted into the next one with Nathan. But now, holding it, it felt a little childish.

I launched myself up the front steps just in time to reach Oliver as Charlie swung open the door.

"Yay, you're all here." She practically glowed as she pulled Oliver in for a hug before throwing her arms around me.

"You look beautiful," I said into her ear.

"Positively radiant," Oliver agreed, grinning. He was right. Charlie's skin popped against her chiffon dress, one that was just as much a soft gray as it was white. Her wild hair had been pulled half up into a braid, while the rest flowed loosely down her back. The smile she wore was positively infectious, and I felt my nerves from earlier slowly start to disintegrate as excitement took over.

"Harrison. Thanks for coming." Charlie gave a small wave in his direction.

He nodded. "Thanks for having me."

I wanted to shoot him a glare, irritated that he was apparently capable of having civil interactions with every person except me.

"I can't believe we're months away from making this official." Oliver sighed and grabbed Charlie's shoulders.

She laughed and rolled her eyes. "It's not like it'll be that different."

We all filed into the foyer of their stunning vintage craftsman, with a large front porch and a completely remodeled interior that still paid homage to the original architectural detailing. While one might think it was modest, considering the amount of money Nathan had, a house like this one in this area of Denver was *not* cheap. Even more so when you realized, despite the wall-to-wall maple floors that appeared to be original, there wasn't a single squeaky plank. That was a sign of wealth if I ever saw one.

"Keep your shoes on. Nathan is on the back patio with

Ben and Skylar, and we've got everything set up there," Charlie instructed us.

"Oh, they're already here?" I asked, trying to sound disinterested.

"Yeah, they had the babysitter all evening, so they stopped by the restaurant to pick up the takeout order for me."

"I could have done that for you," I offered as we padded through the formal living room that Charlie had turned into a room for her cat Edward. I'd laughed when I'd first seen it; only Charlie would take what was supposed to be a classy sitting room and line it with every cat tower and scratching post she could find.

"It was just easier this way. Besides, I'm sure I'll have more tasks for you to do as my maid of honor." She nudged my arm and grinned.

"Right, of course. Anything you need," I said.

"Suck up." Harrison ducked his head and whispered so that only I could hear.

He was right. I was sucking up. Which was ridiculous and unnecessary, considering Charlie was my best friend, but what no one tells you is that when your best friend gets engaged, they also get a whole new set of extended family and friends. Ben was Nathan's college roommate and business partner, and Skylar was his wife. Charlie and Skylar had been spending more and more time together lately, and I felt like the ugliest soul alive for being a little jealous of that. I was terrified of waking up one day and realizing I had become a stranger to someone I once called a close friend.

Oliver slung an easy arm around my shoulder as he led us out the back door.

"You okay?" he asked. And just like that I felt ridiculous about my intrusive thoughts. I fit into this group just fine.

When we passed the kitchen, I set my present on the

island. The last thing I wanted was for her to open it in front of the group so I could get even more grief from Harrison.

"I'm great." I squeezed Oliver's waist and gave him my brightest smile.

Charlie opened the sliding glass door to the patio and eyed us. "Now if you two could stop pretending you're just friends and get together already, we can all be a family," she said.

"Maybe we'll make a marriage pact," Oliver suggested. "Lila, if we're still single at forty, let's tie the knot."

"No offense, but I think I'd let my parents try arranging my marriage before I reach forty without any prospects."

Harrison groaned. "That's disgusting to joke about. You two have total sibling energy. It would be borderline incestuous."

If I'm so similar to your best friend, then why the hell do you hate me so much? I wanted to snap, but I kept my mouth shut.

But as frustrating as Harrison was, he was right again. Because despite loving Oliver as a friend, there had never been anything even remotely close to a romantic spark between the two of us. Probably because we were too similar; we both relished the carefree side of life and tended to push deeper, more meaningful conversations to the backburner. Not exactly a good basis for a relationship with substance.

Charlie and Nathan's backyard had been transformed with hundreds of dainty twinkle lights strung up on poles, making the already-picturesque space look magical. We were still in the city, so their property wasn't massive, but considering the postage stamp I called a yard, this stone patio with an outdoor kitchen that stretched onto a perfectly manicured green lawn might as well have been the Garden of Versailles.

Nathan, Skylar, and Ben stood talking in a semi-circle, but looked up when we all spilled out of the door.

"Brother!" Oliver called, before pulling Nathan into a hug

and clapping his back a few times. Nathan returned the hug easily. Anyone who saw those two could immediately identify them as brothers. They were nearly the exact same height—freakishly tall—and had the same dark hair and features, though the same features that looked stern on Nathan's serious face, his straight nose and expressive eyebrows, somehow looked boyish and relaxed on Oliver's.

"Hi, Nathan. Congrats again." I reached out and squeezed his arm.

"Thanks, Lila." He nodded and shot me a quick smile before I stepped out of the way to let him and Harrison shake hands.

It felt like it hadn't been that long since Nathan had called me up out of the blue. I remember I'd been sitting on my couch, scrolling through the endless movie choices, when his name flashed across my phone. My initial reaction had been panic. Nathan and I did not have a talking-on-the-phone type of relationship. I'd answered in a hurry, worried about Charlie, only for him to ask me to go ring shopping with him.

We'd gone the following week. A best friend waits her whole life for that moment. I knew exactly what Charlie wanted, thanks to a few wine-induced late nights on Pinterest. I'd had to talk him down in price several times, convincing him that Charlie would be stressed out wearing such an expensive ring every day.

I glanced at Charlie's ring finger now, taking in the simple emerald-cut diamond ring. It was perfect.

"Lila! It's so good to see you." Skylar offered me a quick one-armed hug, as she was holding a glass of wine in the other hand. She had one of those perpetually youthful faces, round and vibrant. She'd probably still get carded in her forties.

"I'm good. How are you? How's your little girl?" I asked.

She glanced up at her husband, Ben, before shaking her head. They smiled at each other like they had a secret I could never be in on.

"She's perfect. I mean, she isn't sleeping through the night, and I'm more exhausted than I've ever been in my entire life, but she's perfect."

"What about you, Ben?" I asked, directing my attention to her husband. Benjamin Mead was ridiculously attractive, with that old-Hollywood movie star look about him. "How's retired life treating you?"

Ben had only recently given up his position as CEO of the dating app Nathan and he had started. Nathan had stepped down when he and Charlie first got together; since she'd technically been his employee, their relationship had been strictly prohibited. Both Nathan and Ben still sat on the board, though.

His lip curved up. "I'd hardly call it retired. I'm already trying to get Nathan to invest in this new app idea with me. But it's good. I'm glad I have more time to spend at home."

Skylar rolled her eyes. "He can never stop. I swear, one free minute and he's got a computer out, building a spreadsheet."

"I wish I could say that I didn't relate, but sometimes it feels like my laptop is permanently attached to me as well." I shrugged, smiling at her. I liked Skylar, I really did. The slight jealousy I felt any time she and Charlie had plans that didn't include me was completely unwarranted and petty.

"How's ConnectHer doing? Nathan just mentioned you and Charlie were working on something big."

I filled Ben in on the details of our most recent round of funding and the app updates we were hoping to launch before year end. The speech was so rehearsed I could recite it on command. My job—our company—meant a lot to me.

Charlie and I had built it from nothing, and no one could ever take that away from us. Maybe that was why I chose to pour so much of myself into it. My time. My energy. Sometimes I told myself it was the reason for my nonexistent love life, but I knew that work wasn't entirely to blame.

Technically, my position was Chief Marketing Officer, but I did everything under the sun to ensure ConnectHer had a solid, growing brand. Sometimes, I'd wake out of a dead sleep just to jot down an idea, or to add a task to my never-ending to-do list. Charlie frequently asked me if I wanted to bring on someone at a higher level who could take some of the toppling items off of my full plate. But I knew myself. I could do it.

"Could everyone have a seat?" Charlie asked, standing at the head of the table with Nathan.

Smiling politely at Ben, I stepped away, grateful to have the excuse to drop the conversation. Ben had launched into a line of questioning about our finances, and while I wasn't oblivious about the details, we'd hired finance and accounting professionals for a reason.

The table was beautifully set, with a white runner down the middle and vases with green eucalyptus leaves in the center. The plates were terracotta and looked handmade. I settled into the seat next to Charlie. I expected Oliver—or Skylar, or anyone else—to take the seat next to mine, but I wasn't that lucky. Harrison pulled out the chair instead and sat down heavily, not glancing at me in the process.

"Great," I muttered.

"What was that?" He leaned in.

"Nothing at all." I smiled at him, knowing he didn't buy my sweet charade for a minute. But the funny thing was, even if my smile toward him was fake at the moment, I *wanted* to be nice to Harrison. All he would have to do was give me the faintest hint of a smile, or ask me how I liked the weather, and

I'd have jumped at any chance of civility. If there was one thing I despised more than anything, it was being disliked. Especially by someone with whom I came into such frequent contact.

The sound of a knife tapping against a glass alerted us all to Nathan trying to get our attention. He looked a lot more comfortable in this setting than any other. His chin wasn't tipped down, and his eyes weren't brooding. He even had a soft smile on his lips as he glanced down at Charlie.

"I'm not one for toasts. But I just wanted to thank you all for coming. As you know, we didn't want any extravagant wedding festivities where we'd have to make small talk with people we barely know and haven't seen in years. We just wanted to celebrate with our closest friends."

"I, for one, am thrilled to be here," Oliver said, raising his glass. "I never in a million years thought I would be celebrating my brother's engagement."

"Me either. It's a miracle, honestly," Harrison added.

Nathan scowled at the two of them.

Ben chuckled and said, "I've known this guy since college, and I thought he was celibate for the longest time, until I walked in on him and his lab partner one night."

"Do we really have to bring up the past?" Nathan asked.

"Isn't that what you're supposed to do when someone decides to get married? Break out all their old stories to embarrass them?" Ben pointed out.

"If you do it in front of Charlie, I'll kill you," Nathan deadpanned.

Charlie laughed and nudged Nathan's shoulder. He immediately softened.

"Anyway," Charlie continued. "Since we have you all here, we wanted to make a little announcement." She looked at me excitedly and I tilted my head in curiosity.

Nathan watched Charlie like she was the only person here; like she was the only person who mattered. Seeing them so happy together simultaneously brought a huge smile to my face and made my heart do a little anxious skitter.

Would that type of love ever find me? The number of dates I had been on in the past year alone could fill a Starbucks. That might not sound like a lot, but it certainly felt like too many when I could remember sitting down with every single one of them and exchanging awkward pleasantries. Sometimes it even took three dates before they ghosted me, or I realized we had nothing in common despite trying desperately to convince myself that we did.

The truth was, I wasn't good at being single. I didn't know how to date. I had wasted years on my high school sweetheart. Did I still have to use that term now that he'd turned out to be a raging asshole? I had wanted that relationship to work out so badly that I'd ignored the gigantic tote bag of red flags he carried around. Even when he would occasionally drop one, and someone like a friend or my parents would pick it up and wave it in my face, I'd still pretend they didn't exist.

And then, once I finally got out, I'd had no interest in dating. I'd longed to be by myself, with no one tracking my movements or trying to bring me down.

Which all meant that when I'd dived headfirst into the dating world a couple of years ago, expecting to meet my perfect match after kissing a few frogs, I hadn't been prepared for just how hard it would be.

"—and we're taking you all on a trip!"

Skylar gasped and clasped her hands excitedly while Oliver gave a whoop at the other end of the table. I realized I had been zoning out and tried to catch up on whatever announcement Charlie had made that I missed.

"Neither of us wanted a bachelor or a bachelorette party,

so we figured a little trip with our favorite people was exactly how we wanted to celebrate."

"Where are we going?" Ben asked.

"That's a surprise." Charlie looked at us all mischievously. "You'll find out the day we leave. Of course, I'll provide a packing list and all the information you'll need."

"This is on you, right, bro?" Oliver clapped once and pointed a finger at Nathan, who rolled his eyes.

"Of course."

"Yes, don't worry about any of that. We're inviting you, so of course it's our treat." Charlie waved her hands. "But this is why I asked you all what weekends you had free."

"That's going to be so much fun!" I exclaimed once I had put it all together.

Harrison groaned softly next to me, and I shot him a dirty look. He had the audacity to raise an eyebrow and mouth, "What?" before I turned away to resume ignoring him.

"A trip sounds amazing," I continued, letting the excitement build in my chest. I never got to go away; sometimes it felt like work was my only meaningful personality trait.

A vacation was exactly what I needed.

TWO

Harrison

SOME OBLIGATORY VACATION WAS THE EXACT OPPOSITE OF
what I needed right now.

"I'm not going to do this," I whispered to Oliver, who was
seated to my right.

"Uh, yeah, you are." Although he said it with a smile, his
eyes didn't crinkle and the tendon in his neck flexed. A sure
sign the smile was forced, and a warning that he wasn't
messing around. To everyone else, Oliver might seem like he'd
never had a bad day in his life, but I knew how to spot his
subtle signs of exasperation. After all, I was typically the
reason behind them.

Plates of food were passed and silver cutlery clinked
against the serving plates, thick white ones with pastel flowers
on them. They were hideous, if you asked me. And too expensive to be holding the Mexican takeout I knew Charlie had
picked up from the family-owned restaurant down the street.
When had we become too good for plastic plates? It was a
backyard party for Christ's sake, not a Michelin-star
restaurant.

Nathan, Oliver, and I had grown up in the same lower middle-class neighborhood—well, we had until my dad got laid off and my family had to post up in a motel for a while. But as much as I would have loved to sit and stew in my bitter thoughts about how money could change a person, I knew Nathan wasn't like that. He'd always been relatively the same person, and he certainly didn't give a shit about impressing anyone. Don't get me wrong, the guy had a sick car and a nice house, but he wasn't flashy.

"What if I just back out at the last second?" I asked, spooning some rice onto my plate. "I could say something came up at the shop."

"I swear to God, you better be there," Oliver said ominously, still through a smile. His commitment to the bit of being the most positive guy in the room always made me want to push his buttons. Usually it didn't work, but he hated when I tried to bail on things. "We're family, and you're *not* bailing on Nathan."

Rolling my eyes, I turned to my left to try and get under the skin of the person seated on my other side. At least with Lila it worked. That's what made it fun.

"A joint bachelor and bachelorette party? That's not weird at all," I said to her in a low voice.

Her spine stiffened as she jerked her eyes toward mine. The dress she wore was cut low on her chest, and I had to fight to keep my gaze from falling to that soft skin that looked just a little too inviting.

"It's not that uncommon." Her words were clipped. A warning to me to drop the subject immediately. Unfortunately for her, that just fueled my fire.

"I've never heard of it."

"Oh, because you're just being invited to bachelor parties

left and right? Remind me again how many friends you have, outside of Oliver."

"Hey, Nathan and I are close," I pointed out with a hint of sarcasm. While it wasn't entirely the truth, Nathan and I had arrived at some sort of relationship after years of stalemate. Oliver was where my loyalty lay, but Nathan was like family too.

"Then why are you being a jerk about it?" She huffed out a sigh and set her fork down next to her plate. "Besides, can you really picture Nathan, of all people, having a bachelor party?"

"Shots, strip club, and all," I said, carefully picking the words that would bother her the most. "Don't let the stiff demeanor fool you. Nathan's a total party animal."

Her nose crinkled with disgust. "Gross," she mumbled before trying to turn away from me.

"At least we'll get to finally spend more time together," I continued, unable to help myself. Her green doe eyes always flared up when she was mad. It was almost imperceptible, but after a year of exchanging jabs I could now spot it every time. I was addicted to it.

"You'd be so lucky to go on a trip with me. I actually know how to have a good time."

"Is that what all your dates say?" I asked, poking her in a known sensitive spot. She was always going on one online date or another, despite never seeming to have success with any of them.

Instead of answering with a venomous retort, Lila moved back an inch as if slapped and her whole face went pale.

Fuck. I had pushed her too far. Something I frequently did. She brought her right elbow to the table and rested her rosy cheek in her hand, so that she was turned completely away from me. She and Charlie started talking in hushed tones, and I knew anything I said to her now would be met with an attempt to ignore me.

Pushing someone too far was my specialty.

I was rough with everyone; it was just the way I carried myself. Growing up, I'd had the misfortune of being the small, slightly introverted kid who would rather pore over a comic book than get dragged into whatever sport or game all the other kids were playing. Didn't exactly win me any popularity contests at school. It also didn't help that my family was piss-poor, on top of it all. Oliver was the only person to ever give a shit about me. So this carefully crafted guard I kept around myself had been built for a while. People like Lila were just casualties of my defenses.

Since I had already aggravated the two people seated on either side of me, I moved on to Nathan, who sat at the head of the table, watching Charlie but not participating in the conversation.

"I'm surprised you're having an engagement party at all. It doesn't really seem like your thing," I said, leaning forward so he could hear me.

Nathan met my eyes before looking at Charlie again.

"It's for Charlie. It's important to her."

"Why wouldn't we use every excuse to celebrate?" Charlie pulled herself out of her conversation with Lila to chime in.

"And you just let her run your life?" I asked, not intending to come across as an asshole. But, judging from Oliver's sharp elbow digging into my side and the dirty look Lila shot me, I probably had.

Nathan didn't look offended. He just shrugged and said, "Basically."

Charlie beamed up at him and shook her head slightly. "Please, you're insanely stubborn."

"I think you're thinking of you."

They continued to banter back and forth. Even though they were just talking, it felt like I was eavesdropping on some intimate moment, so I turned away.

I guess, theoretically, Nathan had a point. There were probably worse things in life than letting a beautiful, intelligent, strong-willed woman take control. Personally, it wasn't for me. I couldn't even fathom what that would be like. A serious relationship that lasted more than a couple of months had never found me—or, more accurately, I guess I had never sought one out. As far as I was concerned, you could pry my independence out of my cold, dead hands.

"Did you two have a big wedding?" Oliver asked Ben and Skylar.

Ben shrugged. "Just over a hundred people. It was back when we were still in San Diego, so we did it at a venue right on the water."

"It was perfect," Skylar added.

"That sounds amazing," Lila said next to me, her voice far away, as if she were drifting in and out of a daydream.

"I thought the whole wedding thing was stupid, to tell you the truth. But it turned out to be a fucking blast. It was one of the best days of my life." Ben lifted the fork he was holding to point at Nathan. "Nathan was there. Although I'm pretty sure he managed to dip out before the reception even got started."

Nathan shrugged. "I saw the ceremony. I left a card. What more was there to do?"

Ben's head shook with laughter. "So heartfelt. Damn, this guy never changes. I hope you aren't writing your own vows."

Oliver tilted his head back and laughed. "Could you even imagine? No way Charlie puts him through that."

"I don't know. I'd kind of like to see what he'd come up with," Charlie teased.

"We're just doing something small," Nathan insisted. "We talked about just eloping."

"If I'm not there, I'll hold a grudge until the day I die," Oliver said. "And Mom will hold one even longer than that."

Nathan glared at his brother. "Good thing she still has you to throw a big spectacle of a celebration."

Oliver rubbed his hands together. "Oh, you better believe it'll be a spectacle whenever I get married. I'm thinking at least three hundred guests. We'll do it somewhere in the mountains with a sick-ass view. Maybe I'll even parachute into the ceremony. Or snowboard in, if it's in the winter."

I snorted. "Parachuting and snowboarding? Might be kind of tough when you're finally ready to settle down at sixty."

That got a laugh out of the rest of the table, but most noticeably from Lila. Her laugh was almost sickeningly sweet and contagious, the kind that drew you in and made you want to be a part of the joke. Usually, her laughter was something I only experienced at a distance.

"He's got you there, Ollie," she said.

"Hey! I could meet the right girl tomorrow. You never know."

Oliver was a huge flirt. He liked women, and certainly saw enough of them, but he'd never been serious about anyone in his entire life. He had—what did they call it—Peter Pan syndrome. He was like a kid trapped in a twenty-seven-year old's body. I highly doubted he'd be walking down the aisle in the next decade.

Lila and I shared a knowing look, maybe the first one in our entire relationship. I tore my eyes away quickly and threw my hackles back up.

"What about you, Harrison?" Ben asked.

"What about me?" I asked gruffly.

"Do you want a big wedding?"

"Doubt I'll ever get married." Marriage was something I had given absolutely zero thought to. My parents had been happily married for thirty years, so I had no reason to be outright against it, but I couldn't fathom ever meeting a girl who would make me want to commit to her like that. The guard I had built around myself was an impenetrable fortress. The only person I had ever really let past it was Oliver, and that was only because he'd gotten through when I was six and I'd only had a few crumbling bricks up at the time.

"You'll be alone forever if you only keep dating those scary women you're always bringing around." Oliver shuddered.

"What can I say? I have a type." I took another slow pull of my beer, smirking at the thought.

I knew exactly what kind of woman my demeanor attracted—intense, daring, the kind not easily scared off. I wore my standoffish look like armor, and the ones who braved it were often just as inked and no-nonsense as I was. They were the type who liked a challenge. The type who just threw me a simple "fuck you" when it inevitably didn't work out, instead of writing me a sonnet about how heartbroken they were.

They weren't soft. Unlike the red-headed cinnamon roll currently seated to my left.

"Well, your type is terrifying. You should find yourself a *nice* girl. Preferably one who doesn't attempt to vandalize my house when you don't call them back." Oliver got up to retrieve another bottle of wine for the group, stopping by Lila's chair in the process. He wrapped an arm around her shoulders and leaned down so he could press the side of his face against hers. "Someone like this little ray of sunshine."

"Shut up," she whispered, but a smile remained plastered to her face.

A small fire lit in my chest watching them so at ease with each other. It was a feeling that had become more and more frequent as I watched them interact, but I couldn't quite pinpoint the underlying motive. Was I jealous that my best friend was getting closer to someone else? Or was I just irritated that she was around?

As if she could read my thoughts, Lila's gaze flitted to mine before I quickly dropped it.

Wherever the feeling of frustration was coming from, I just ignored it like I always did.

"You know, you two really should talk." Oliver pointed between Lila and me. "Harrison here is having some website issues. He could really use your help."

"What kind of issues?" Nathan and Ben both looked up.

"It's nothing." I flashed a warning look at Oliver, urging him to drop it. The last thing I wanted to do was discuss my business issues in front of a table full of start-up-crazy tech fanatics. The tattoo shop I'd owned for the past three years had been experiencing a bit of a downswing the past few months, but it was nothing I couldn't handle. And it certainly wasn't something I was going to go begging for help with.

"More of a branding thing," Oliver continued, clearly not oblivious to my irritation, but choosing to ignore it all the same. "He's trying to make it more user-friendly or some shit."

"Branding." Interest painted Lila's face at the word.

"It's nothing," I repeated, this time more sternly.

"I could take a look if you want," Lila offered.

"Lila, are you serious? You're so busy right now." Concern filled Charlie's voice as she eyed her best friend.

"I'm not *that* busy," Lila said defensively.

"Where are you hosting?" Nathan asked.

"You own a tattoo parlor, right? What's your current demo like?" Ben pressed.

"Like you know anything about tattoo parlors." Skylar snorted with laughter.

Heat rose to my face as chatter about websites and branding flew from all sides of the table.

"Can we just drop this," I said loudly, unable to keep my cool.

Silence fell over the group. One fork hit the table and the sound reverberated around the whole yard.

Oliver, finally taking the fucking hint, backed away from Lila and resumed scanning the bar. "Should I open a white or a red?"

Grateful for the distraction, everyone resumed their mindless chatter and I sat there, still stewing. Weakness wasn't something I took lightly, and Oliver parading my problems around for everyone to see infuriated the hell out of me. But when he sat back down and poured more wine in my glass first, offering me an apologetic half-smile, I knew I'd already forgiven him.

Because when push came to shove, I couldn't alienate him for meddling in my life when he was the only person who cared enough to even try. A consequence I had brought upon myself, but a consequence I still felt the weight of, nonetheless.

"I really could help," a small whisper floated up to my ears. "If you wanted, that is."

Lila's cheeks reddened when I glanced down at her, but she forced herself to keep eye contact. God, why did she have to be so *nice* all the damn time? Made it a lot harder on me to keep this divide up between us when it was so painfully obvious that all she wanted was my acceptance.

"I'm good." Keeping my tone curt, I resumed staring straight ahead.

"Can we get back to discussing this all-expenses-paid trip you're apparently taking us all on?" Oliver asked.

Great. Just what I needed.

THREE

Lila

"How many fourteeners have you summited?" Dave, a clean-cut guy who liked to talk about himself a little too much, looked at me expectantly from across the white-clothed table. The restaurant was entirely too fancy for a first date, but Dave had turned down all of my other suggestions. The scents of roses and linen wafted through the air instead of sizzling meats or pastas, and the whole sensation was making me a bit dizzy.

"None yet." I forced a smile. "I find it a little hard to breathe when the elevation is that high. I do like to hike, though," I added quickly.

Conversation wasn't exactly flowing, but I had to admit that he was even better looking than his profile picture promised he'd be. While I didn't want to be shallow, I also didn't want to write him off before our waiter even had a chance to deliver our menus to the table.

Dave pursed his lips in disappointment. "Man, there's nothing like a fourteener. The challenge. The climb. It's breathtaking up there." He said it like somehow every four-

teen-thousand-foot-high mountain offered the same experience, instead of being completely separate and distinct places.
"It's like seeing a whole different side of the world. You really
haven't experienced hiking until you've done a fourteener."

The grin stayed frozen across my face as he continued
listing each fourteener he had summited since he'd moved to
Denver two years ago. When the yawn came bubbling to the
surface, I did my best to cover my mouth to hide it.

"I'll have to take you on one someday."

"Oh, that's alright." My voice fell flat as I tried to
discreetly check the time on my grandmother's vintage watch,
the one I always wore for luck. In hindsight, given how dread-
fully these dates typically went, maybe it was cursed. I made a
mental note to experiment with leaving it behind next time.

Dave seemed a little put off at my response. He took a
large sip of the beer in front of him as he searched for another
topic of conversation.

Dating was hard, but dating in Denver when you were
eager to settle down and move into something serious? Impossible. Every man I met had just moved here to find themselves
and live out whatever outdoorsy fantasy they had curated.
Usually, a girlfriend was the last thing on their minds, and
despite my profile explicitly stating, "Looking for something
serious," that somehow didn't deter every self-proclaimed
smooth talker with extensive commitment issues from asking
me out.

You'd think I'd be better at weeding them out by now. But
nope. Here I was, still stuck going out with the same cliché,
over and over again.

"So," Dave continued, tapping his fingers against his glass
before his eyes lit up at whatever just crossed his mind. "I'm
thinking about buying an old van and fixing it up. You know,
people live in them nowadays."

VOICES DRIFTED OUT OF MY BUNGALOW AS SOON AS I WEDGED open the door with my hip. The scents of lavender candles and buttery popcorn were the first things to hit me.

"Um, help, intruders!" I pretended to lean outside and yell as Charlie and Oliver sat on my tiny plush-pink loveseat, deep in conversation, tossing popcorn into their mouths. "That key was for emergencies," I scolded half-heartedly, reaching down to slip off my black heels. I padded barefoot across the wood floor before they finally looked up.

"It *was* an emergency," Charlie said.

Oliver flashed me a smile and waved. "Yeah, we were bored."

I had rented this place for a couple of years before my landlord—a sweet, elderly woman who, despite referring to me as her surrogate granddaughter, never could remember my name—offered to sell it to me. It only had two bedrooms and one bathroom. Two people could barely squeeze into the tight kitchen, and the front door opened straight into the small living room that couldn't even fit a three-seater couch. But I loved this place more than anything. It was home.

I ruffled Oliver's hair on my way past them to the end of the room that led to a small hallway. The door to my bedroom was already open, so I slipped in. The pair of sweatpants I had been wearing earlier lay on my bed where I'd tossed them, along with a few T-shirts I had just washed but not yet folded or put away. I unzipped the dress and let it fall to the floor before tossing on the comfortable clothes. The cotton grazing my skin made me shiver with contentment.

"What are you two really doing here?" I asked when I came back into the room and dramatically flung myself over my vintage floral-print armchair.

"Oliver came over looking for Nathan," Charlie explained.

"But only Charlie was there," Oliver said.

"Nathan's off with Ben. Ben's trying to talk him into a new business venture or something."

Damn, couldn't those two just relax? I guess I was one to talk, considering I had mountains of work to do on several projects myself.

"Then I suggested we pop over to your house and see what you were up to," Charlie finished.

"And when you saw that I wasn't here you just thought you'd make yourself comfortable?"

"We knew you'd appreciate seeing our faces the moment you walked through the door." Oliver blinked a few times while smiling at me in an attempt to look adorable.

"Where were you, anyway?" Charlie asked. "I figured you were out grabbing groceries, not out and about in your little black dress."

"Oh, you know, just wrapping up the Friday night usual— a date from hell." I tried to keep my tone light and free of guilt, but I saw the way Charlie's eyebrows pulled together.

"Why didn't you tell me?" she asked.

"It was super last minute," I lied, sitting up and reaching for the popcorn bowl that sat on the coffee table between us. "Anyway, there won't be a second date. He spent twenty minutes showing me pictures of used vans for sale," I said dryly.

Oliver snorted. "You're kidding."

"Nope." I popped a piece of popcorn into my mouth.

I had actually set the date up last week. I couldn't pinpoint exactly why I hadn't wanted to tell Charlie, but feeling pathetic certainly had something to do with it. Ever since the engagement party and our constant chatter about weddings, shame brewed in my gut at the thought of mentioning to her that I was headed out on *another* first date. I had begun to fantasize about meeting someone and keeping it quiet until we hit it off and started officially going out. Then I could mention it to my friends when it had become something stable. I'd come to Charlie and tell her I had a boyfriend, and she'd look at me with shock at first, but then we would excitedly jump around and celebrate. Then I could invite everyone to a happy hour where I'd introduce him, and he could be my date to the wedding, and——

"Why do you keep doing this to yourself? I think you need a dating break." Oliver interrupted my thoughts, and my daydream came crashing down around me. That fantasy felt delusional even to me at this point. Especially after how tonight had gone.

"What, so I can be alone forever?" I narrowed my eyes and dug my hand into the bowl of popcorn. "No, thank you."

"You're exhausting yourself," Charlie pointed out. The worry etched on her forehead made me want to dive under the covers of my bed and never resurface. How hopeless was I if even my friends didn't think I could find someone?

"The right guy will come along eventually. Maybe you're searching in the wrong places. You should just take a break," she added.

"I already took a break and look where that's left me. If I'd known it'd take this long to meet someone, maybe I would have started sooner," I said, thinking about the few years I'd spent single and avoiding men like the plague. My ex had done a number on me, and I'd needed to just be on my own for a while.

"You needed a break after the last jerk." Concern shone in Charlie's eyes, and I resisted the urge to chuck a plush pillow at her.

"Let's not talk about him." My tone was harsher than

intended, but the last thing I wanted to do was recount tales of my nightmare ex in front of Oliver. I had mentioned to him I had a shitty ex-boyfriend, but I hadn't gone into detail. I knew I shouldn't be embarrassed about the situation, but it was hard not to feel a little ashamed about wasting so many of my good years on a narcissistic asshole.

"You're trying to force it," Oliver said, moving the subject back to the present and kicking his feet up to rest them on the edge of the coffee table. "I bet if you just chilled out on the dating apps, you'd meet someone organically."

I laughed bitterly. "Where? At work, like Charlie and Nathan? We run a woman-centered networking company. We have thirty employees—all of whom are women or *not* interested in women."

Oliver shrugged. "You could meet someone outside of work."

"Outside of work I'm just hanging out with the two of you. And sorry, but I can't believe you, Mr. Perpetually Single, are trying to give me dating advice right now."

"Perpetually single *by choice*," he added, like it made all the difference.

"So, you could just meet the perfect girl tomorrow if you wanted to?" I challenged.

"I mean—" He flashed me a huge grin. "Probably."

This time I didn't resist the urge to throw a pillow. It landed square in his face and his shoulders shook with laughter. The annoying part was, he was probably right. Oliver was gifted with more natural charm than one human should possess, and the face of a nineties boyband heartthrob.

"You're so annoying," I said through my laughter.

"Maybe I could set you up again." Oliver stuffed the pillow behind his back and tapped his chin.

"With who, Harrison?" I mimed gagging. Oliver

constantly made jokes about the two of us being perfect for each other, despite Harrison's open hostility toward me. I knew he was just messing around, but I hated the little flutter in my stomach at even the thought of going out with Harrison. "Speaking of him, I've actually been meaning to kill you," I continued. "Why the hell are you talking to him about my dating life?"

"I'm not," Oliver insisted.

Charlie and I exchanged a look of disbelief before training our attention back on Oliver.

"Really? That's funny. Because he seemed to know enough to throw a few jabs at me last weekend." His comments from the engagement party still tortured the back of my mind.

"I just mentioned you were doing a lot of online dating." Oliver threw his hands up as if caught. He did that a lot—played innocent so you couldn't really be mad at him, because of course, at least according to him, he always had the purest of intentions. "I didn't know it was a secret."

"You're just giving him ammunition," I groaned, covering my face with my hands.

"Harrison is all talk. He's completely harmless." Oliver stuck up for Harrison with the same gumption as an up-and-coming criminal defense attorney eager to prove their worth.

"Speaking of your other half, where is he tonight?" I asked, feigning disinterest as I stuffed more popcorn into my mouth.

When it came to Harrison, I would always have some lingering curiosity. Maybe it was his aloofness, or maybe it was because, no matter how hard I tried, I couldn't make myself ignore my attraction. Either way, asking about him had become a bad habit that I really needed to break.

"He's working on shit for his shop. He's been trying to

redesign their website for weeks now, and he won't admit that he can't do it."

"He's trying to rebrand, right?"

"Lila." Charlie's tone had a heavy note of warning to it.

"What? I'm curious."

She threw a piece of popcorn at my head, but I snatched it out of the air and tossed it back at her.

A lot was happening with ConnectHer right now. I was juggling several new app integrations, and despite Charlie begging me every week to hire extra help, I refused to delegate. I knew her concern wasn't about controlling my time; it was about trying to prevent me from burning out. But I just couldn't help myself. As a trained graphic designer, branding was my bread and butter.

I pulled out my phone. "What's his shop called again? I want to see what he's working with."

"You're impossible." Charlie stood up and padded into the kitchen. The clicking of cabinets opening and closing signaled she was searching for more snacks.

Instead of answering me, a slow smile spread across Oliver's face.

"What?" I demanded.

"Look, I know he was all defensive about it the other day, but he really needs some help."

Rolling my eyes, I keyed "Harrison" and "Denver Tattoo Shop" into my search bar instead of waiting for Oliver to answer.

"He literally looked like he'd rather get a root canal with no anesthesia than get any help from me," I mumbled, pulling up what I assumed to be the website for Harrison's shop. The black screen featured dark, sporadically placed text that was almost impossible to read. When I scrolled down to click on the photo gallery, the link didn't even work. My hands were itching to get into the backend of this site and make a few simple updates.

"Harrison is the most stubborn person you'll ever meet, but that's just his gut reaction. Literally, when we were driving home, he told me he wished he'd just sucked up his pride and asked for your help."

I arched a brow and looked up at him skeptically over my phone. "*Harrison* said that?"

"I swear." Oliver held up his hand like he was pledging an oath or something. I still didn't buy it.

"Look, let me talk to him. If you'd even be able to help him one evening after work, it could make a huge difference."

"There's no way he'd want my help," I insisted.

"I promise you, he will. Let me just talk to him." Oliver pressed his hands together in a pleading motion. "Look, he's stressed as hell about this. And he's my best friend. If you won't consider doing it for him, consider it for me?"

"Oliver." His name came out like a groan. He knew a guilt trip was the perfect way to get me to do whatever he wanted. Disappointing people wasn't in my nature.

"Can we change the subject?" Charlie interjected, coming back in and plopping on the couch. Packets of candy rained from her hands and onto the coffee table.

"Hey!" I protested. "I was saving those."

She shrugged and tore open a bag of Peanut M&Ms. "Oops."

Oliver snagged a Snickers. "Could we perhaps talk about this mysterious trip you and Nathan are taking us on in a few weeks?"

"Nope." Charlie held up her hand. "I've told you everything you need to know. You're not getting anything more out of me."

A few days ago, we'd all received an email with a simple

"save the date" for the pseudo bachelor/bachelorette trip, and a brief packing list. Beyond that, nothing—no itinerary, no hints. The thought of a surprise trip was honestly thrilling. I never got to go anywhere, despite always having an urge to travel.

"Please," I begged, swiping up and closing Harrison's website before setting my phone face down on my stomach.

"We won't tell anyone." Oliver winked at me.

Charlie's head fell back with laughter. "You can't keep a secret to save your life," she said.

"Not knowing *is* kind of exciting," I admitted, caving and grabbing a piece of chocolate from the table.

"I guess." Oliver tapped his fingers together, before snapping and leaning forward. "Hey, speaking of this trip and Harrison—"

"Were we still speaking of Harrison?" I asked.

"You helping him with his site would be the perfect way to bury the hatchet between the two of you before this trip."

"I'm not the one wielding the hatchet in the first place," I argued. "I would love nothing more than to get along." *Understatement of the century. I'd like to do a lot more than just get along. . .*

I shooed the unwelcome thoughts away.

"Then help him. Please, Lila." Oliver rose from the couch. Dropping to his knees on the floor, he clumsily shuffled his way toward me before taking both of my hands from my lap and looking up at me with his best puppy dog expression. "*Please.*"

"Oh my gosh." I took my hands back and playfully shoved him in the shoulder. We were both laughing now. "You're desperate."

I glanced up at Charlie, who simply shrugged with a casual "Do what you want" expression.

Maybe Oliver had a point. Helping Harrison with his site

wouldn't be all that challenging for me, and then maybe he'd finally realize that I wasn't as bad as he'd made me out to be in his head. Then, we'd go into this trip as civil acquaintances and maybe even get the chance to bond, or something.

It seemed far-fetched, but, honestly, it kind of drove me crazy that Harrison couldn't stand me. I valued being liked. I was a people-pleaser, through and through. Maybe that wasn't the healthiest trait, but I thrived on it. I loved seeing grateful smiles when I brought the good coffee to work, or the relief on my employees' faces when I stayed late to help them meet a tight deadline. And I couldn't help but bask in the appreciation whenever someone called me a lifesaver for doing them a favor.

So, for those reasons, I found myself telling Oliver, "I'll *think* about it."

FOUR

Harrison

"HEY, BOSS, ANY OTHER CLIENTS TODAY?"

Shane poked his head of spiky blond hair into my closet of an office, the only contents of which were an ancient desktop that took twenty minutes to power on and a couple of chairs.

"Done for the day."

Shane whistled. "Wow. It's only seven on a Friday." He held up his hands when his eyes met my glare. "I'm just saying," he said defensively. "It's a bit slow this weekend."

"I don't see you flush with business either," I grumbled, even though I knew the shop was partially to blame for that.

While the artists at my shop were responsible for taking their own bookings, the shop's website typically drove at least thirty percent of their traffic. The website that was currently down because of an error I'd made trying to set up new links. I had been on the phone with tech support for an hour yesterday trying to fix it. My technological ineptitude knew no bounds.

I followed Shane out of the office and into the main—and

only—room of the shop. It was just a giant square, with each artist having their own station in a corner of the room and a small desk and waiting area at the front. Aside from that, we had a small piercing room in the back. The other artists had already gone home for the evening, and I was about to pack up.

"This is the deadest we've seen it in months," Shane mused, tossing a few papers into a brown leather backpack.

"Why do you keep feeling the need to point out the obvious?" I asked.

Shane had been here the longest, so I knew he wouldn't take my brusqueness personally. We'd apprenticed together at the same shop south of the city for a few years, back when I'd first moved here. Oliver and I had always known college wasn't in the cards for either of us, and moving to Denver was something we'd talked about all through high school. I, for one, couldn't get away from the town we'd grown up in fast enough.

It was bad enough that my peers already thought I was too shy and too poor; as time went on and I found my passion for drawing, I also became the "weird art kid." Despite my size—and despite Oliver always begging me to try out for whatever sport he was playing—I'd preferred spending my free time in the cramped studio, sketching in silence alongside the school's ancient art teacher, Mr. Coleman. It hadn't done much for my popularity, but aside from a few snide remarks, most people left me alone.

That was probably because of the time Kyle Rogers, football star and all-around asshole, cornered me in the hallway with one of his lackeys. They'd ripped up one of my portraits, so I hit him right in the face. When they'd started to fight back, Oliver jumped in, and we started wailing on them both before some teachers broke up the fight. I got suspended for a week, but it had been worth it to see Kyle's crooked nose for the rest of high school.

Tattooing was art in its most badass form. Who was going to fuck with someone covered in ink from head to toe? Maybe it wasn't the most noble reason to enter the profession, but eighteen-year-old me had longed for a way to pursue my art in a way that ensured I wouldn't be messed with. And by now, I'd grown to love the form of expression. Saving up for and starting my own shop was my biggest accomplishment to date.

"I'm just saying, a year ago, we were booked months in advance, and now we're desperate for a walk in."

"The climate was different a year ago," I insisted, but I wasn't even sure if my statement was accurate. Business wasn't my expertise, but I had still managed to do well for myself. I had always been financially responsible, at least. Growing up the way I did had given me no choice.

"I just got drinks with Jack from the old shop last week. He said they're booked solid," Shane said.

"Jack does sloppy work," I grunted.

"Hey, watch it." Shane rolled up his sleeve, showing off a bulky gray skull piece. "I got this piece from him last year."

I just shrugged. "You should have asked me to do it."

Shane winced and examined his arm. "You're probably right." He rolled his sleeve down before slipping one of his arms through his backpack and shouldering it on. "But isn't that even more reason why we should be getting more business than him? No one does cleaner line work than you, and my shading is impeccable."

"It's just an off month," I said.

"It's been an off *few* months," Shane mumbled under his breath.

"Is that helping?" I barked.

Shane snorted with laughter. "You know, I think it's the

charming owner that has people beating down the doors to get in."

"Piss off." I halfheartedly waved my hand to brush his comments away. Business had been undeniably slow and I wasn't sure what to do about it, hence the reworking of the website. Web design and running a business weren't my God-given talents, but no one could ever say that I didn't work my ass off to make up for that. I grabbed the disinfectant cleaner from the back cabinet and started to wipe down my area.

The chime of a bell sounded through the shop, signaling someone walking in.

Shane perked up first and spun around on his feet. "Why, hello there. What can I help you with?"

"I'm looking for Harrison."

My head whipped up at the sound of that familiar soft voice.

"What the hell are you doing here?"

"Hello to you, too," Lila greeted me. She wore a confident smile, but I could practically see her shaking in her perfectly white tennis shoes. And. . . *overalls?* What kind of grown ass adult wore overalls?

"Oliver told you I was coming by, right?" Her voice faltered this time.

Fucking Oliver. I should have predicted he'd do something like this.

Shane looked between the two of us with a spark of interest.

"And who would you be?" he asked, returning his attention to Lila.

"I'm Lila." She offered him an outstretched hand and Shane shook it enthusiastically.

"And you're here to see Harrison?" he asked, disbelief evident in his voice.

"She's Oliver's friend." My comment was meant to be dismissive, but Shane just looked all the more interested.

"Oliver's girlfriend?"

"Just friend," she quickly corrected.

"So, you're saying you're single?" Shane leaned against the glass desk and placed his chin in his hand.

"Um, well. . ." Lila glanced nervously back and forth between Shane and me. It took all my willpower not to roll my eyes. She was so desperate for a boyfriend that she'd go on a hundred online dates a month, but the second someone covered in tattoos showed interest she practically clutched her pearls.

"I'm sorry, when did this become a singles mixer?" I demanded, glaring at both of them. "Oliver didn't say shit to me. What are you doing here?" I asked, although I already had a hunch. Oliver was hellbent on getting me help, whether I wanted it or not.

She cringed. "Oliver really didn't mention it to you?"

After a few moments of letting her sit in her discomfort, I finally blew out a breath and slumped on the front counter next to Shane. The glass needed to be wiped down, anyway.

"Did he tell you I need help?"

"He told me you *asked* for help."

"Does that sound like me?" I arched a brow and her cheeks reddened before she dropped her gaze to her feet.

"He told me you knew I'd be stopping by today."

"Oliver can't keep his damned nose out of my business." I glanced at Shane who raised an eyebrow.

Lila chewed on her bottom lip. The black clock that hung in the entryway ticked loudly, as if signaling each passing awkward second.

"Sorry, I-I can go—" She finally stuttered.

"Wait!" Shane said. "What are you here to help with?"

"Shane, drop it." I shot him a look that implied he should mind his own goddamn business.

"Um, well. Oliver mentioned your website was down. I was going to take a look at it."

"What are your credentials?" Shane asked, his tone more curious than condescending.

"Um, I own a company with my friend. ConnectHer? It's an app that lets women create meetups and networking events."

Shane pursed his lips and nodded. "That's badass."

The air felt thick with her here; I felt exposed for reasons I didn't care to dive into. Admitting I needed her help was like rolling onto my stomach and waving a flag that said, "I'm vulnerable, fuck with me however you like."

"Right. Sorry for the mix-up, but we're good here," I said, gesturing to the door behind her. "You can blame Oliver for wasting your time."

"You should let her help, boss."

"We're fine."

"We are *not* fine." Shane turned toward Lila, like the two were already in some secret club formed only to undermine me. "If I have to watch him peering over that ancient computer in the back, mumbling to himself for one more day, I'm going to lose my mind," he said with a smile.

"I've almost got it," I bit out.

"She's already here," Shane protested. "Stop being so fucking stubborn and let her look."

Lila shifted from foot to foot, looking like she wished she could teleport straight out of here.

"I already looked at your website. It'll probably only take a minute," she said. "Sometimes, when you make changes to a page or update the source, the link can break. Anyway, I'm not sure if that's exactly what's going on, but maybe, if I could just take a look, I'd know for sure."

She was rambling, nervous energy radiating off her. While the entire purpose of my harsh demeanor was to make people nervous, I did feel a small sense of obligation to Oliver to at least attempt to put Lila at ease.

"Fine," I said, inhaling slowly through my nose. Stubbornness had no place when it came to ensuring my business ran successfully. Even an asshole like me could see that Lila offering to help was more than generous. It was far beyond anything I deserved after the callous way I continued to treat her. "Sorry. Yeah. That would actually be great."

Lila's lips parted in clear shock. This was the gentlest tone I'd ever used with her, and guilt surged through me at the realization. Pushing people away had become second nature, even when I took it too far. Lila was just collateral damage in the endless internal war I waged with myself.

"It would?" she finally choked out.

She looked so small and unsure of herself, standing there in her overalls and pink shirt. . . a far cry from the confident, talkative woman she usually was. I had done that. I had bullied her into feeling self-conscious in my space, in my presence. And nothing disgusted me more than a bully.

My shoulders deflated at the thought, and I forced myself to let go of some of the tension I always held.

"The computer is in the back."

FIVE

Lila

"YOUR SHOP IS NICE," I SAID, STEPPING INTO THE CRAMPED office Harrison led me to. The walls were covered with tattoo sketches, framed art, and shelves holding everything from ink bottles to strange knickknacks. His desk looked more like an artist's den than a place to handle business. Organized chaos, much like Harrison himself.

"It's a mess. You don't have to be nice." He brushed past me to sit at the small, battered metal table in the corner of the room. It looked like it had been dragged out of a thrift store; one leg was shorter than the others, a book wedged underneath to compensate.

"Is this it?" I eyed the ancient desktop that sat atop the table. It looked like the prototype Steve Jobs himself created.

Harrison ran a hand along his jaw and stared at it. "I have a laptop at home. I just didn't want to leave a nice computer in here. There was a break-in down the block a few months back. Nothing serious, but I don't want to deal with replacing anything expensive."

The monitor came to life with a loud whirring sound.

"That's what insurance is for. Besides, this thing is ancient. You should probably upgrade to something from this century." I tapped the top of the machine. The heat caught me off guard and I snatched my hand away. "This thing is more likely to catch fire and burn your shop to the ground than it is to send an email in a timely fashion."

The corner of his mouth ticked up and I felt a surge of pride that I'd *almost* made him smile.

"I'll look into it," was all he said.

"May I?" I gestured to the chair in front of the computer.

"Be my guest." He pulled out the chair and I slid into the worn seat.

A loud buzzing sound rang from the computer while it booted up. I eyed Harrison when the vibrations grew so intense that the metal desk began to rattle.

"I'll look into it," he repeated, rubbing the back of his neck. His chin-length dark hair fell forward. He often wore it pulled back into a small bun, but I liked it down. It made him look less intense, somehow. Or maybe his new hint of approachableness was a result of the uncertainty behind his eyes. Harrison never looked uncertain.

When the browser finally loaded, the site used to host his website was already pulled up. An angry red error message popped up. I clicked into it to investigate.

"Yeah, it's been doing that all week. I tried chatting with the support team, but it was useless."

"It looks easy enough," I said, clicking around.

"Really? Because it's been giving me a hell of a time." His voice held a hint of doubt, but it was overshadowed by his obvious hope.

I typed something into a box before copying and pasting a new link. Harrison braced his hands on the edge of the metal table, leaning closer to the screen to get a better look at what I was doing. Tension coiled in my stomach and my heart rate shot up. I made a few typos, rushing to delete them and correct my mistakes.

"One of your page references was broken," I said, purposefully steadying my voice. "That's all the error was saying. I just reconnected it and refreshed the page. Let me just hit publish and. . . there." I pointed to the screen. "It's back up."

"Seriously?" He looked from the screen to me. "Damn, that was fast."

Pride coursed through my veins.

"Told you I could help."

"Yeah, yeah." He waved off my comment, but he maintained eye contact, and not in that menacing way he usually did.

"Thank you," he said.

The sincerity in his voice melted right into my chest. It made me want to lean in even closer. Damn. Why was him saying the bare minimum so ridiculously attractive? And what did it say about me that I had a crush on a guy who made me work so hard for the tiniest scrap of approval?

Not a crush, I reminded myself for the hundredth time. I'd have to bring this up in therapy.

"You're welcome." My voice came out like a squeak, and I tried not to wince when he tilted his head in amusement.

One of those old swivel stools sat untouched in the back corner of the room. Harrison went over to grab it before scooching it right up next to me and straddling the seat.

"What do you think of the rest of the site?" he asked with his eyes trained on the website that I was now scrolling through.

"Honestly?"

"Give it to me straight."

I smiled and turned toward him, momentarily forgetting that there had ever been a time when he'd seemingly disliked me.

"It's a little dark," I said.

He let out a loud sigh. "I knew you were going to say that."

"Because it's true," I insisted, pointing to the homepage that looked like it could be a tour announcement for an old death metal band.

Harrison pinched my bright pink blouse between his fingers and held it up as if to show me. "Be objective. I own a tattoo shop. I can't just make everything pink and call it a day. Think about my target market."

"I obviously know that. Don't insult my marketing capabilities." The skin underneath where he'd just touched my shirt felt branded. I was acutely aware of it even though his hands now rested on the table. "First off, you're trying to attract a wider market, no?"

He ran a hand over his face. "I guess. But—"

"And even for your current target market, there is such a thing as too dark. I mean, come on, Harrison. Dark gray font over an almost-black background? Who do you expect to be able to read this?"

He squinted at the screen. "I can read it."

"Because it's easy for you to read, or because you typed every word yourself and you already know what it says?" I challenged him. "And this font. Did you just select the first choice and run with it?"

"It looks fine."

"It's Times New Roman. Of course it's fine, but it's also a hundred years old. Here." I clicked around as Harrison angled himself closer so he could see every change I made. The deep furrows between his brows warned me he was ready to object if the cursor even hovered near a shade resembling pink. Instead, I updated the header font to a blockier choice, with a different one in the same family for the paragraph text. I left the background dark, but changed the font to a light gray that was about as close to white as you could get without being too stark.

"See? Isn't that better already?"

He shrugged stubbornly. "Doesn't look that different."

I smiled and swatted his shoulder. "You're a liar."

"Fine. It looks better. Thank you."

Something flickered across his face that I couldn't quite place—but it looked like intrigue. A lock of my hair fell forward and I tucked it behind my ear, brushing past the piercings that lined my lobe. His eyes lingered there, and I could practically see the judgment forming. He probably thought I got them done at some cheesy teen store or something.

"I didn't get them pierced at the mall, if that's what you're thinking," I said, unable to keep my mouth shut.

He blinked a few times, looking guilty. "Why so many?"

"Because despite what anyone else thinks, I like them," I said simply, not caring to get into the story of how my ex made me take out my first piercings in high school because he said they looked "trashy."

"I like them too." Harrison studied me but didn't say anything more. The air felt heavier in the room. Part of me wanted to make an excuse and get the hell out of there, but I forced myself to push through.

"What about this section?" I pulled up the "about me" page that was painfully bare.

"What about it?"

"It's just a picture of you with your name and how long you've been tattooing. It's basically empty."

He just stared at it before returning his gaze to me. "Right. About me."

A small laugh escaped my throat at his seriousness. "You can't include one singular personal detail? Getting a tattoo is personal. Some people want to know something about the artist who will be etching something permanent into their skin." I poised myself at the keyboard, ready to type. "How did you get into tattooing in the first place?"

His eyes scanned my face. My skin grew hot under his stare, and I shifted in my seat to break the tension.

"Um, hello?" I said, hoping on everything that my cheeks weren't as bright red as they felt. "Earth to Harrison. I asked you a question."

"How I got into tattooing?" He blinked a few times before repeating my words. "Why would anyone care?"

"It's interesting. Plus, I care, you dummy. I'm genuinely asking you."

His leg bent slightly under the table as if he were stretching it out. It bumped my knee, and he moved it so swiftly I was almost convinced I had imagined the contact.

"Um, like everyone does, I guess. I had an apprenticeship. Just some divey shop downtown."

"What does an apprenticeship entail? Like, you draw tattoos and learn how to use the little guns?"

The corner of his lip curled up. "Yes, I eventually learned how to use the *little guns*." He looked at me the same way one might look at a puppy—mild amusement, perhaps he even found me slightly adorable. While my first instinct was to bask in the glow of not being outright disliked, the harsh reality hit me straight in the gut that *adorable* was certainly not Harrison's type.

"Apprenticeship is code for shop bitch," he continued. "I cleaned everything and ran errands. I was basically a glorified assistant."

"But you got to learn."

"Exactly."

"You must have liked art before then, right? I mean, I'm assuming you don't get into tattooing unless you have some sort of inclination toward drawing."

I had tried to connect with Harrison in the past about our possible shared interest. I had been doodling in sketchbooks for as long as I could remember, long before going into graphic design. But the last time I'd asked him if he liked to draw, he'd looked like he wanted to bite my head off and called graphic design a pointless waste of potential. I hadn't revisited the subject with him since.

"I guess," was all he said. Funnily enough, those two words were a notable improvement.

"I've always loved to draw," I offered. I wasn't sure why I was being so generous with my conversation, especially since he hadn't given me any reason to be. "My parents begged me not to get an art degree, though. That's why I went the digital route instead and went into graphic design. Honestly, at first I thought I'd be disappointed, but I ended up falling in love with it. I guess I have more of a business acumen than I originally thought, because every marketing problem or branding misstep feels like a fun challenge." His blank stare sent my self-consciousness into overdrive, so I ducked my head. "Probably sounds stupid. I know it's nothing like tattooing."

The tendon in his jaw pulsed a little, like he was trying to work through something. He ran both hands over his black jeans before finally breaking eye contact.

"I wasn't going to say it sounds stupid. Maybe a little trivial, but. . ." His words trailed off, but they had done their job.

I straightened up and frowned. That's what I got for letting my guard down around him. He'd never change.

"Right, of course. Nothing could compare artistically to jabbing a needle into some drunk biker's forearm. What you do is truly on another level." I let hostility coat my words, letting him know just how irritated I was that he had to turn a civil, almost friendly, moment into another cheap shot at me.

His lips parted and I swore I saw something that looked like remorse in his eyes. But he blinked and it was gone, replaced by a smirk. "You know, you should come by sometime. Get yourself a tattoo. I can be your first."

"Thanks, but I'll pass," I said. "I'd rather go somewhere a little less condescending."

"So, you do want a tattoo," he pressed.

"Maybe I do. It's none of your business."

"Where would you get it?" His eyes roamed over my body.

My face was probably a shade of scarlet at this point. "Wouldn't you like to know."

"A tramp stamp, right?"

My lips parted at the tactless phrase. "A lower back tattoo is just that, Harrison. A tattoo on someone's back. I can't believe that you'd use that kind of sexist language as a tattoo artist. No wonder your business is struggling. No woman in her right mind would come in here."

Anger flared in his eyes at that, confirming that I'd prodded at a sensitive spot.

"With all those dates you go on, a tramp stamp would be a pretty fitting placement," he muttered.

My ears rang. "That's it." The chair screeched against the floor as I stood up sharply, sending it backward.

He inhaled sharply and tried to grab my wrist. "Wait—"

"Don't touch me." I yanked my arm away and glared

down at him. "And good luck with your website. Honestly, I hope it's a bitch to figure out."

His footsteps hurried behind me as I pushed the door to the office open and stormed back out into the shop. Shane looked up from his phone, eyebrows lifted in surprise.

"I'm sorry—" Harrison tried to say.

"No, you're not."

"That was too far. It was a dumb joke."

"I know," I spat, turning around just so he could see how completely and utterly pissed I was. "But it's my fault. I was stupid for coming here in the first place. Everything about me is a joke to you, and that will never change. I shouldn't have wasted my time."

"Lila—"

"Bye." I glared at him before spinning around and getting out of that shop as fast as my feet would carry me.

"Fuck," I heard him mutter behind me, right as the door slammed shut.

Oliver was a dead man for sending me here, and I intended to tell him so. This whole charade had been some kind of weird, twisted plan to get Harrison and me to get along, but it had been an epic failure. Harrison would never like me, and I was done trying.

A biker came zooming down the sidewalk, forcing me to step aside and interrupting my rage-fueled walk home. Hot tears welled up at the corners of my eyes, and I cursed myself for letting someone who cared so little about me affect me. I swiped at them and continued on my way, eager to put as much distance between this shop and me as possible.

And as for this little surprise trip we'd all be taking in a couple weeks, Oliver would just have to live with the fact that we wouldn't all be sitting around a bonfire singing kumbaya together. Of course I'd put on my best smile for Charlie's sake, but I wouldn't say two words to Harrison if I could help it. Maybe I couldn't ignore him completely on a trip with only five other people, but I could certainly limit our interactions.

Harrison would not get the best of me, and he certainly wouldn't be getting even a second more of my precious time. As long as it were up to me, I'd avoid him like the plague he was.

SIX

Harrison

A SHOULDER BUMPED INTO ME AS I CLUTCHED MY SMALL duffel closer to my chest. If there was one thing I hated more than the Denver airport, it was the packed train to get there. Crowds were decidedly not my thing, and I had yet to see the Denver airport *not* overflowing with obnoxious, likely incompetent, travelers.

Patience was not a virtue I held dear. Witnessing someone struggling in the TSA line, their baggage spilling out as they held up the people behind them, made me see red every single time.

The train pulled into the airport station, and I lingered near the doors, ready to step off as soon as they opened. From the moment I hit the walkway, I used my long strides to my advantage to distance myself from the throngs.

One thing I could be grateful for was that I was doing this part of the trip alone and not with the rest of the group. At least I didn't have to make idle small talk. Oliver had been a little pissed when I told him I couldn't leave yesterday with everyone else, but I'd had an appointment on the book with a long-time client that I didn't want to reschedule. Nathan couldn't care less, though, and the travel agent had booked me on a later flight without any issue. Now I got to navigate the airport alone. The idea might not have appealed to some, but to me it was a huge fucking relief.

The security line was surprisingly short. It was a good thing, too, because the whole area smelled strongly of some sort of disinfectant. Although it should have been an indication of cleanliness, it just made me feel sick.

"Boarding pass." A middle-aged woman in a blue TSA uniform looked right through me as she held up her hand.

I scrolled through my emails before selecting the one that had my travel information, but I couldn't find one with my trip confirmation and boarding pass.

I muttered a curse under my breath as I stepped to the side and checked the time.

Charlie had been adamant that this whole thing would be a surprise. I couldn't even imagine being so disgustingly rich that I could just book my friends a bunch of first-class tickets to some exotic destination, where we'd surely be staying at some five-star accommodation. But the lack of information meant this whole surprise trip thing had gotten old. I just wanted to get to my gate and get settled in.

I could feel eyes on me. I whipped my head around only to see a familiar redhead. We made eye contact before she tore her gaze away to pretend like she hadn't been staring at me.

Fantastic. What an unfortunate turn of events.

Lila stood there, just behind the security belt barrier, wearing a fuzzy, light pink hoodie and matching sweatpants. I hadn't seen her since that painfully awful encounter at my shop, and the deep frown on her face now told me she wasn't thrilled about this unexpected reunion.

That day at my shop, she'd been trying so hard to connect

with me—it had been written all over her face. That hopeful look, tossing out small details about herself, waiting for me to respond with a friendly 'I know what you mean,' or 'I've been there.' And I'd had no reason to deny her that simple courtesy. She'd been nothing but kind and helpful from the moment she'd walked in. Her smile had been genuine, a clear sign that her usual irritation toward me was entirely my doing, not hers. Lila would've gladly been my friend if I'd let her.

And for whatever reason, the impenetrable forcefield I had spent my entire life crafting saw that as a threat. I'd lashed out.

I could admit that I had been an ass that day, and I knew I should apologize. But despite what Oliver thought, the two of us didn't have to be friends. I was more than fine with never speaking to her again. But here we were, apparently both late to this spectacle of a trip.

I closed the gap between the two of us.

"What are you doing here?"

"Are you serious?" She lifted her gaze for a moment only to roll her eyes before looking back at her phone. "I'm obviously here for the same reason you are."

"I meant, why didn't you leave yesterday with everyone else?"

"A work thing. I had to present something to a new investor this morning," she said dismissively.

I shifted from foot to foot. "Were you really planning on ignoring me?" I asked, even though I knew I completely deserved it.

"I didn't see you."

"Yes, you did," I challenged.

She glanced up at me for a moment, only to narrow her eyes. "Fine. Yes. I was planning on ignoring you. Now can you just go be somewhere else so I can have some peace?"

Discomfort surged through my body. My bad behavior

had gone too far last time. She knew it. I knew it. But apologizing was not a skill in my wheelhouse. Still, I had to say something.

"If this is about what happened at my shop, I'm sorry, okay?"

"Great," she mumbled dismissively.

I looked up to the high, pitched ceilings and sighed. "I'm serious. I'm sorry."

I waited for her to respond, but when it was clear she was done talking to me, I held up my phone instead.

"Any idea how we're supposed to board the flight when we haven't gotten our itineraries yet?" I asked, hoping her shell would crack a little. Lila wasn't an angry person by nature. Grudges weren't her thing.

She continued scrolling on her phone, still refusing to look at me. "Charlie wanted it to be a secret until the last possible minute."

"It's stupid, is what it is. We're just supposed to wait around until we get our boarding information?"

Lila huffed and shoved her phone into the black belt-bag slung across her chest. "It's not stupid. It's fun. Ever heard of the concept?"

"Oh yeah, it's real fun standing around waiting like an idiot with no direction."

"If you had bothered to read the emails, you would have known that we'll receive our itinerary two hours before take-off, which she told us was at five-thirty." Lila paused to check her phone. "So based on that information, we should get it in approximately four minutes."

The color-coded, two-page email Charlie had sent through the travel agency had, unsurprisingly, gone straight to my trash folder. I had fully planned on just gleaning all the details from Oliver, a plan that had worked out well for me historically and would have been fine for this, too. Until I had to stay back an extra day.

"Why are you even here so early, anyway?" She pursed her lips and gave me a once-over. "You seem like the type to roll up to the gate right as they announce last call for boarding."

"I don't fly much," I admitted. Lila's assumption about me couldn't have been further from the truth. Control was something I had difficulty relinquishing. And because this whole scenario made me so anxious that I had a rash creeping across my neck, I'd made sure to get to the airport early.

"Huh," was Lila's only response as she continued to assess me, her gaze lingering on my beat-up duffel.

"What?" I asked, agitation creeping into my voice.

A large group of people swept by us to enter security. The line snaked as it got busier. It was torture having to sit back and watch it while we waited.

"You got a bathing suit in there?" she asked.

"Yes." Oliver had at least been able to give me the highlights from the packing list.

"Interesting."

"Why?"

"I'm just trying to imagine you relaxing on a beach, and I can't do it." She looked past my shoulder as if there was a screen there portraying the scene she was imagining. A smile crept onto her lips.

"Believe it or not, I do own a bathing suit." Just one. I'd only worn it on two occasions. Both had involved Oliver dragging me paddle boarding last summer.

"Hmm. . . I'm still struggling to picture it." Lila stroked her chin with her dainty fingers. "Be honest. Have you ever relaxed a day in your life?" She was goading me. Honestly, it was an improvement to being ignored. Although I could sense the resentment underneath her teasing tone. I probably owed her a better apology, but I didn't know how to go about it.

"I'm always relaxed."

She tilted her head back and laughed. "I find that very hard to believe."

Our phones dinged. I pulled mine out of my back pocket, hoping it was my itinerary and boarding pass.

"Finally," I grumbled, when I saw the new email from the travel agency.

Before I even had a chance to open it, let alone read it, Lila gasped, throwing a hand over her mouth.

"No way!" she exclaimed, so loudly that a few people near the TSA entrance turned their head to look.

"Don't make a scene," I hissed. I hated having eyes on me, especially in a large public space.

I opened the email to see what had set off this flurry of enthusiasm. It took me a second to look past all the numbers and times to find the actual destination on the pass. When I did, my jaw went slack.

A round-trip ticket to Santorini, Greece.

"Europe," I said, eyebrows raised. This was unexpected. While this whole display had seemed overly elaborate from the start, I still hadn't envisioned us traipsing all the way across the Atlantic Ocean.

"This is absolutely insane," Lila gushed. "I've always wanted to go." Her soft green eyes glistened.

A patter started up in my chest when I absorbed her genuine delight. I couldn't remember the last time I'd seen anyone that excited about something. A tiny tear brimmed at the corner of her eye before trailing down her cheek.

I nearly shot back. "Are you *crying?*" I asked, horrified.

"Shut up! I'm happy." She swatted my chest, her glassy eyes immediately hardening as they trained on me. "Geez, are you going to suck the fun out of everything for the entire travel day?"

"I'm not the one crying."

Her eyes squeezed shut and she blew out a breath before gripping the handle of her pink carryon-sized suitcase. She rolled it past me without looking up. This was arguably not off to the best start.

I slid into the line and lingered behind her. Voices buzzed all around us, but her silence was so loud it left a ringing in my ears.

"You know, the words fun and travel day should be an oxymoron." I couldn't stop myself.

She turned, brow crinkling. "Are you kidding? What's more exciting than an airport?" She said the words without a hint of sarcasm. "Everyone here is excited to be going somewhere different, taking a break from their lives. They could be visiting a family member, going on the trip of their dreams, moving somewhere new." She pointed at a family outside the security line, hauling a cart brimming with luggage. "The possibilities are endless. There's energy everywhere."

I snorted. "That's the most romanticized bullshit I've ever heard in my entire life. The airport is stressful." Aside from the occasional trip home to see my parents, I didn't travel much, and I preferred to keep it that way.

"It's thrilling," she shot back.

"No, it's not." I stepped forward so that she was next to me. "Because even people who are excited about the end destination don't want to deal with the hassle of the airport."

"Well, I happen to like the airport. Hassle or not, it breaks up the monotony." Lila rolled her suitcase next to her with a little more aggression as we came to the front of the line.

"I'd take monotony over this, any day," I insisted. She

either didn't hear me or chose to ignore me. I'd bet on the latter.

The TSA agent waved us forward and Lila walked up.

"Families can come up together," the agent said in a bored voice. Lila turned her head back to look at me before realization sank in. She frowned.

"We are *not* together," she said with a little more disgust than I liked.

The TSA agent just shrugged, looked at her ID, and let her continue.

I followed suit, the whole time trying not to look at the sliver of stomach that poked out from under Lila's sweatshirt as she shifted her backpack off her shoulder and onto the conveyer belt.

Before she could reach down and get her suitcase, I moved into the spot next to her and grabbed the handle. I grunted as I lifted the small but shockingly heavy luggage onto the belt.

"Christ, what do you have in here?" I asked as I threw my own duffel behind it.

"I didn't need your help," she said stubbornly.

I scanned her frame. She came up to my chin, which meant she couldn't be more than five foot three, even with her chunky white sneakers. "You been training with powerlifting or something?"

She jutted her chin and tilted her head down, an obvious display of her lack of amusement.

"I got it here," she grumbled.

We walked robotically through the scanner before grabbing our bags and heading toward the shuttle to the terminals, which like the rest of this hellhole, was overly crowded.

I leaned against the wall and held onto the bar overhead. Lila could barely reach, and when the train started to move, she lurched forward. Without thinking, I reached out and grabbed her waist to steady her. My fingertips brushed the tiny sliver of skin exposed by her cropped sweatshirt. Her skin was so soft I had to fight the urge to stroke it.

"Careful," I said, before she stepped hurriedly out of my grasp.

"I'm fine." Her flustered appearance indicated otherwise, but I wasn't about to mention it. Not when I was already skating on paper-thin ice.

At our stop, we rode the escalator up to the terminal in silence. My brain scanned over any and all possible conversation topics to repair this uncomfortable crack between us. Lila and I weren't friends, I had made sure of that. She'd always found me irritable and likely a displeasure to be around, but now I was concerned her feelings were developing into outright revulsion. And for whatever reason, I didn't want that.

The terminal greeted us with giant boards displaying departure information. People moved in every direction, rushing to get to their gates. While I stood by what I said earlier—airports were a nightmare and stressful as hell—Lila's perspective had me seeing it through a new lens. Each person there was on some sort of journey, whether it be mundane or once-in-a-lifetime. I felt that energy now, the one that whirred through everyone that passed. We were all in the same place, yet everyone's lives were so completely different I couldn't even fathom them. Like, who the fuck was going to Charleston on a random Tuesday evening?

Lila twirled around without warning, nearly causing me to crash into her. I hadn't realized how closely I was trailing her.

"We don't have to stick together." Her tone was curt and her narrowed eyes were arctic.

I winced, feeling guilty that I had ostracized Lila so badly that she wanted nothing to do with me. Usually that was the goal. Keep my guard up to distance myself from anyone and everyone. But Lila really didn't deserve all of the insensitive comments I'd thrown her way in our yearlong acquaintanceship. Not even close.

I slung my duffel over my shoulder and scratched the back of my head. "Look, Lila. Can we just—"

"It's no big deal, okay? We're just two people with mutual friends who happen to be on the same flight. It's not like we have to make small talk, or hang out together."

Her voice shook slightly despite her upturned chin. She was nervous. The realization made me feel like an even bigger prick. Intimidation was my signature style, but making Lila uneasy felt a lot like terrorizing a bunny rabbit.

I tried again. "What if we just—"

"We'll be on the flight soon enough," she cut me off, looking down the terminal as if she were searching for the quickest escape route. "Then we'll land and be reunited with the rest of the group. Then we hardly have to speak to each other."

Lila's face contorted into an expression of indifference, but I didn't buy it. She hated that we didn't get along. It was written all over her face. She likely wanted nothing more than to have an airport buddy to grab dinner with before the flight, one who would match her energy and be content chattering away about all the possibilities for the upcoming trip.

But she was also obviously over trying to connect with me, and I couldn't blame her in the slightest. I should be grateful that she was finally letting me off the hook, but instead, I felt a sinking sensation in my gut.

"Okay," I said. "I guess I'll see you when we land."

SEVEN

Lila

"You've got to be kidding me," I groaned.

"Hello again," Harrison said, as he stuffed his ratty duffel into the overhead compartment and tossed a sketchbook onto the first-class seat next to mine.

"I should have known they'd stick us together." Even though the seats were massive up here, I still curled myself toward the window to distance myself from him even further.

"I'm so sorry. Am I cramping your first-class style?" He gave me that smug closed-lip smile that I wish I loathed but instead gave me butterflies.

"Not even you could ruin this for me," I shot back.

And it was true. After we'd separated, I had gotten a few snacks and a new book. The prices at the airport were expensive, but I couldn't resist. I loved the ritual of wandering the terminal before a flight and picking out a new vacation read. If I hadn't ditched Harrison, I'm sure he would have droned on about how it was a waste of money.

"You aren't going to want to talk the whole time, are you?" Harrison asked gruffly as he sat down in his pod-like seat.

I pulled the airline-provided blanket over my lap.

"Nope."

"Really?" He questioned, arching a brow. "Because you seem like the type to talk my ear off the whole time and never take a hint."

My cheeks stained pink. Why was he always so insistent on sparring?

"Sorry that you're going to be subjected to me for an entire flight," I said, the sweet sarcasm dripping from my tone. "But I promise, despite what you might think, my obnoxious personality won't rub off on you."

I let his comment wash over me, but it still stung a bit. *Of course* I liked talking, especially on airplanes when I was all excited about the end destination. If Charlie had been in Harrison's place, you'd have been hard pressed to get us to shut up for at least the first hour or two.

To Harrison, however, that was apparently the most annoying trait imaginable. Much like every trait I possessed, it seemed. Despite the promise I'd made to myself after that day at his shop, to not let him get under my skin, his taunts still hurt. It would always drive me a little nuts that I wasn't his cup of tea, especially since that tiny little flutter in my heart refused to fade. It was even worse now, sitting next to him without the divider up, leaving it all too easy for him to inch into my space at any moment. Plus, he smelled *good*. Like distractingly good.

I shuddered and turned toward the window.

"Nothing else to say," he probed as he picked up his leather drawing pad.

"Look who's the chatty one now. I'm just trying to enjoy this." I made a big display of opening my book and pressing it close to my nose. The pages had that new book smell. "Why don't you just keep to yourself the rest of the flight?"

His deep sigh sparked my curiosity, and I glanced up. His hard expression made him impossible to read, whereas my own face tended to show every emotion like I wore a sign across my forehead. I didn't mind it, usually. Had it made my dating life challenging? Sure. But overall, I liked my vulnerability. People like Harrison could call it a weakness if they wanted, but I knew it was one of my biggest strengths.

"I'm sorry." The words sounded like they were physically painful for him to deliver.

"For what?"

"For being a jerk. You can talk if you want to."

"You said it five seconds ago. How can you already be sorry?" I asked, giving up on pretending to read and setting the book back down in my lap. "I get it. You've made it abundantly clear that everything about me is a giant joke. But no worries; in just ten short hours we'll be landing in Munich, and then just one more short flight to Santorini, and then the two of us never have to be alone in the same room again. I can promise you that."

I turned away again as the burly bear next to me shifted uncomfortably in his seat.

"Hey," he started. But I opened my book back up aggressively and placed it over my face, using it as a barrier so I wouldn't have to look at him. If he made some sexist comment about the pink cover or the fact that it was obviously a romance novel, I might lose it.

"Look—" Harrison breathed.

"Let's not talk," I snapped, pulling my book down for a moment to level him with a glare before returning it to eye-level again.

He sighed as if he had just completed some sort of physical labor.

"I'm trying to apologize," he said.

I lifted the book higher.

"Are you listening?" he asked before his hand slid over the top of my book and lowered it gently.

I caved in and lowered it the rest of the way before eyeing him warily. His dark eyes looked sincere. I could honestly say in the entire time we'd known each other, he'd never given me a look like that. When I glanced behind him, I noticed our elderly seatmates across the aisle look away quickly.

"Fine. Get it over with." The last thing I wanted was every person in the first-class cabin eavesdropping on our drama.

I shifted in my seat so that I faced him and he wouldn't have to talk as loudly. My heart rate kicked up a couple of notches at the prolonged eye contact. Man, I'd thought he was attractive when he was being a jerk; I would have been done for if he'd shot me one of these looks every once in a while. I stuffed my sweaty palms into my sweatshirt and hoped he wouldn't notice that he had any sort of effect on me.

"I'm really sorry for the last time we were together, okay?" He said the last word while searching my eyes, begging me to take him seriously. "That was an asshole thing to say, and it wasn't true."

I lifted my chin up. "Go on."

"I shouldn't have said anything," he admitted. "You were helping me out, and I was a dick. I'm sorry. Unfortunately, it's just my nature. Sometimes, I find myself saying the worst possible thing to. . . I don't even know. Get the upper hand, maybe? I've been doing it my entire life and I'm sorry you were caught in the crossfire."

Attempting to analyze the sincerity in his words was tough. On the one hand, I didn't know that I'd ever be able to fully trust Harrison. But on the other hand, he'd never been so earnest with me before. This felt like a different person.

"Crossfire? Seems more like any time we're together, I'm

in your direct line of attack," I pointed out, still not prepared to let him off the hook.

"And it's fun, right? A little friendly banter?" His guilty grin caused me to snort.

"Oh, that's what you're calling it? No wonder Oliver is your only friend if that's what you consider 'friendly banter.'"

"Look, I don't do apologies," he said tersely, jaw clenched.

"Shhh." I held up my finger and nodded forward, indicating we'd gain an audience if he kept that up.

"I suck at this." His voice was now just above a whisper. "But I know that you deserve an apology—a real one. And you're right. I do always give you a hard time. I can't change how I've acted in the past, but I'll try to do better."

I dipped my chin.

"I *will* do better."

I paused for at least thirty seconds, letting him sweat. Did I believe him? I mean, he hadn't said he was going to try and be my best friend or anything. He just said he'd try to be less of a jerk. Which, let's be real, was not a very high bar to reach. But this awkward repentance was miles more than I had received in the past. Maybe he'd never accept me, or want to be friendly, but we could at the very least coexist. Plus, it wasn't like I had to completely open myself up to him. Calling a truce was not going to leave me vulnerable.

I hoped.

"Fine. I'll accept that."

His shoulders dropped.

"Thank God," he grunted and turned away from me.

And just like that, the hairs on the back of my neck bristled. "Wow, apologizing to me really took that much out of you?" I whispered. "Grow up, Harrison."

He ran a hand over his face but didn't look fazed.

"Apologizing in general is hard for me. But I can admit when I'm wrong."

"Must be easy to admit it when you're always in the wrong," I fired back, unable to help myself.

"Hey." He tore out a blank piece of white paper from his sketchbook and waved it. "Did we not just have a nice moment? We can't ruin it already."

"I didn't start it," I insisted, rolling my eyes and snatching the paper out of his hand. A smile snuck onto my lips looking at his exasperated face.

His eyes shone with relief when he noticed my shift in demeanor. If he was truly going to try and be a little nicer to me, then I wasn't about to be the one holding on to any bitterness.

"Let's just have a nice trip with everyone," he said.

"I'm planning on it." My shoulders sagged. This was the first time I had been away from work since. . . since. . . well, since I couldn't even remember. But it had been too long. "I've needed a vacation for months, and I'm not about to let any animosity between us ruin it," I added.

"No animosity here," Harrison insisted.

"Good," I said, picking my book back up.

"Good." Harrison opened his worn book and produced a pencil that had been lodged behind his ear. It was one of those nice artist's ones that was so satisfying to sketch with. My eyes itched to sneak a glance at his drawings, but something told me he wouldn't appreciate that.

I tried to focus on my new book, but the words blurred together on the page. My mind wandered to the trip ahead instead. Freaking Greece! We'd be there in just a few hours. Well, it was more like twenty hours of travel, but still. Less than a day away. I assumed our hotel had a pool, and the first thing I wanted to do was drag Charlie and Oliver out for a swim. My mental calculations informed me we wouldn't get there until dinnertime, local time, but what a magical way to start a trip. A little evening swim. Maybe I could even convince everyone to go.

My thoughts drifted back to Harrison and the bathing suit he apparently definitely owned. A small chuckle escaped my lips.

"What?" Harrison demanded, jerking away from his drawing. It was like he was attuned to any trace of joy, ready to squash it instantly.

I bit my lip, trying to keep my smile from growing.

"Tell me." He set down his pencil and eyed me with the tiniest hint of impatience.

"Just still trying to picture you on vacation," I admitted. "Do you have sandals to match your bathing suit?"

He rolled his eyes. "I hope this is making you feel better."

"It is," I said, turning back to him and smiling. The corner of his lip quirked up ever so slightly.

"Sorry for the short delay, but we'll be taking off soon." The flight attendant peered over at us from the aisle. "Anything to drink?"

"No thanks," he grunted.

"We'll have two champagnes, please," I said at the same time.

The woman winked and went back to the front.

When Harrison glared at me, I just shrugged in response. "What? It's going to be a long enough flight as it is. We might as well try to enjoy it."

"I don't drink champagne."

"Too girly for you?" I fluttered my eyelashes.

"It's too sweet."

"Anything is too sweet when you're filled to the brim with bitterness."

He scowled, which just made me laugh.

"You'll live," I said just as the flight attendant returned and handed us two glasses.

He ignored me, but he took the glass before shutting his book and setting it to the side of his tray table.

I nodded at it. "You draw a lot?"

"Oh, uh." He eyed the sketchbook and then eyed me. His brow softened slightly when he took note of my genuine interest. "Yeah, I do. It's always the quickest way to pass time for me."

"I take it you wouldn't let me see any of them?" I asked carefully.

His dark eyes widened, but he didn't get angry like I worried he might. Instead, he just gave a quick shake of his head. "Sorry, I don't really like sharing them."

Instead of pushing, I just smiled. "I get it. I used to sketch more in high school, and I never liked showing anyone. It's personal."

We sat in silence for a moment before he tipped his head toward my book. "You read a lot?" he asked.

"I try to. I wish I had more time, but I'm always working. Do you read?"

"Sometimes," he said. "Usually heavier stuff."

I rolled my eyes exaggeratingly at that. "I read all sorts of books, Harrison. And I can promise you, this—" I held up the colorful book and shook it at him. "—this is exactly what you want while soaking up rays in the Mediterranean."

"Looks really educational," he mused. Thankfully, there was no condescension in his voice. Was Harrison actually teasing me?

I snorted. "You're such a snob."

At this, he turned his whole body to face me. "You're telling me that's the height of literature?"

"What does that even mean? It's fun. It's compelling. I love the characters. Plus, reading a fluffy romcom is a great distraction from my own depressing love life. Do you ask yourself every time you pick up a book if it's going to be *the height of literature?*" I said the last words with a bad British accent.

"Yes," he said flatly.

"Harrison," I said, unable to contain my bubble of laughter. "That's the saddest thing I've ever heard."

He scowled at me before reaching over and plucking the book from my clutches.

"What are you doing? Give that back." I tried to retrieve it, but he held it high, just out of my reach.

"No. Apparently I need to broaden my views," he said.

"You're seriously going to read my book?" I asked, trying not to gape.

"I can't critique something I haven't tried."

"Why do I feel like that hasn't stopped you in the past?"

Harrison held my book in front of him and held up a finger to his mouth. "Excuse me. Can you please keep it down? I'm trying to read."

I let out a laugh at the sight.

The flight attendants came through to prepare us for take-off. Soon our plane was taxiing out of the gate, and we were airborne. I glued my face to the window, keeping an eye on the ground. As it got farther away, so did my real life.

"You really do like flying."

I turned back around to see Harrison staring at me openly, my book sitting forgotten on his lap.

"I love it."

He frowned in a pensive way before nodding. "I think I'm going to watch a movie and pass out. It's a long flight."

"Enjoy," I said, knowing that I'd probably be up for hours savoring every second of this experience. I mean, business was doing well, but realistically, when could I expect to fly first-class again?

Harrison shifted in his seat, his expression hard as ever. I tried my best to tune out his presence, but the heat crawling up my skin wasn't going anywhere. Could this little crush be any more humiliating? The urge to peel off my sweatshirt hit me, but it was actually freezing in here. The last thing I wanted to do was draw attention to the fact that I was nearly combusting.

Instead, I slipped on my giant noise-canceling headphones, selected whatever latest comedy the airline had to offer, and settled into my seat, pretending I didn't even notice my very attractive, attention-consuming seatmate.

Warily optimistic. That's how I would describe my feelings toward him. Our newfound truce was unexpected and welcome. But knowing Harrison, his mood could shift as easily as a leaf floating gently to the ground could be whipped back into the air by a rogue gust of wind.

He might change his mind about all this, or simply forget the second an opportunity arose to make a snide remark directed at me. Even if he did revert, though, only two international flights separated us from our friends. Charlie, Oliver—even Nathan. They'd be the buffers we desperately needed. Once we were all reunited, Harrison and I would barely have to interact.

For the sake of my racing heart and the nervous energy swelling inside of me, I was immensely grateful for that.

EIGHT

Harrison

APPLAUSE RATTLED THROUGH THE CABIN THE INSTANT THE wheels hit the tarmac in Munich. Annoyance simmered in my chest. Maybe it was the lack of sleep, but something about clapping for a landing—especially on such a smooth flight, with close to zero turbulence—irritated the hell out of me.

The commotion caused Lila to lift her cheek from the window where she'd been passed out and blink her eyes open. Almost as soon as she snapped to attention, she smiled and clapped along with everyone else.

"Stop that," I said, my face unintentionally contorted into one of disgust.

She narrowed her eyes before dropping her hands to her lap. "Can you just let me be excited? It's not like it's affecting you."

"It's obnoxious and it's in my vicinity," I grumbled.

Not my best line, but I was irritable. Well, more irritable than usual. While I should have had no issue sleeping, given this lavish setup, I couldn't get a certain perky redhead off my mind. Her presence was like a magnetic field. I could sense her, and for whatever reason, that kept me wide awake.

And surprise, surprise—I didn't do well on lack of sleep.

"Someone woke up on the wrong side of the bed," she muttered under her breath before stretching her arms above her head and letting out a big yawn.

"Try no sleep," I said. "I can't wait to get to the hotel and crash."

She looked appalled at the thought.

"You can't go straight to bed. You have to stay up at least a few hours so you're not completely jet-lagged."

"I'll be fine."

"I'm telling you, you'll regret it. You better take a power nap on the next flight."

Only one more short flight to Santorini and I'd be able to put some much-needed distance between Lila and me. I felt guilty about giving her the brunt of my bad personality, but it couldn't be helped. Soon, Oliver's smiling face would be between us, and I could just sit back in silence. Which was my preferred strategy when it came to socializing.

The plane pulled into the gate and the fasten-seatbelt sign flickered off. I moved into the aisle and opened the overhead compartment before pulling Lila's suitcase out and setting it on the ground, followed by my own bag.

"Such a gentleman," she said.

I knew there was sarcasm layered into that comment. How could there not be? No one in their right mind would refer to me as a gentleman; making sure Lila never had to carry her suitcase wouldn't suddenly grant me the title.

She was likely just as eager to be done with me as her only travel companion as I was. In fact, she was probably a lot more excited. The thought made me feel guilty and a little frustrated. I didn't want to ruin this trip for her by always being in a shitty mood.

Why couldn't I just be excited, for once in my life?

The feeling simmered deep in my gut, but I couldn't bring myself to let it boil to the surface. Excitement had always felt like a weakness to me. Maybe it had been getting bullied by those little assholes in school. Or maybe it was just the way I was always meant to be.

Growing up, we couldn't even afford to drive to the closest theme park in Ohio, let alone fly somewhere. I hadn't even been on an airplane until I turned nineteen and Oliver and I had moved out to Colorado.

My ability to suffocate any emotion that even resembled enthusiasm frustrated Oliver quite a bit. But he let me be me. He must've understood, at least on some level, why I was the way that I was. He had seen me get relentlessly bullied when we were too young to do anything about it, watched as any little spirit I'd had slowly iced over. He'd stood by me through everything. Sometimes I felt guilty for not having any real friends aside from him, like I was asking too much. Sure, I was friendly with the other artists at my shop, but we didn't connect outside of tattooing. Letting people in, it seemed, had become impossible for me.

"Do you think there's Wi-Fi here?" Lila held up her phone as we exited the plane.

"You didn't spring for the international plan?" We emerged out of the loading bridge. The gate at the Munich airport was packed with people, and every seat was taken.

"I'm too cheap," she said.

"Isn't it only, like, ten dollars?" I asked, even though I hadn't bothered to do it either. If anything, I was looking forward to being less available for the next few days.

She continued to click through the settings on her phone. I

grabbed her arm and pulled her closer to me to keep her from walking straight into a pole.

"Can you watch where you're going?"

"Shit, sorry." She finally looked up. "I was trying to get ahold of Charlie."

"Charlie is still going to be there after we get to the next gate."

"You're right." She offered me an apologetic smile and slipped her phone back into her belt bag. "I just want to let her know we made it to Munich."

Our next flight boarded in an hour, and while I forced myself to remain calm, I wouldn't be able to truly relax until we physically sat down at the next gate.

"I'm sure they already have a driver ready to come pick us up," I said. "It's not like she needs a play by play."

"I still want to update her." An information desk sat in the center of the terminal. Lila pointed to it. "Let's ask about the Wi-Fi there."

"Lila," I snapped. Her eyes widened and she halted in her tracks. I sucked in some air to steady my voice. "We need to get to our next gate."

She eyed me up and down. "You're stressed." She looked pleased with herself for arriving at that conclusion.

"I'm not stressed. But I didn't fly halfway across the world only to miss my connecting flight." I knew I sounded exasperated, but I didn't care.

"Okay, okay. Fine." She chuckled before looking up at the signs that lined the ceiling, all pointing travelers in the correct direction. "That way," she said definitively, pointing down one of the long, wide halls.

Without waiting for me, Lila set off with surprising speed, lugging her suitcase behind her. Maybe it was her small stature, but she easily dodged people walking in the opposite direction. I quickened my pace to keep up with her, not wanting to risk losing her in the crowd. When I finally caught up, I grabbed her forearm lightly as she made another rapid turn.

She halted and looked back at me. I dropped her arm.

"Sorry. I didn't want to lose you."

A hint of a smile tugged at her lips before she continued leading us to the gate, this time at a moderately slower pace. Even though she tried to stop on two separate occasions to get a snack and a magazine, I only allowed her to deviate from our mission once the gate was in sight. By the time we got settled in seats, we only had fifteen minutes until boarding.

"Okay, screw it. I'm just going to pay for the international plan. It's only a few days." Lila clicked around on her phone. "I'm going to text Charlie."

"Fine, whatever," I said, picking up the book that I had stolen from her on the plane, and thumbing to the chapter I was on.

"You're not *actually* reading that, are you?" She lowered her phone and stared at me, eyes wide with disbelief.

I hadn't meant to read it, but I had felt self-conscious about drawing with Lila right next to me, and movies usually failed to capture my interest. So, I'd read her book. Two friends forced to fake date because of some bizarre stipulation in a will. Then, they arrive at a hotel and—of course—there's only one bed. It was cheesy, and a total cliché. And yet I hadn't been able to stop myself from turning each page, desperate to know how two people with such seemingly different personalities were going to make it work.

"So what if I am?"

She leaned back in the worn leather seat and set her phone on her stomach. "I never thought I'd see Harrison Porter reading a romance novel." The carbonation of her soda made an audible fizzing sound as she twisted open the plastic bottle and took a sip.

My full name danced easily off her lips. "You know my last name?"

"Obviously. We've known each other for a year." She arched an eyebrow. "Do you not know mine?"

My mind sifted through every scrap of information I'd picked up about Lila since we'd met, but honestly, it wasn't much. Maybe that was why I had kept reading this book. I wanted to understand what she saw in it, get a glimpse into her mind.

She might wear her emotions on her sleeves, but that only made her more of an enigma to me. How could she be so comfortable being herself?

"I don't," I admitted after a second. "I'm sorry." The apology came easily this time, and I hoped she could see it in my eyes. Asking people questions wasn't one of my strong suits. But now, as I caught a glimpse of the disappointment flash across her face before she masked it, I felt a twinge of regret.

"It's Cornell."

"Got it," I said.

Lila Cornell. I knew without a doubt it was committed to my memory now.

She threw me a half-smile before resuming scrolling on her phone. Nearby, people began crowding around the gate agent, passports in hand, even though boarding hadn't started yet. As impatient as I was, I never understood that. Being first in line didn't get you there faster.

I patted my back pocket to ensure my passport was still securely in its place before pulling out my phone from the pocket of my hoodie. Lila's phone chimed with incoming messages, and I briefly considered powering mine on. But we'd be boarding any minute. The only people who might have called me while we were in flight were Oliver or my parents, and both could wait until we were in Greece.

Instead, I watched Lila as her eyes danced across the screen. Her pink cheeks grew noticeably paler as she brought her other hand to her phone and started typing furiously.

"Are you okay?" I asked, sitting up. She looked like she might pass out right there on the dirty airport carpet.

"No," she whispered. "What? There's no way."

The phone fell out of her shaky hands and slid between the cracks in the seats. "Shit!" she hissed, scrambling to see where it fell.

"What's going on?" I demanded, sliding my arm between us and retrieving her phone. "You're freaking me out." She snatched her phone back before standing and pacing back and forth in front of me.

"This can't be happening."

I stood and gripped her shoulders, gently but firmly, forcing her to meet my gaze. "Lila. What the hell is going on? What happened?" She was starting to freak me out. I had never seen her lose her cool like this.

She froze for a moment, her breath catching, before turning the phone in my direction. All I saw was a blur of messages, but I wasn't close enough to actually read them.

"They're in Fiji." Her voice came out like a shocked whisper.

"What?"

"Fiji," she repeated.

I gave up trying to get a complete sentence out of Lila and leaned in so that I could scan the conversation she had pulled up. She had texted Charlie back in Denver, right before we'd gone through security, about being excited for Santorini.

Charlie's response came in later. Just a lot of exclamation

points and question marks, starting with, "What are you talking about!" followed by, "Call me as soon as you get this," then, "You're joking right?" And finally: "We're in Fiji. YOU'RE SUPPOSED TO BE FLYING TO FIJI!"

"What the fu—"

But my words were cut off by the sound of Lila's ringtone. Charlie's name appeared across Lila's phone. She quickly pressed answer, and her best friend's face filled the screen. Charlie's eyes were bloodshot and it was clear she'd been crying.

"You're joking right? You're not in Europe! You've got to be joking."

"Um, nope." Lila caught my eye and frowned. "We're definitely in the Munich airport right now, waiting at our gate for a flight to Greece."

I raked my hands through my hair. *Shit.* I knew this stupid surprise trip was a horrible idea.

"No, no, no. I can't believe this."

"It's alright." Lila glanced at me but tried to keep any anxiety out of her voice for Charlie's sake. "What do you think happened?" she asked.

"The travel agent must have gotten it mixed up," Charlie said, choking on a small sob as she rambled on about where it could have gone wrong.

Lila's pale face and panicked expression had vanished. Talking to Charlie had flipped a switch. Now, she looked calm, focused, ready to problem-solve. I knew Lila must have it together—she owned a business, after all—but watching her transform like that in real time was almost uncanny. You would have thought Lila was in on the plan all along, considering how coolly she listened to Charlie's explanation, nodding along slowly.

While they talked, I got out my own phone and accepted

any international charges. Almost immediately after getting service, Oliver's name flashed across my screen. I debated pressing the red button. He knew how much I hated video calls. But I answered and held the phone up.

Oliver flashed his ever-present smile at me. He already had a tan from being in Fiji for two seconds.

"Europe? Are you serious?" His head fell back with laughter. I could see Charlie in the background of his video and glanced back at Lila's screen.

This wasn't the reunion I'd pictured.

"—I switched the locations at the last minute," Charlie said. "I knew you always wanted to go to Greece, so that's why I picked it originally, but then I thought that was a selfish thing to do, to bring you on *your* dream trip for *my* bachelorette party. So I rebooked it to Fiji instead. The boutique hotel we booked through had a sister location here. I figured we could go to Greece on our own another time. To celebrate a business milestone, or something. God—I'm so stupid. The travel agent must have forgotten to rebook you and Harrison, since your reservations were made separately and for a day later. I should have called her to double-check."

Lila glanced at me with an expression that ever so subtly said, *Oh shit.*

"Let me say hi," Oliver said through my phone.

"Is now really the time?" I glared at him.

"Come on," he begged.

I held up the call so that he could wave at Lila. She gave him a weak smile in return.

"It's alright," she said, once Charlie came up for air.

"No, it's not," Charlie cried. "Fiji is a thirty-hour flight from Munich. I already looked it up. And they don't have anything available until tomorrow night. If you tried to make it here, you'd only get here for the last day."

Oliver whistled. "Sounds like you two are stuck there."

Charlie whipped her head around and called to Oliver, off screen. "Are you helping right now?" she demanded.

Oliver held a hand up and yelled an apology before walking a little further away from the upset bride-to-be.

"Say hi to Nathan," he said before pointing the camera at his brother. Nathan sat slouched, his head resting heavily in one hand. Without asking, I could tell he'd been trying to talk Charlie off a ledge; likely for hours at this point.

"Hey," I said. "Having fun?"

"Loads." The tiniest trace of a smile formed on his lips. "You?"

"The time of my life."

"Get a room, you two. I swear, you'd talk for hours if I let you," Oliver said, laughing and turning the phone away from Nathan. "Be honest, H. Did you plan all this just to get some alone time with Lila?"

Lila jerked around in her seat just as I scowled and said, "Of course not."

She snorted. "Right. Spending time with me is the absolute last thing Harrison would ever volunteer to do."

I winced. But before I could say that I didn't mean it like that, Lila had already turned her attention back to her call with Charlie.

Oliver chuckled and I wished I could reach through the screen and smack his shoulder. "Why do you always have to say the wrong thing around her?" he asked, this time more quietly.

"That's it. I'm hanging up," I hissed. He stuck out his tongue right before I pressed the *End Call* button.

"I just feel so awful about all this," Charlie continued to apologize. "You could just enjoy Greece. You should still have your hotel and whole itinerary booked since the travel agent didn't change you over to this trip. I'm so sorry." She sniffed. "Or I could just get you booked back to Denver if you'd rather do that."

"That would be great," I said at the same time Lila said, "Absolutely not."

She glared at me and held her chin high. "One sec, Char," she said before muting the call and holding the phone camera away from us.

"I haven't had a vacation in *years*. I am not about to get on a plane back to Denver when I'm in freaking Europe right now."

"But—" I started.

"No. I've never been to Europe. Have you? How could we just turn around when we're already here? I worked my ass off these past few weeks to take this trip. I'm not letting that all go to waste."

Even as she made one solid point after another, I still couldn't picture us continuing on.

"Look," I said, "I only came on this trip in the first place because Oliver begged me to, and I didn't want things to be weird with Nathan. Now that we're on our own, what's the point?"

Her lips parted slightly before a maniacal laugh bubbled to the surface. "What's the point? *What's the point?* You can't be serious."

She regarded me with such contempt that I couldn't bring myself to admit that I was, in fact, serious.

"Can't you ever just enjoy anything, Harrison?" she prodded.

She couldn't have known it, but that hit me right in the chest. Enjoyment felt too much like vulnerability to me. Much like excitement, or humor, or anything really.

Which is maybe why I'd glommed onto Oliver for all these

years. Of course, my loyalty to him ran deep, but it was more than that. Having a best friend who loved life so much was almost enough to make my own less miserable. I had the luxury of standing in the background, pretending I was above it all, because Oliver was always a step ahead and dragging me along. I still got to experience everything, albeit at half-mast.

But without that crutch I couldn't even stand straight.

Rubbing my forehead with my left hand, I let out a deep sigh.

"I'm tired, Lila. I just want to go home."

"Fine," she said easily. Too easily. "Then ask Charlie to book you on the next flight back."

"Can't you ask her to book us *both* on a flight home?"

All the water in the Mediterranean Sea couldn't extinguish the fire in Lila's eyes.

"I'm getting on that flight to Santorini."

My eyebrows shot up as I looked from her to the gate. One worker sifted through papers while the other prepared the microphone to announce the start of the boarding process.

Frustration surged through me as I looked back at my accidental travel companion.

"I'm not letting you go by yourself," I said.

"Well, you can't stop me." She stood and straightened her sweatshirt. "I *am* going on this trip, Harrison."

I tipped my head back and groaned. There was no way I was getting on that plane, knowing no one from our group would be waiting for us when we landed. But there was also no way I was letting Lila out of my sight.

"I'm not just going to leave you in a foreign country by yourself."

She arched a brow and tilted her head toward the waiting plane. "Then you really only have one option."

NINE

Lila

WE SAT SIDE BY SIDE ON A HALF-EMPTY SHUTTLE BUS, OUR knees brushing with every jolt. Charlie had forwarded us the old Santorini itinerary from the travel agency, and when we landed, we'd expected a private ride to be there to take us to our accommodations. But after twenty minutes waiting at ground transportation, no one came. Harrison insisted that it seemed a little strange, but I had already researched the bus options and found us the quickest way into town. We were staying in the cliffside city of Fira, which was on the western edge of Santorini.

Our flight in had been quiet.

Harrison had finally, very begrudgingly, agreed to join me. You would have thought I was asking him to help clean farm stalls for the week or plan a family funeral, not jet-set off to a Greek island. I think it helped my case that boarding began almost immediately after I had insisted on going, giving him quite literally seconds to make a decision.

Now he sat next to me, all big and looming, with a permanent glower on his face.

Outside the window, a rocky landscape whizzed by, dotted with scrubby vegetation and whitewashed buildings with blue shutters. As the bus climbed higher, I caught a glimpse of the sparkling dark blue water in the distance.

I elbowed Harrison,

"Look, the water!"

He leaned over me to look for two seconds before saying, "Yep," and setting his dark eyes straight ahead again. If this was going to be his attitude the entire time, I almost wished he hadn't insisted on going with me.

I turned away from him to lean my head against the windowsill. My eyes drooped ever so slightly. Despite not wanting to miss a thing, the exceedingly long travel day and the whole trip switch dilemma had caught up with me. My whole body both ached with exhaustion and burned with anticipation simultaneously.

The thought of missing Charlie's bachelorette trip did sting, but I'd already promised her we'd make up for it another time. It wasn't like this was the only chance we'd ever get to travel together. The fact that Skylar and Ben were there did spark the tiniest, microscopic pang of jealousy. Irrational, I knew, but it was hard to watch your best friend grow this whole new community of people that didn't include you. I mean sure, they were always great and welcoming toward me, but soon they'd be making plans for only the four of them, leaving me with empty weekends. A bitter, illogical part of me wondered if having a significant other would somehow turn those hypothetical plans into six instead of four.

And after this trip? They'd have all these core memories together—inside jokes I'd never be a part of, even though they'd try to tell me the story over dinner. They'd laugh and reminisce, all the while telling me, "You just had to be there."

And what did I have? Harrison. The thought of us making any inside jokes on this trip was so ludicrous it was laughable.

"I can't wait to see the caldera," I said, my forehead now fully pressed against the glass.

"The what?" Harrison asked.

His bulking frame pressed against mine in our cramped seats was my only hint that this was reality and not some bizarre fever dream. Because Greece was a dream; a bucket list item of mine, in fact. And now I was finally here, but with a virtual stranger. Actually, worse than a stranger. An acquaintance who barely even tolerated me.

After this shocking change of events, who knew where our truce stood? He didn't seem pleased about the new circumstances, but at least he wasn't being openly hostile. Perhaps a little inadvertently hostile, but that seemed to just be his personality.

Regardless, Harrison Porter would not ruin a single second of this trip for me. If he thought I was too bubbly on a normal day, he was in for a treat. Vacation Lila was a whole different breed. I wasn't about to dim any bit of my glimmer just so he could look cool—or whatever the hell his motive was for always being so salty and disagreeable.

"The caldera," I repeated brightly. "It's basically this giant circle depression that forms after a volcanic eruption. I read about it in a travel guide. Santorini is the only inhabited caldera in the world. That's why some people call it Atlantis."

He cocked his head, studying me, but didn't say anything.

"And the food," I said, practically moaning. "I can't wait for the food."

Harrison remained silent and resumed staring straight ahead, not even interested in the views rushing by. Unable to take his weird silence anymore, I elbowed him in the ribs.

"Aren't you even the tiniest bit excited to be here?"

"Not really." He said it so easily. Smacking me in the face would have stung less. My face must have looked all kinds of wounded, because Harrison's brow knit together. He pinched the bridge of his nose and muttered, "Shit."

"It's fine," I said woodenly. If that's where he stood, that's where he stood. I could still have the time of my life while he wasted away in whatever five-star accommodation Charlie and Nathan had originally planned for us.

"I didn't mean it like that. I guess I'm just. . ." His voice trailed off and he shot me a pained look. "I'm stressed, okay? I hate feeling out of control. The surprise trip was bad enough, but now all this?" He waved around, too exasperated to continue the thought.

The cardboard wall I'd crafted to protect myself from Harrison bent easily. I was never very good at having a guard up. Just ask my ex how he was able to manipulate me so easily for all those years. Perhaps I should have learned my lesson. I was sure Harrison's hard demeanor would be back any minute, but he looked so genuinely anxious, it just made me want to help him.

"Anxiety is worrying about a future outcome that you can't control. It doesn't actually serve you at all. Live in the present, be prepared, and deal with things as they come."

A particularly violent bump in the road sent me flying toward the aisle. Harrison caught me easily around the arms and steadied me. "I don't have anxiety."

If that was what he chose to believe, then it wasn't worth arguing over.

The shuttle made an abrupt turn into a parking lot and came to a sputtering stop. I jumped up with enthusiasm that someone else might describe as incomprehensible, considering

I'd just had a twenty-hour travel day. But it was only seven p.m. local time, and the sunset had just started to brush the evening sky.

"Go. Go. Go." I grabbed Harrison's arm and hoisted him up and out of the seat.

"For someone so tiny, you've got a good grip," he said, rubbing his arm where I'd just let go.

"And for someone who looks so fit, you move at a glacial pace," I countered.

He looked back at me, the corner of his lip quirked upward. "You think I look fit?"

Flames burned behind my cheeks. "You know what I meant," I said as we moved down the aisle.

"I think I need you to clarify," Harrison continued, snatching my suitcase from my hands and lugging it behind him. "Did you mean that I'm strong? Attractive, maybe?"

Stepping off the bus felt like the first real stretch I'd taken since leaving my house in Denver.

"Don't let it go to your head," I huffed as I turned around, only to see a playful gleam in Harrison's dark eyes.

Was he. . . was he *flirting* with me? The thought nearly made me pass out. While I was sure Harrison had no issues attracting women—though I really didn't want to dwell on that—I had always assumed the word 'flirting' wasn't in his vocabulary.

I had pictured him disarming a woman with a withering glare, leaving her weak-kneed as the two of them disappeared into the night for some hate-fueled, intense sexual encounter that in no way resembled real intimacy. No, Harrison definitely didn't flirt. And I was grateful for that, because that meant I'd never have to put my weak resolve to any sort of test.

I had a pulse, after all.

As if mocking my internal dialogue, Harrison's bicep bulged as he lifted both of our bags and carried them over the rough cobblestones.

"This has to be the most impractical luggage for this terrain." He struggled with my pink rolling suitcase before setting it down again and dragging it along. The wheels didn't glide smoothly over the uneven surface, and it made a loud rattling noise with each step.

"It's not like I knew our destination," I snapped back. "And I can carry it if you're going to be a jerk about it." But when I reached for my suitcase, he snatched it away.

This man was truly insufferable.

"Let's just get to our hotel," I said, pulling up the maps app on my phone. I had downloaded the entire island so I could use it offline. I punched in the saved address Charlie gave us, and turned directly left. "It's only a few hundred feet this way."

"Only a few hundred feet this way" wasn't exactly a short trip when you were with me and I was in a new place. The bus had dropped us at the edge of town, and our first obstacle was a bustling square filled with people waiting in lines for dinner. The aromas wafting through the air were utterly mouthwatering. In one stall, a vendor spun a spigot of savory meat, expertly shaving it off and sliding it into pitas for eager customers. I rarely ate meat, but I would definitely be trying that.

Much to Harrison's dismay, I had to stop and gape at every stall we passed. Every few steps, I paused to check out a menu, or admire a cute trinket in a gift shop. Harrison, on the other hand, kept moving ahead until he eventually looked back, stopped and dropped his head back in frustration. His patience was already worn so thin you could see right through it, but I didn't care.

Instead of rushing to meet up with him, I stepped into the line for the gyros, looking at Harrison and blinking innocently. His exhale was laughably loud as he trudged back the few feet to stand next to me.

"Are you serious? Can't we just get to the hotel first?"

"Let's just get a snack. It's right here."

"This line is going to take forever."

But just as he said it, two people paid and received their food, bringing us only a few people away from the front.

"It's moving fast. Besides," I poked his belly. "Maybe you're hungry too, and that's where all this anger is coming from."

"I'm not angry." He let go of my suitcase and folded his arms. "I'm just exhausted."

"All the more reason to get this now while we're still standing. First rule of avoiding jet lag, don't crash until you have to."

"I feel like you're just making that up on the spot." But he didn't move out of line, and he didn't protest further once he eyed someone walking away with a stuffed pita in hand.

"So what if I am? Doesn't make it a bad rule."

"Sorry I'm not built with more energy than a wind-up toy."

"If you think I'm not going to be insufferably enthusiastic the entire time we're here, you are sorely mistaken."

"You've got the insufferable part right," he muttered.

My cheeks reddened as I whipped around to glare at him. "Was it my imagination or did we forge a little truce on the flight over here?" I demanded.

Harrison's eyes widened, clearly not expecting me to turn on a dime like that.

"We're good," he said gruffly. It took everything in me not to reach out and strangle him. If this was good, I would hate to see what his bad side looked like.

"You insisted on following me here," I continued. Maybe it was the long travel day talking, or perhaps the emptiness in my stomach, but either way, I couldn't just brush off his negative attitude and grating comments anymore.

"No, you insisted on going and I wasn't going to leave you by yourself," he argued.

"Like I said. *You* insisted on following me here," I said again.

He blew out a breath like I was the most exhausting person on the planet. *Me!* He truly had zero idea how unpalatable he was. Actually, he likely did, he just didn't give a flying shit about it.

"You are not ruining this trip for me, okay? We can either go about each day and do our separate things, or you can put on a fake smile and be civil for four goddamn days of your life. We are on vacation, on a trip some can only dream about. Buck up and stop acting like you're being dragged to a prison sentence, or something. You're coming across like an entitled ass."

He regarded me with raised eyebrows, the only thing that gave away his surprise. But instead of saying something snarky in response, he simply nodded and said, "You got it, boss."

I snapped my fingers. "Boss. That's the perfect way to look at me on this trip. Think of me as your champion of fun. Your leader of good times. You, Harrison Porter, are about to have more fun than you could even imagine. All you have to do is follow me and be just the teeniest bit open-minded, got it?"

"Whatever you say."

Ten minutes later, we were each clutching our own pitas. Harrison wasted zero time sinking his teeth into his for a huge bite.

"Wait, let's take a picture." With my free hand, I struggled with the zipper on my bag for a second before prying it open and carefully pulling out my phone.

"Are you serious?" He asked, still chewing.

"For the memories," I insisted. "It's our first meal in Greece."

"And you want a picture of this?" He eyed himself before looking down at me. "What are you even going to do with a picture of the two of us?"

My eyes fought not to roll into the back of my head. Why did he insist on making everything so difficult? But I decided not to push him any further tonight.

I lifted my phone and smiled, snapping a quick selfie that didn't include Harrison before dropping my phone back into my bag and diving into my sandwich. We devoured them in silence, clearly a lot more ravenous than we originally thought.

Harrison's eyes were practically red from exhaustion and I felt a little guilty for dragging him around. But we were in Santorini, for crying out loud! How could I not savor every second we were here, even if we were basically dead on our feet?

"Alright, onward," I instructed.

"No more pitstops." Harrison fell into step next to me, still lugging around our suitcases.

We walked down a narrow alley. After some steps up, I caught a glimpse of the shimmering blue sea just beyond. Despite the allure of the winding alleyways that we passed, filled with incredible shops and charming restaurants, I quickened my pace, eager to reach the view that waited for us, just out of sight.

Then, we were there. I laid my hands on the protective stone wall that separated me from the cliffside.

"Holy crap," I whispered, letting the scene wash over me.

Stark white and blue buildings clung to the edge of the cliff, cascading into the mesmerizing depths of the sea below. It was even more breathtaking than any picture I had seen. Glancing to my right, I marveled at the island curling gracefully around us. I felt immediately overwhelmed, in the best way possible—like there were so many amazing things to see and do and explore, and I couldn't wait to just dive into all of them.

"This is incredible. Isn't this incredible?" I turned to Harrison, who, despite always having to be the most unimpressed person in every room, looked just as mesmerized by the view as I was.

"It's alright," he said, that playfulness back in his tone.

When I shoved his chest, his lip curved up into an actual smile for a moment before he corrected it back to neutral. He could try to play it cool all he wanted, but I could tell he was captivated too.

"I can't believe we get to stay somewhere down there." I peeked over the edge.

"Come on. Let's go find it," he said.

But I made no move to leave. Instead, I kept my eyes glued to the horizon.

"Let's stay a few more minutes."

Although the sun had already dipped below the water, colors still blotted the night sky. The first stars began to emerge, barely visible against the deepening backdrop.

"I'm sure the view is good from the hotel," Harrison pointed out, but he joined me, leaning against the wall without any real protest.

"I know. I just want to take it in for a second."

The air felt so good here, not like the dryness in Colorado. It wrapped around me, breathing life back into my body. It was the perfect temperature. I could wear either a sweatshirt or a tank top and still be comfortable. I pulled my hoodie off, desperate to feel more of the air directly on my skin.

Standing there, shoulder to shoulder with Harrison, wasn't as strange as I'd expected it to be. Traveling somewhere so completely different than what you're used to almost makes you feel like you're in an alternate universe, and with each passing minute, our old reality seemed to drift further away. In this universe, maybe Harrison didn't hate me. Maybe here, we could be friends. A girl could dream, right?

"Let's go find our hotel." I clapped my hands.

"Finally."

The address in our itinerary wasn't far at all from where we lingered. Just a few turns, and a staircase that descended the cliffside.

The boutique hotel was jaw-droppingly beautiful, and screamed 'quiet luxury.' Every surface was spotless, and the furniture was crisp and leather. The lobby was lined with dim ceiling lights that gave off the perfect relaxing ambiance. The back wall of the lobby was floor to ceiling glass windows, overlooking a stunning deck with views of the water. I nearly gasped when I saw the infinity pool. It took everything in me not to rush right out to it and jump in, fully clothed.

I turned to Harrison, and gave him a look of disbelief. He just shrugged as if he had arrived at a roadside motel instead of a five-star luxury resort.

The front desk attendant, who was just as striking as the rest of the hotel, waved us over with a warm smile.

"Hello," she said with a subtle accent. "Welcome to Hotel Caldera. Do you have a reservation?"

"Yes. It should be under Shaw," I said as I stepped up to the counter and gave Nathan's last name.

"Of course. One moment while I look that up." Her red manicured fingers typed away at the keyboard in front of her while her expression grew confused.

"Shaw, you said?"

"Yes," I answered, growing wary. Charlie had been adamant that, since the travel agent hadn't rebooked our flights, the rest of our itinerary should have remained the same too. "S. H. A. W." I spelled it out while Harrison shifted next to me, stroking his jaw.

"I see a reservation for five rooms, but it was canceled last week," she said apologetically.

"Shit," Harrison said next to me. "I told you it was weird that no one came to pick us up."

My smile remained frozen in place as I ignored him. "Is there any way to get two of the rooms back? You see, there was a bit of a mix up with the plans. We need a place to stay until Sunday."

She frowned and clicked around. "I'm sorry, but we're almost completely booked. We can't do two rooms."

My face fell before she continued. "We do, however, have one of our king suites available. It has a private plunge pool."

Breathing a sigh of relief, I turned to Harrison with a look that said, *see? Everything works out.*

"Perfect. We'll take that one."

"One bed?" Harrison raised an eyebrow. "Isn't that the beginning of every bad romance novel?"

"I think you mean beginning of every *beloved* romance novel," I said, as the clerk typed away. "You read a few pages of my book on the plane and suddenly you're an expert?"

He shrugged but didn't look sheepish. "I'm just saying. I'm not sleeping on the floor."

"We're adults. We can build a pillow wall if we need to."

"Alright, I just need a credit card for the room," the hotel agent continued.

I fished around for mine. "What's the price?"

When she told me the figure, my heart nearly sprang straight out of my chest.

TEN

Harrison

"THIS IS BETTER. WAY BETTER, ACTUALLY." LILA WAVED HER arms in a frenzy as she led us back up the cliffside. "Who needs to stay in one of those fancy hotels? They're total tourist traps. Real travelers don't stay in those over-the-top luxury rooms."

"You were fine with the luxury room when you thought Nathan's endless pockets were paying for it," I said, hurrying to keep pace with her. For someone with such short legs, Lila could really move.

"That was before I knew how much it cost," she said, cheeks flushed. "That's basically robbery."

As soon as we'd heard the price, Lila had zipped her bag shut and laughed awkwardly before telling the front desk agent that we wouldn't be needing the room after all.

I had suggested we call Charlie to sort it out, but Lila wouldn't even consider it. It had been hours since we'd spoken, and it was already the middle of the night in Fiji. Lila had refused to be a burden on her friend, insisting she would find a solution.

I'd gratefully let her take charge. Being in an unfamiliar city in a different country with nowhere to stay should have sent me spiraling, but watching Lila handle everything was both fascinating and oddly calming. For all the things I had given her crap about, her competency in a crisis certainly wasn't one of them.

After we left the other hotel, Lila undertook a rather impressive mission of problem solving while I stood there, holding the bags. I wished I could say that I was good for more in this situation, but honestly, I was already in way over my head. I hardly traveled and had only been out of the country once, when I was fourteen and my parents had saved up for a road trip. My mom had insisted on going to the Canadian side of Niagara Falls—said it was more exotic, or something like that. The memory made me smile. I had already promised Mom I'd video-call them so she could see some of the views in Greece. She couldn't even fathom I was here when I'd shot her a text from the airport.

Money wasn't something I had an abundance of—either growing up or now. My dad had been working construction my whole life and my mom had a hard time keeping a job because she suffered from chronic migraines. Thankfully, she'd finally found a medication that worked for her. It was expensive, but I'd figured out how to get them on a better insurance plan—after hours of arguing with them about it, of course.

I worried about my parents. They hated accepting help from me, but despite that, I tried to push every spare dollar I made from the shop in their direction. In response, they'd started sending money back. So instead of sending it directly to them, I'd opened a retirement account in their name. My dad was getting older, and he wouldn't be able to work a manual labor job for much longer. It meant that between my meager savings account and trying to make sure my parents were covered, I didn't have a lot for extras. Like, say, a fancy hotel in Santorini.

While Lila was researching a place to stay, I was stressing out about how to broach the subject of money. I had thought this would be an all-expenses paid trip. While I wasn't broke, I didn't have thousands just lying around for fun.

To my immense relief, Lila seemed to be on the same page as me. After a few minutes of searching, she found a modest hotel nearby and presented it for my approval, saving me the awkwardness of admitting I couldn't afford anything nicer. It wasn't luxurious by any means, but it would do the job. And, most importantly, it wouldn't break the bank.

"Those stairs are killer," Lila said when we arrived at the top of the cliff, back at a main road. "I'm glad we aren't staying down there. It'd be, like, a thousand steps anytime you wanted to leave the hotel."

"I think you're exaggerating." I set down her suitcase and adjusted my duffel so the strap wasn't digging into my shoulder blade. At that point, those bags might as well have been my permanent accessories.

Lila's cheeks were flushed as she pulled up her phone again and held it a few inches away from her face to examine the map. The dim glow from the screen cast a soft light over her features in the dark.

"This way." She didn't even wait for me. She glanced up and spotted a gap in traffic, then bolted across the street.

"Hey!" I protested, looking both ways and darting after her. "You can't keep doing that."

"Doing what?" The way she blinked up at me innocently told me she knew exactly what I meant.

"Taking off without warning."

"Maybe you just have to be better at keeping up." She

smiled, and instead of being irritated, I found myself biting hard on the inside of my cheek to keep from smiling.

The other side of the street wasn't the view that was pictured on postcards. I could still make out the dark abyss of the ocean in the distance, but instead of endless white buildings, there was a lot of construction, and no businesses. Lila led us down one of the alleys, checking her phone every few seconds.

"You sure this is the right way?" I asked when we passed another abandoned building.

"Yes," she said confidently, not the least bit fazed. She turned abruptly when we got to a tall copper gate and pushed it open.

Once inside the fence, it was like we were in a different area entirely. A quaint, dimly lit path wound its way between several small white buildings, each with a gated outdoor space and a single chair. In the middle of it all was a modest pool, reflecting the soft glow of the surrounding lights. It might not have been the peak of luxury, but it was a hell of a lot more charming.

An orange cat waltzed right up to us and Lila cooed before dropping to her knees and scratching under its chin. The cat moved on to rubbing against my leg, and I stepped away instinctively.

Lila stood up, looking appalled. "Don't tell me you're afraid of cats," she accused.

"Afraid?" I balked. "I'm not afraid. I'm allergic."

She sighed heavily as if this was some terrible character trait I had just revealed.

"What? I am," I insisted as Lila led us to the only building with an open door. Inside was a small desk, an old computer, and one of those wooden racks that held a bunch of tourist brochures. Stairs at the back of the room, behind the desk, led upstairs and out of sight.

"Hello?" Lila called.

"Ahh, hello. I'll be right down." A friendly voice boomed from above.

A few seconds later a woman, her graying hair swept up into a bun, descended the steps. She wore what looked like a permanent smile, as demonstrated by the faint lines by her eyes and lips.

"I'm Maria," she said in a thick accent, offering her delicate hand to Lila.

Lila shook it. "Lila. And this is Harrison."

"Hello," I said.

"I just made a reservation online." Lila waved her phone. "I hope it went through alright. We're in a bit of a bind. We just got here, and we don't have anywhere to stay."

"I saw it," Maria said, gesturing for us to sit in the chairs on the other side of the desk. "Just in time. I stop reservations at ten so I can go to bed."

"I'm sorry we're keeping you up." Lila sat in one of the seats and I plopped down next to her, relieved that we were about to finally have a bed for the night. This had been the longest day in recent memory.

"Oh, it's no trouble at all. My husband used to stay up and take the later check-ins, but now it's just me." Maria plugged away on the computer as I looked around the modest room. I reached for one of the travel brochures and thumbed it open.

"Where's your husband?" Lila asked in a gentle voice.

"He passed away."

I snapped the brochure shut and bumped Lila's knee with mine so that she could see my dirty look. This woman didn't want to talk about her life to two strangers.

Lila's eyes narrowed when she met my gaze, but she kept her voice soft when she said, "I'm so sorry to hear that."

Maria was still focused on her computer screen and didn't notice our exchange. "That's life. It was a few years ago; I'm just happy to still have this place."

"Your hotel is beautiful," Lila gushed as I shifted in my seat uncomfortably. Small talk with strangers wasn't my strength.

"Thank you." Maria looked up from the computer to smile at the both of us. "We bought the place thirty years ago."

"Wow," Lila breathed. "It's great. You should be proud."

Maria nodded, her eyes glassy as she looked around herself. "I am. This area wasn't a big one for tourists, but now all the big companies are coming in and building hotels around us. So much construction."

"And your hotel will stand out because it's long-established and family owned," Lila said.

Maria sighed. "I hope so."

"It will," Lila insisted.

Lila spoke to Maria like she knew something I didn't. We hadn't even seen the inside of our room yet and Lila was already singing this hotel's praises. Her desire to convince a total stranger that they had something special baffled me. It struck me that, if I had been here alone, I likely would have taken the room key from Maria without exchanging more than three words.

"Once I get you set up, I'll give you some ideas for things to do. Do you have any plans for your trip?" Maria asked as Lila took the brochure from my hands and opened it up.

"I guess not," she said. "We had this whole itinerary with friends—it's a long story—but we're on our own now."

It struck me again how odd it was that we were here. I had

hardly ever been alone with Lila, and now we were on this trip together, checking into a room and figuring out travel plans. I was almost convinced that, when I finally went to bed after being awake for nearly twenty-four hours, I'd wake up to find that this was all an exhaustion-induced hallucination.

"Oh," Maria looked surprised when she saw our booking. "I have you two in the shared room. Usually, couples prefer a private room. Are you sure I can't move you?"

"We aren't a couple," Lila said at the same time I said, "We're not together."

We looked at each other quickly before looking back at Maria. "We also don't have a giant budget for this trip," Lila added, before leaning into me and whispering. "The shared room was a third of the price."

"I don't mind sharing," I chimed in. I had never stayed in a hostel myself, but Oliver had stayed in a bunch during snowboarding trips. They were probably livelier than my usual antisocial preferences, but I had earplugs.

"If you're sure." Maria eyed us both, not looking convinced. "Alright, then. Passports please." We handed them over while she continued the rest of the check-in process. Once she explained that our room would be a right turn out of the office and down at the end of the property, she handed each of us a key before spreading out a map on her desk. She uncapped a pen and circled the hotel.

"Here's where we are. Just across the main road is the heart of Santorini. I imagine you'll want to explore that area quite a bit." She circled a second spot on the map. "You must eat here. There will be a line but it's worth it." She drew another line. "These steps will take you to the water. There's also a gondola you can take back up, or donkeys. But that's a little stinky," she laughed and continued. "I highly recommend the hike to Oia. Time it for sunset, it's perfect over there. Are you planning on renting an ATV?"

Lila bit her lip and tilted her head. "We weren't planning on it. Is that safe?"

Maria shrugged. "Up to you. You'll see a lot of people driving them around. There are a lot of accidents, but if you have any sense, you should be okay. If you do rent one, it's a good way to see the island and some of the beaches."

Lila's eyes lit up at that suggestion, but she still looked uneasy.

"Where should we rent one?" I asked. Maria leaned over the map and circled another spot.

Lila turned to look at me. "*You* want to rent an ATV?"

I shrugged. "How else are we going to see the beaches? I can drive us. I used to have one of those things in high school." That was a partial lie. Oliver and I had a part time job one summer, bailing hay at a farm. The owner had let us drive his around.

Lila still looked uncertain, but ultimately smiled at me gratefully. "If you think it's alright. . ."

Seeing her relief tugged at my chest a little. My taking the reins on this one thing had put her at ease. It really shouldn't have. What had I ever done to earn even the tiniest grain of her trust? Yet I somehow had, and that fact made me sit up a little straighter.

"Breakfast is served from seven to nine in the room next to this one. Please let me know if you have any questions and I'll be happy to answer them."

"Thank you so much, Maria," Lila beamed. "We're so happy to be here."

"I'm happy to have you." Maria chuckled. "Get some sleep. Hopefully you're tired enough that the jet lag won't be a problem."

"It definitely won't be," I said, already knowing I'd pass out as soon as my head hit the pillow.

Lila went to grab her bag, but I snatched it before she could get it. I let her lead the way, following the dim lights illuminating the walkway.

When we arrived at the room, Lila used her old-school key to unlock the doorknob. It wasn't terribly late, so it wasn't likely that anyone we were sharing the room with would be sleeping, but she entered cautiously anyway.

The door opened to a wide, short hallway, with a small table and hooks to the right. On the left was a bathroom. I poked my head in to see a few toiletry bags cluttering the counter, but other than that it was thankfully quite clean. It was also large and covered in white tiles, with two stalls for showers and two stalls for toilets.

"This looks *cozy*," I said under my breath as Lila scurried into the room, a giant smile on her face.

"It's huge," she breathed as we both stepped into the main room. A bunk bed was set against each wall and there was a sofa and chair in the middle of the room. I had never stayed in a shared room like this, but it was much bigger than I had pictured it. I couldn't help but notice the men's shoes that were lined up next to two of the bottom beds as we walked to the only empty bunk.

"I'll take the bottom," I said, slinging my bag onto the lower bunk, one that would barely fit my six-foot-two frame.

Lila folded her arms. "Why do you automatically get dibs?"

"Are you serious?"

"What if I wanted it?" she continued.

"We aren't five years old, arguing about which bunk we want to sleep in," I said.

She snorted, a soft laugh escaping her rosy lips. "Aren't

we? And I've never had a sibling before. This fight is one I've always dreamed about having."

"If you had a sibling, or watched any movie ever, you'd know that the top bunk is the one people argue over. No one wants the bottom."

"Then why do you want it?"

I groaned. My severe lack of sleep was getting to me. It was almost as if she knew I was at my wit's end, and just wanted to mess with me.

"I don't give a fuck which bed I'm sleeping on, okay? But see that?" I pointed to the men's shoes by the other beds. "We're sharing this room with other guys. I'm sure it's fine, but I'd rather be safe than sorry. The top is less exposed. I'm taking the bottom bunk, got it?"

Her smile faltered just a little as she took in my serious expression. "Wow." She bit her lip before nodding and placing her small shoulder bag on the top bunk. "That's actually kind of sweet."

"Don't go reading anything into it." The last thing I needed was Lila giving me those green puppy-dog eyes.

"Relax, Harrison." She sighed. "I would never be stupid enough to think that you were actually going soft on me."

I tensed at the double-entendre in her words. She obviously heard it at the same time, because she immediately burst out laughing.

"Actually, I guess you're technically always *soft* around me." She snorted. "In fact, I think there's probably no one in the world who makes you softer than I do."

She continued her giggle-fit as I glared, taking a deep breath through my nose.

"Are you done?" I asked. Apparently, a long travel day and lack of sleep resulted in a punch drunk, slap-happy Lila.

Maybe I should find her adorable. Objectively, she was.

She literally gave cartoon character energy. But I just couldn't handle it. I needed to change, brush my teeth, and crash as soon as humanly possible.

"You're never any fun," she said, pouting. Thankfully, she unzipped her suitcase and started rummaging through it. I took that as my cue to grab a change of clothes and my toiletry bag out of my duffel and head to the bathroom. While the small twin-size bed was calling my name, the control-freak germaphobe in me absolutely needed to shower the airplane smell off of me first.

This day felt like an entire week.

The shower pressure was weak, but the water was hot. I let it run over me, allowing my shoulders to deflate for the first time since I'd left for the Denver airport an eternity ago. It was now Wednesday night, and we would leave for home Monday morning. That meant this accidental solo trip with Lila would only last four days.

Four whole days.

While that amount of time seemed so short in theory, something told me those days would drag on just like today had. Not even in a bad way, necessarily; it was just the truth.

I'd told Lila I'd be more open-minded on this trip, and while it wouldn't be easy for me, I had meant it. I didn't want to be the asshole who ruined this experience for her. She was a nice girl, and it was time I started treating her with a hell of a lot more respect and decency. I didn't know how to enjoy a vacation, and I certainly didn't know how to enjoy one with a girl I hardly knew, much less one who was also my total opposite. But damnit, I was going to try.

Before I could get too lost in my thoughts, the shower in the stall next to mine turned on. Soft humming filled my ears, and I jerked my attention to the divider that was just barely high enough to block the sight from next door.

"Lila? What the hell are you doing?"

"Um, showering?" she said it in a tone that implied I was being an idiot.

"You couldn't wait until I was finished?" I bit out.

Her laugh was melodic, mixing with the sound of the steady stream of her shower. "There are two showers, Harrison, and I wanted to refresh myself just as badly as you did. Why should I have to wait?"

The subtle scent of her floral shampoo wafted over to my side and made my nostrils flare. I could hear her next to me as she lathered her hair—or was it her body?

Suddenly I was all too aware that a very naked Lila was just a few feet away from me, separated only by a flimsy plastic divider. I bit down on my lip and closed my eyes, trying to get a clear head.

As blood rushed to my dick, I looked down and realized that she had been wrong earlier. I was definitely *not* always soft around her.

Shit. I'd have to chalk this up to exhaustion. I wasn't thinking straight.

I avoided biting out a groan as she continued to shower obliviously next to me.

"Not a shower singer, huh?" she asked in that sing-song voice I was so used to by this point I could pick it out in any crowd.

"Nope," I grunted, trying everything to hide my internal battle from her. If she knew she had affected me this way, I'd never live it down. Suddenly I was eternally grateful that we wouldn't be living out the one-bed trope. Earlier today I would have sworn up and down that I could share a bed with this woman without batting an eye. But now. . . now I wasn't so sure.

But I couldn't allow there to be confusion. I quickly

switched off the shower and toweled dry. I needed to get the hell out of there and back into the room, where I could breathe and think more clearly. Lila was a beautiful woman, there was no question about that. My body had just been thrown off because she was literally naked right next to me. It didn't mean more than that.

Because one thing was for sure: Lila was undoubtedly, indisputably, *not* my type.

ELEVEN

Lila

"Charlie, it's seriously fine. Don't even worry about it."

"Are you sure? We can get you a reservation someplace else. I feel terrible." The video shook as she threw on her sunglasses. I saw a flash of a stunning turquoise pool behind her as she readjusted on a chaise lounge.

"I'm positive. The woman that owns this place is so sweet; she's already given us a million recommendations. And you know me, I love to support a small, family-owned business. Seriously, I want to stay."

When I woke up this morning, just after seven a.m. local time, I removed my sleep mask to find that I'd already received several texts from Charlie instructing me to call her immediately. The only message I'd sent her last night told her there had been a slight change of plans, but we'd figured it all out. She still panicked, though.

I'd padded out of the room quietly, careful not to wake Harrison or the other sleeping forms in their beds. For being stuck in a room with strangers, there was surprisingly little snoring—either that, or I'd been too tired to notice.

Now, I sat on the pool deck, watching the sun rise over the horizon. It was official: you definitely didn't need to be at some fancy hotel to appreciate the beauty of this place.

"Is that Lila?" I heard a woman say before Skylar poked her head onto the screen. "Hi." She waved at me and smiled.

"Hey." I smiled back, ignoring the dull ache of jealousy I felt while I heard Skylar say something to Charlie off-camera.

Charlie laughed before saying, "I'll be down in a sec."

For the longest time, it had just been Charlie and me. That's why we'd started a business in the first place: to connect with other women. But through it all, the two of us had always been more like family.

But now here Charlie was, marrying the love of her life, adopting his friends as if they were her own. Even Oliver. He was one of my closest friends, but soon he would be Charlie's new brother. She was growing and expanding her world so much, while I was just the tag-along.

It made me feel a little queasy.

"Is Harrison being an ass? Be honest. I can have Oliver call him and sort him out." Charlie's question pulled me down from my escalating thoughts.

"He's fine. I think we have an understanding." I hoped that he would at least attempt to have a good time on this trip. "It's weird being here with just him, though. It feels so intimate to be on vacation with someone, and now here I am with Harrison, of all people." I kept my voice low even though I knew that Harrison was still completely passed out. When I had tiptoed out of the room, he had looked so dead to the world that I had stopped to place a hand over his nose to check for breathing.

"Maybe, after being stuck together for a few days, you two will start a torrid affair," Charlie whispered teasingly.

My lips fell open before I snapped them shut again. "What?" I asked, trying and failing to sound both casual and confused.

Charlie and I told each other *everything*. But I would never admit to her that I felt anything other than total and utter indifference toward Harrison. In fact, I couldn't think of a more embarrassing revelation. Which was why I'd thought my little secret crush was just that—a secret. If I hadn't so much as hinted at the subject to her, the person to whom I told my most embarrassing truths, then I figured no one would ever be the wiser. If a thought was never spoken, did it even truly exist?

"Come on. I know you," she pressed.

I shook my head. "Exactly. You know me. So you'd know that I've never said anything about being interested in *Harrison*."

She waited for a moment, waiting to see if I'd reveal more before letting out a sigh. "I know, but Oliver and I were talking—"

"You were talking with Oliver?" I snapped, now sitting straight up. "Why would you two be talking about Harrison and me?" Something like horrified interest washed over me.

"Well, obviously we were talking about how weird it is that you two ended up all the way over in Greece just by yourselves. Then *I* joked that you'd definitely murder Harrison, or that Harrison wouldn't even last half a day before leaving. But Oliver. . ." Her voice trailed off as she looked behind her.

"Oliver what?" I demanded.

"I don't know. He mentioned that maybe there's something there."

"Oh, and Oliver is the expert on my love life? I can't believe you'd talk about us like that."

At least she had the decency to look guilty.

"Well, you can't deny that Harrison is attractive. You even admitted you thought he was hot—that one night we were out for wine and cheese plates."

"I was tipsy and that was months ago," I said, offended that she'd hold that against me.

"Friends don't forget." Her sheepish smile turned devilish.

"Well, please do me a favor and forget that thought. Absolutely nothing will be happening between Harrison and me, so you and Oliver can drop the subject immediately. I don't even find him attractive anymore," I lied. "How could I, with that attitude of his? It's a total turn-off." Another lie. The part of me that needed to be liked by everyone was the same part that wanted to try just a little harder every time Harrison came at me with a rude comment.

"If you say so." Charlie looked at me over the top of her sunglasses.

I gripped the phone tighter. "I do," I said through clenched teeth. "Can we talk about literally anything else? What amazing Fiji adventure am I missing out on today?"

Charlie smirked, but obliged me by dropping the subject and describing the catamaran they had chartered. We finished chatting, and promised to call every morning with updates.

I set my phone down and picked up my forgotten espresso that I'd gotten from the small breakfast spread earlier. It was ice cold at this point, but I needed something to quell the sickening worry blooming in my chest that everyone was talking about me and Harrison behind our backs. I'm not sure if they saw the idea of us as a joke or some weird science experiment, but either way, I hated it.

My mind raced through every conversation I'd ever had with Charlie or Oliver, desperate to ensure I'd never unintentionally incriminated myself. No one could know about my minor inkling of a crush. The embarrassment would be unbearable.

"Enjoying the view?" I turned to see Maria waving at me as she walked to the small main office.

"Yes!" I called back. "I hope it's alright that I brought my breakfast out here."

"Of course," Maria waved off my comment. "Please enjoy it."

"Thank you." I turned back and pulled out the map she'd marked up for us last night. If anything could take my mind off Charlie's words, it was planning the day ahead. It was still early, but I already knew I wanted to head back into town. I'd hardly had a chance to see anything yet.

Would Harrison want to join me, or would he be bored by the idea of spending a few hours walking around and enjoying the sights? We hadn't explicitly said we'd stick together, but at the same time, I didn't want to start this trip by ditching him if he did want to tag along. Selfishly, I wanted him to come with me. Sure, he was a grouch, but he was kind of warming up to me. Plus, while I felt confident I could have fun in any situation, I preferred to have company. It was likely the reason I was so dead-set on finding a serious boyfriend. It was laughable to think back to my early twenties when I thought I'd be married by now.

"Eh, good morning. Are you our new roommate?" A younger blond guy with a British accent of some sort approached me, followed by two boyish-looking guys with brown hair. They all looked a bit disheveled from sleep.

"Um, possibly," I offered. While I had noticed three of the beds were occupied this morning, I hadn't exactly gone over to inspect what the other inhabitants of the room looked like. "I'm in the shared room over that way."

"I think she is," the shorter of the two brown-haired guys piped up. "She's above the big bloke."

"That would be us," I said.

"I'm Nigel," the shaggy blond said. "And this is Mark and Will."

"How's it going?" They said in unison. They didn't look identical, and one had several inches on the other, but judging by the strong resemblance they had to be brothers.

"Lila," I said, extending my hand and shaking Nigel's.

"Whereabouts are you from, Lily?" Nigel asked as he sat down in the seat next to me while Mark, the shorter one, leaned against the chair. Will stood in the back.

"Um. . . it's Lila, actually. And we're from the U.S."

Nigel brightened. "Eh? I've been there. Only to New York City, though."

"I've actually never been to New York," I said, his friendly smile instantly making me feel comfortable. "We're from Colorado."

"No way. The skiing there is supposed to be great," Will said.

"Oh, it definitely is. Although I wouldn't know much about that personally." Aside from one misguided attempt from Oliver to teach me last winter, I'd never gotten into the sport.

"Are you just here on holiday?" Nigel asked.

"Um, kind of? Yes. I guess we are. We're only here through Sunday."

"You'll be able to see a lot in a few days. We only just got here the other day and we've already done loads. We're down for Mark and Will's birthday."

"Twins?" I guessed.

"Yep," the two said in unison.

"Fraternal, obviously," Mark added.

"Well, happy birthday, then."

"Thanks," they said again before Will added, "We just turned twenty. Turning into old farts."

My smile froze before I burst out laughing. "Right; talk to me when you're approaching twenty-seven."

"You don't look a day over twenty-two." Nigel smiled and winked at me.

"Sure, thanks for trying," I said, still laughing. "I suppose you're twenty as well."

"Nah, I'm only nineteen," Nigel said, grinning.

Infants.

I shifted my posture, hoping my back didn't creak in the process.

"What's on your agenda for the day?" Nigel asked.

"I wanted to head into town soon. We didn't get to see much last night."

"We're about to head that way now. Care to join us?" Nigel sprang to his feet and offered up his hand.

"Oh, um, well. . ." I hesitated, my hand hovering over his. Would Harrison want me to wait for him?

"We can wait a bit, if you need to grab something from the room," Will offered.

"Just let me get my bag."

I could leave Harrison a note if he was still sleeping. It was already almost nine, after all. I had been up for hours at this point and I was itching to get moving. He would understand.

As I entered the room, I quietly approached our bunk bed, noting a lump under the covers. I grabbed my shoulder bag and threw in some sunscreen, my wallet, and a few other necessities. I scanned the shelf by my bed for a pen and paper so I could leave that note.

"What are you doing?"

I nearly jumped out of my skin and whipped around to see Harrison standing behind me, fully awake and dressed for the day. I tried not to stare at the thigh tattoos that poked out of his black cutoff shorts.

"You scared the shit out of me," I accused.

He furrowed his brow. "I've been standing here this whole time."

"I thought you were still asleep." I gestured to his bed. Upon closer inspection, the lump I'd noticed turned out to be just a pillow and a rumpled comforter.

"Nope. I'm up."

"Oh, well. Were you interested in going into town? I know you just woke up, but I met the other guys from our room, and we were all about to head out."

He scowled at me, and I swore I saw a vein bulge in his muscular neck.

"*What?*"

"I said, me and the other guys from our room—"

"No, I heard you the first time. I'm just in disbelief that you'd traipse off with men you don't know in a country you've never been to."

I fought the urge to roll my eyes. When the hell had he become so protective?

"They're hardly *men*. They're basically boys. I felt like a corpse just breathing the same air as them."

"Young men are still men. And you shouldn't just trust them because they seem nice. Haven't you ever seen *Taken?*"

I sighed, knowing he was probably right, but still irritated that he was questioning my judgement. "Yes, I've seen *Taken*. I don't need a lecture."

"You sure? Because I'll give you one."

I waved away his comment. "Do you want to come, too?"

I asked, hopeful. "Because I wasn't sure if you'd want to do your own thing, or—"

He arched a brow and shook his head. "Do our own thing? Lila, no. We're here together. We're sticking together. Got it? No running off on your own. Jesus, I didn't realize that I was at risk of losing you if I took my eyes off you for a second."

"Alright, enough," I said, holding up a hand. "I appreciate the concern and the attempted chivalry, but let's not act like I'm a dog you let loose in your front yard."

To my surprise, a quiet huff of laughter escaped him. "You know what I meant," he said, the tiniest of smiles etched into his features.

"Let's go, then," I said, holding out my arm, elbow bent, gesturing for Harrison to thread his into mine. I'd meant it as a joke, of course, but it still stung a little when he just stared at it before shrugging and moving toward the door.

"Let's go," he said, without turning back.

TWELVE

Lila
———

THE WALK INTO TOWN STOLE MY BREATH AWAY MORE TIMES than I could count. With each step, the view transformed before us, revealing vibrant blue water and cascading white-washed buildings that seemed to glow in the sunlight. The scents of blooming flowers filled the air, and the distant sound of waves lapping against the rocky shore added to the allure.

Every fifteen feet or so, I had to stop and snap a new picture. I couldn't resist. Nigel and the other boys were right alongside me, holding up their phones and gaping at the spectacular views. Harrison, on the other hand, hung back. While he did take one quick picture at the first stop, I could tell he was getting a little irritated. To his credit, though, he didn't make a single snarky comment.

Honestly, after spending more time with our roommates, he was probably thinking twice about how annoying *I* was. Nigel, Mark, and Will were a bundle of energy, and then some. They even asked Harrison to get in a group shot with them while I took it. He said no at first, but when they begged loudly and dramatically, he finally moved beside them, frowning. I giggled when I snapped it.

Had I ever been that energetic? I could hardly remember myself at twenty, and what memories I did have usually involved my ex sucking the joy out of my college experience. Maybe sometimes I had a hard time grappling with the fact that I was still single, but I said a silent prayer that at least I wasn't still with that nightmare of a human.

Everyone we passed on the walk—myself included—was dressed in light blue and white linens. Even though I hadn't known we'd be going to Greece, I had packed a blue and white checkered sundress that felt perfect for wandering the narrow streets of Santorini. Harrison's all-black outfit of a T-shirt, shorts, and Converse stuck out ever so slightly, but it did make him look more like a local than a tourist.

Just on the walk over alone, three different people had approached him speaking Greek. His dark features probably hadn't helped their confusion. Or the fact that he looked like a Greek god. . .

"Go on, you two," Nigel waved at Harrison and me. "Go stand over there for a picture."

"I'm good." Harrison lifted up a hand.

"What? You don't want a picture with your girlfriend and that epic background?" Mark asked.

"We aren't together," I offered weakly, as Harrison cringed. Why that thought unsettled him so much was something I'd never understand.

The boys should have known we weren't together; I'd already mentioned it twice on the walk over here. But they seemed to have the collective short-term memory capacity of a goldfish. Either that, or they really weren't all that interested in conversation.

122 • TRIP SWITCH

"Whether you're together or not, it's silly not to get a picture," Nigel insisted before lightly grabbing me by the shoulders and placing me in front of a short stone wall, with the cliff below descending into the water as a backdrop. He held out his hand for my phone.

I smiled in defeat and gave it to him. Nigel turned around and handed it to Harrison. "If you won't pose for the picture, mate, I'll do it for you. Lily needs something to remember this by."

They also either were convinced my name was Lily or had decided it was a cute nickname. I chose to believe the latter, and had stopped correcting them the second time they called me that.

To my surprise, Harrison pushed my phone away and brushed past Nigel to stand next to me.

"You don't have to," I mumbled, a little embarrassed by the whole display.

"If I let that dingbat near you, he's probably going to try and cop a feel," he whispered.

That broke the tension, and I laughed.

"That's beautiful," Nigel said. "Get closer together. Look like you like each other."

I only came up to Harrison's chest. I went to reach my arm around his waist, but then at the last second, I hesitated, leaving my arm hovering just behind his back. He glanced down at my awkward position before shaking his head and placing an arm around my shoulder, tugging me into his side.

I had never felt my stomach do an actual cartwheel before, but the instant his body pressed against mine I almost lost my composure.

"Smile," Nigel said, with a big grin as if to demonstrate.

I complied, tilting my gaze up to see if Harrison would as

well. While no teeth were shown, the corner of his lip did tilt up. I supposed that was the best I would get.

"Brilliant. That's a good one." Nigel snapped a few more before walking back over and standing next to me. "Now, just a quick one of the two of us."

"Oh, uh."

I smiled instinctively as Nigel leaned into me and snapped a few, strategically angling the phone so Harrison was out of the shot.

"Um, that's a good one," I said when Nigel finally handed me my phone again.

"Something to show our future kids." He winked at me again before crossing the path to join Mark and Will, gawking at one of the vendors.

I chuckled as I scrolled through the photos Nigel had just taken. When my eyes lifted to meet Harrison's, I found him scowling at me.

"You know this isn't some romantic comedy, right? You're not here to meet your future husband and move to Europe on a whim."

"Are you jealous?" I taunted, keeping my voice confident even though my whole body quivered at the thought.

His frown deepened. "Not even close. I'm just reminding you that dipshit over there is not a viable option."

"Be serious," I snorted. "I feel more like I'm chaperoning a high school field trip than meeting the love of my life."

"Well, knowing you—"

"I'm a romantic, not delusional." I shoved his chest and the deep lines between his eyebrows finally softened. "Do you want to see the picture or not?" I held up one of the shots of the two of us and he studied it.

"That one's getting framed, for sure," he said.

We certainly looked like an odd pair, him with his dark outfit and me with my bright sundress. My smile was almost embarrassingly huge as Harrison smirked nonchalantly next to me.

"I'll send it to Oliver," I said, firing off a text.

Harrison chuckled. "He'll love it."

Almost immediately after I'd sent the text, I had a response.

Now that's an attractive couple.

I clutched my phone to my chest, but it was too late. I knew Harrison had seen it. I didn't know why I was embarrassed, though. Oliver always made jokes like that; I was sure he'd made plenty to Harrison while I wasn't around.

Still, the implication had me blushing so hard I hoped it looked like a sun-kissed glow instead of my obvious unease. But Harrison said nothing, and we resumed wandering the streets.

When we got to the food stand Maria had suggested, we all fell into line. Apparently, Nigel, Mark, and Will had already eaten there, and informed us it was indeed well worth the wait.

When I finally took a bite of the warm sandwich, my eyes closed in pure pleasure.

"This is so freaking delicious," I said, covering my mouth with my hand.

Harrison nodded in agreement, yet remained as aloof as ever. His constant composure left me feeling a little deflated. Why couldn't he ever just let loose?

"Mmmm," I moaned exaggeratedly, leaning closer to Harrison.

"Everything alright?" he asked, brow furrowed as he took another gigantic bite of his pita.

"Is this not the best thing you've ever eaten?" I pressed.

"I'm already planning on coming back a third time," Mark chimed in, and Will agreed.

"It's good," Harrison said, as we all raved. I gave him a pointed look. "What? It's a sandwich. What do you want me to say?"

"Could you be any more bloody serious?" Nigel asked, laughing and nudging me in the ribs. "How do you get on with this guy?"

"You met me five seconds ago. I'm not always serious." Harrison's glower made us all burst into laughter.

"Five seconds, five months, five years, it's all the same, I reckon," Nigel continued.

"It's true," I said. "I've known him nearly a year and I don't think I've ever seen him laugh."

"I laugh," he insisted, although he looked like he barely believed that himself.

To be fair, I'm sure he laughed sometimes. Like maybe once a year, in the safety of his shared living quarters, with only Oliver present as a witness.

Making Harrison laugh felt like a challenge now. One I would likely fail, but a challenge nonetheless.

We continued on, in and out of the winding alleys and stores. There were a few times I held up a souvenir to Harrison to get his opinion, but he would just shoot me a harsh look.

I insisted on stopping at one of the jewelry vendors while Mark, Nigel, and Will moved ahead. I was enthralled by all of the delicate necklaces on silver chains. Many of them held a dainty charm depicting an evil eye with white and blue crystals, a symbol I'd seen everywhere since arriving in Greece. I wanted one to commemorate the trip and this looked perfect.

The shopkeeper appeared next to me, having noticed my

interest in the necklace. "It's to ward off evil spirits, you know."

I smiled as she returned to the counter.

"She's lying. She's just trying to make a sale," Harrison said, leaning against the door frame of the shop. He was already glancing down the narrow street, obviously eager to leave.

My smile fell, but I tried to keep my resolve. "I think I'll get this one." I held it up to my neck and looked at my reflection in one of the many mirrors.

Harrison snorted. "You can't seriously be one of those people who gets taken in by tacky, overpriced trinkets," he said.

My face flushed. I set down the necklace and made a mental note to come back to the shop by myself later.

To Harrison's credit, aside from the occasional snide remark, he followed us around without much of a struggle. I even caught him staring out at the view a few times. Maybe he wasn't a ball of excitement, but he seemed to be warming up nonetheless.

After another hour I finally checked the time.

"It's already past one," I said to Harrison. "Maria mentioned today would be a good day to do the hike to Oia to see the sunset. We should probably get back and get changed if we want to make it there in time."

"You lot are on your own for that," Nigel said.

"Yeah, we did that yesterday and my legs are still on fire," Mark added.

I looked at Harrison, who winced, but didn't say anything against the idea. He would probably do anything if it meant getting away from our new upbeat travel companions.

"I guess this is where we leave you," I said, and waved to the guys.

"We'll see you later tonight, eh?" Nigel nodded. "We can all go out. It'll be fun to have a group."

I glanced at Harrison who gave a subtle shake of his head. "We'll see how we're feeling," I said with a bright smile. I'd pretend to placate Harrison for now, but seeing the nightlife was a must for me. He'd have to suck it up, or let me go alone with our new acquaintances.

We navigated the winding path back to our hotel from memory.

"I can't believe I left you alone for five seconds this morning and you took in a pack of stray puppies," Harrison said.

"They're fun."

"They're *young*," he retorted.

Giggling, I stepped over a particularly large hole in the cobblestone path. "They do make me feel ancient," I admitted. "I never thought I was getting old at twenty-seven, but they've proven me wrong."

"All that energy. I bet they don't even stop back at the room for a nap before their night out."

"Definitely not. They're going to keep it going until the early hours of the morning."

The tension melted away from Harrison as we walked and made casual small talk about the day. Seeing his obvious shift in comfort made me swell with pride, just a little bit. Because despite feeling like Harrison's least favorite person sometimes, it was obvious now that I was in his circle. Whether he admitted it or not, being around me wasn't draining him like being around strangers had been. And that felt good.

As soon as we stepped through the archway of the hotel, Maria greeted us with a wave and a warm smile.

"Welcome back. How was town?"

"It was lovely," I said.

Maria approached us, her gauzy top flowing in the breeze, one that was getting increasingly stronger as the day went on.

"I wanted to ask you two something."

"Sure," I said, stopping and feeling Harrison come to a halt directly behind me. He wasn't touching me, but my body could feel his presence all the same.

"I've got three guests arriving today; they just called and were hoping to find a shared room. Only problem is, I only have one bed left in the room you all are in."

Furrowing my brows, I waited for her to continue.

"But I have a couple of open private suites." She gestured to the other side of the small property. "I was hoping I could convince you two to take a different room."

"Oh," I started awkwardly. "We totally would, but you see, we're on a bit of a tight budget. . ."

"It would be at the same cost," Maria added quickly. "You'd be doing me a favor." She winked and smiled again. Why did it somehow feel like she was trying to do *us* a favor, and not the other way around?

"Well, if it's okay with you. . ." I trailed off, glancing up at Harrison.

He shrugged. "Doesn't make a difference to me."

While he said it didn't matter, I knew on the inside he was dying for some privacy.

"Sounds good, then," I said.

"Fantastic." Maria clapped her hands. "You get your things, and I'll get you your new key."

We went back to the shared room and gathered all of our belongings. It didn't take long, since we'd barely had a chance to unpack anything.

Just ten minutes later, Harrison pushed the key into the lock of our new room and turned it before pushing the door open.

The inside was beautiful, all white just like the last one had been, but there was an archway separating the bedroom from a small sitting room that led to the bathroom.

"Well, isn't that something," Harrison said gruffly, dropping his duffle and circling the singular queen-sized bed that was staring us in the face. "Looks like we'll be living out that one-bed trope after all."

THIRTEEN

Harrison

"Could you slow down?" The wind whipped the fabric of my T-shirt around my body as I stopped to catch my breath.

"Could you hurry up?" Lila countered, in an infuriatingly not-out-of-breath voice.

"You're practically sprinting," I argued as I looked up at her small figure, perched on a hill just fifty feet ahead of me.

She tossed her head back and laughed. She had pulled her hair back into a long braid, but several stubborn tendrils had fallen loose around her face. She struggled to keep control of them as the wind increased in intensity.

We were on the edge of a cliff, walking a popular trail between the towns of Fira and Oia, the one Maria had recommended last night. Lila had assured me it would be an easy hike, but after the first thirty minutes, I'd insisted on knowing how long it was. To which she had replied, "About six miles."

Was I a fit guy? Yes. Did I spend more time at the climbing gym than working on my endurance? Also, yes.

Meanwhile, Lila had neglected to mention that she was

apparently a professional trail runner. She zipped along the path like it was some casual stroll, hardly needing to stop for water or oxygen.

"We're from Colorado, Harrison. This should be a piece of cake for you."

"I don't hike that much." I started walking again, looking straight down at my feet to avoid tripping over any loose rocks.

"That's obvious," she said with a laugh before sighing. "Would you look at this view? It's incredible."

"I can't look anywhere except my goddamn feet, or I'll slip off the side of this cliff."

"Come up here, then, and take a second to look."

Taking a few more strides, I stopped where she stood. I took off the worn baseball cap I was wearing before fanning myself twice and placing it on my head backwards.

"Damn," I breathed. Trying to play it cool was too much trouble when I was already physically exhausted. Plus, she was right. This was arguably the coolest view I had ever seen in my entire life. Crossing my arms, I leaned back on my hip, scanning the ocean that lapped at the cliff's edge. To my left I could see Fira in the distance, and to my right, I could just make out a smaller city.

"I'm sure Fiji would have been amazing, but there's nowhere I'd rather be right now," Lila said.

"Same." I found myself agreeing too quickly to take it back. Lila looked over at me and I briefly met her eye for a second before dropping my gaze. "I'm sure that group is partying and being obnoxious. I'm glad not to be a part of it," I added.

Lila let out an exasperated sigh, before turning on her heel and marching away from me.

"Wait up," I called out, hurrying to scramble behind her.

Lila twisted around without warning and glared up at me. "Why do you always do that?" she demanded.

"Do what?" I seriously didn't have a clue what she was talking about.

"Act like you don't care. About anything." She lifted her arm and pointed to the expansive view. "You couldn't even enjoy this for five seconds before belittling it. Why do you always do that? You told me you would try, and I expect you to keep your word."

My mouth parted slightly, and I licked my bottom lip. Lila was growing fiercer by the second. Sure, she'd always shot back with snark to match mine before, but this felt different— raw, unfiltered. She was genuinely done with me, and she wasn't about to hold back. It was just us two out here, and as temporary as that was, in this moment it was real.

"I don't know." I shrugged, but judging by the glare she gave me, it wasn't good enough. I dragged a hand across my face. "I'm sorry. I've always been like this. I can't even help myself."

Her eyes softened at my distraught tone. As much as I didn't want to let my guard down, I knew I couldn't keep interacting with her in these close quarters without chilling out a little bit. It was exhausting, always pretending to be above everything. Usually, Oliver was the only person I trusted enough to let in, even just a little. But now, out on this trip, and completely outside my comfort zone, I needed to give this girl at least an inch.

"It's a beautiful view," I said again, looking back at the ocean. "I meant it the first time. There's nowhere I'd rather be. I'm not even thinking about anything else right now, other than how surreal this all is."

Lila looked me up and down. Despite her short stature, I felt small under her gaze.

"Good," she finally said. "Now let's get to the end of this hike and get a well-deserved drink. Because if you don't loosen the hell up on your own, I'm going to do it for you."

I nodded and that seemed to appease her. Instead of stalking away again, she put her hands on her hips and gazed out at the water.

I pulled out my phone to check the time. "Hey, mind if I do something real quick?"

Lila narrowed her eyes and a skeptical glint appeared in them. But she ultimately shrugged and said, "Sure."

I pressed the green call button and let it ring a few times before the call was picked up and my mom's smile came across the screen. She held the phone so close to her face that I couldn't even see anything behind her. Despite being a relatively young mother, she was completely inept with technology.

"Harrison. Is that you?"

"It's me, Ma."

"It's not too expensive to call from Greece, is it? How are you doing? Is it safe there? What's it like?"

I chanced a glance at Lila, who was staring openly at me. When I made eye contact, however, she immediately looked away and suddenly became fascinated by the view.

"You'd love it here. I just wanted to show you something." I pressed the button to flip the camera so she could see the incredible view in front of me.

"Oh Harrison, that's stunning. I can't believe that's real. You're really there? Gabe, come look at this." She called my dad over, and soon both of their faces were pressed close to the camera.

"Why the hell are you holding the phone so close to your face?" he complained before taking it from her and setting it farther back.

"Wow, Harrison, that's just amazing," my mother continued. "I hope you're enjoying every second of that. I'd never think my son would be all the way over in Greece. What day is it there?"

The corner of my lip tugged up. "Same day as it is there, Ma. Just later."

"Wow, you feel a world away. You'll have to come visit when you get home and show me all the pictures."

"I'll plan on it."

"Are you by yourself?" My dad asked. "I thought you said in your text that a friend was with you."

I cringed at the word 'friend' and glanced up again at Lila, who was still looking enthralled by the view.

"Lila is here too, but—"

"Let me say hi," my mom insisted. Before I could even object, Lila was at my side, grinning into the camera.

"Hello, Harrison's parents," she said brightly, because of course she would be the type of girl who loved meeting parents.

"Hi sweetie. Nice to meet you. I hope you're taking care of my son."

"Ma," I scolded, but they both ignored me.

"I'm trying my best to get him to let loose and have a little fun."

My dad snorted. "Good luck with that. He's always been like this."

"We gotta go," I said flatly.

"Wait," Mom said. "I wanted to tell you that you sent way too much money for my birthday last week. I'm sending some back."

I squeezed my eyes shut in frustration. The two of them were too proud for their own good.

"I wanted you to have it. Do something fun. Get yourself something you've been wanting."

Lila side-stepped away from me and the conversation.

"We don't need it," my dad said more sternly.

"Well, I don't want it back."

"You should put it into a savings account," my mom added.

'You should put it into a savings account,' I wanted to argue, but I bit my tongue.

"We can talk about this later," I said. "I gotta go."

"Okay, sweetie. We love you. Have so much fun!"

I waved at my parents before pressing the red end button. When I turned back to face Lila, she was studying me.

"What?" I asked warily, not liking the look in her eyes.

"That was sweet of you to call them," she said.

"I promised I would." I started walking down the trail, knowing she'd keep up with me easily.

"Your dad looks just like you, you know," she said, falling into pace next to me.

"We've been told."

"And you could have called them any time, but you picked in the middle of the hike because. . ."

I blew out a breath. It felt like she was prodding me under a microscope.

"Because I knew my mom would want to see the view."

She smiled and looked straight ahead.

"What?" I demanded.

"Nothing."

"Tell me."

"You do care about something," she said. Then she winked at me before taking a few quick strides, leaving me to follow in her footsteps for the rest of the hike.

FOURTEEN

Harrison

"WE DID IT," LILA SHOUTED VICTORIOUSLY AS I TRAILED A few feet behind her.

"We did it," I repeated, sucking in a breath. Lila looked out at Oia with a smile before holding up her hand.

I straightened up and eyed it. "What?" I asked when she waved in my face.

"What do you mean, what? Ever heard of a high five, genius?"

"Was that really high-five worthy?" I asked, finally catching my breath and arching an eyebrow at her.

"Was a strenuous hike in Greece from one stunning city to another *really high-five worthy*? Are you serious?"

Reluctantly, I held up my hand and she slapped it gleefully. There were few things I hated more than high fives. It was almost impossible to look cool doing them. But I was sick of seeing Lila's disappointed face because I had made yet another blunder, or snide comment. She would enjoy this trip, I would make sure of it, and if her enjoyment meant I had to lower my guard and match even the tiniest iota of her energy, then so be it.

"Let's go explore." She tugged on my arm and dragged me down to the quaint village of Oia, and I felt a little lighter as I let some of my reservations go.

But after we walked through the small town and arrived at the spot that promised the most breathtaking sunset in the world, I'd already had enough.

"This is not happening," I stated as soon as I saw the crowd that had formed at the edge of town. We were shoulder to shoulder with other tourists, some even sitting on the ground as everyone prepared to wait the hour until they could watch the sun set.

Lila stuck her tongue out the side of her mouth as she assessed the situation. While we technically would be able to see the sunset from our spot, we were at least fifteen people back from the railing and wedged in like sardines. Tourists all around us were getting their cameras ready, and even more were piling in behind us.

Up until this point, the crowds had been relatively thin, and I'd been grateful we weren't here in high tourist season. The streets of Santorini weren't nearly as packed as the travel blogs Lila had looked up warned us they could be, but it seemed the sunset at Oia was just too good to pass up. There had to have been at least a hundred people gathered at this small edge of town.

Lila pointed to our right, where a small cobblestone path led away from the heart of town.

"Let's go that way," she suggested.

"What's the point?" I argued, but she was already moving. I caught up to her in a few strides and lightly grabbed her arm, not willing to lose sight of her in this crowd.

"The sunset should be amazing from this entire side of the island. I'm sure we can find someplace better to watch it."

"Everyone wouldn't be standing up there in that crowd if there were a better place to watch it," I pointed out.

She laughed. "Oh, please. One person waits in a spot and then everyone else does. It's human nature. Why should we follow the crowd when there's always a better path?"

"Not always."

"Always, Harrison. Speaking from one fellow business owner to another, we know how to follow our own paths, do we not?"

She had a point there. I had never for a minute thought about joining someone else's shop when I could open my own and have the control. It was what I had been working toward since the day I started my first apprenticeship. It was funny how Lila brought that up—us having that in common. I wasn't something I'd thought about often, but maybe I should have.

The path went through an area that was mostly residential. We passed a few businesses here and there, until it was almost all houses. The noises of the crowd had completely faded away by this point.

"I don't know. It seems pretty dead over here. I feel like we're in someone's back alley," I said, wishing she'd just give it up and turn around.

"There," she said excitedly, pointing to what looked like a resort hotel perched right up on the edge of the cliff. The pool deck had the perfect view of the ocean and the lowering sun. A few people sat in loungers by the pool, but it was pretty empty otherwise.

"That's a private hotel," I insisted. "We can't just go in."

Lila ignored me. "I'm going to ask."

"Lila," I hissed. But it was too late, she was already ambling toward the entrance of the pool deck. I followed her, muttering under my breath about what a pointless idea this was.

By the time I reached her, she was already talking with a smiling woman at a host stand.

"Great, thank you so much," Lila said cheerily, before turning to me. "Let's get those seats over there."

I couldn't hide the surprise on my face. "We can stay?" I asked. This place felt too good to be true. It was only a fifteen-minute walk from that crowded cliffside and had an even better view.

"Yep. She just asked that we buy something from the bar, which isn't a problem for me because I'm starving. And you look like you could use a drink."

Drinking didn't loosen me up in the ways it did for other people. I always had control over myself. Always. But I didn't argue with her.

"Here, you sit." Lila practically pushed me into a chair. "I'll go order for us. Any preferences?"

Before I could say anything, she gave me a thumbs-up. "Great. I'll be right back."

With that, she sauntered over to the tiki bar behind the pool, and I was left by myself.

Clenching and unclenching my fists, I tried to ignore the mild discomfort I felt. What the hell was even wrong with me? I was just sitting here, like every other tourist watching the sunset. A group still in the pool behind me laughed loudly, and the sound caused me to bristle. Slumping down further in my chair, I tapped my foot anxiously waiting for Lila to return.

"Here you go." Her bright voice sounded just two seconds before a neon blue drink was placed in front of my face.

I recoiled at the sight of it, and did not pick it up.

She narrowed her eyes and hurt flashed across her face.

"What's wrong?" she asked.

"I can't drink that."

"Why not?" she pressed, sitting down in the seat next to mine and sipping her own bright blue cocktail. "It's delicious."

"It's blue."

She snorted. "Obviously."

Lila kept her green eyes fixed on me, but I said nothing else. "I don't get what your problem is." Her shoulders slumped in defeat.

"My problem is that I'll look ridiculous holding that," I snapped, hating the disappointment I kept putting in her eyes.

"You've got to be kidding me. Who the hell cares? You're on vacation, playing tourist, drinking a fruity drink. Who. The. Fuck. Cares?" She sat up and pointed behind me. "Do you think that couple using the selfie stick cares? Or that group, drunk off their asses in the pool? Or all the workers who literally make their living off of silly tourists like us? I can promise you, Harrison, literally no one is looking at you. Except me. And I *will* judge the hell out of you if you don't pick up that blue drink and enjoy yourself."

Her outburst had my spine straightening. I swear, for such an adorable package, Lila had a sharp tongue on her. But her words hit as I looked around and saw everyone else simply enjoying themselves. With a sigh of resolve, I picked up the offending drink and sipped it.

Damnit. It was delicious. Sugary and citrusy and exactly like what sitting by the ocean and watching this sunset should taste like.

"Now was that so hard?" she asked.

I winced.

"Why are you like this?" she murmured, relaxing back in her seat. She clearly didn't expect a response, but that just made me want to give her one. Lila had been nothing but kind to me even when I didn't deserve it. If I was going to open up to anyone, it might as well be her.

"It's not easy for me to enjoy myself," I admitted stiffly.

Her ears perked up at that and she leaned over to look at me. "You don't say?" she said, a slight teasing tone to her voice. But she didn't say anything else, clearly not wanting to scare me out of talking.

"I. . . I feel like I always have to be on. I don't like anyone thinking they can look down on me for anything."

She wrinkled her forehead and turned completely in her chair so that she was sitting sideways and facing me.

"Why would anyone look down on you for enjoying yourself? And even if they did, screw them. You shouldn't care what anyone else thinks."

I cringed inwardly, because she was right. But I had crafted my entire persona out of being someone untouchable.

"I just. . . I would just prefer it if people didn't look my way."

"Or you'd prefer they be scared of you," she added.

"I'm not scary," I insisted.

She smirked and shook her head. "Think again. You're incredibly intimidating."

While that was usually my goal, I hated the idea that I intimidated her.

"I'd rather people mind their own business," I said.

"Except Oliver."

"He's my best friend."

"He's your only friend."

I paused. "We've been through a lot together."

She sighed, and I felt bad that even my attempt to open up was coming across as cryptic. I took another sip of my drink to distract myself.

"We've known each other since kindergarten," I continued. "I didn't have the easiest time making friends." That was an understatement, but I couldn't bring myself to divulge all of the vulnerable details. Even when she was looking at me like that.

"That was probably hard," she offered, even though I was giving her nothing.

"It stuck with me, I guess."

"Whatever happened then, you shouldn't let it have all this control over you now." Her eyes bored into me, and I shifted to look at the ocean.

"You're always so full of life. It's like you don't care what anyone thinks," I said. "I'm jealous."

She laughed softly. "I haven't always been like this. Or at least, I had someone try to dim my light before."

That made me tune in more closely.

"My high school and college boyfriend. We dated for forever. He. . . let's just say he wasn't the nicest."

My whole body heated up at her words. Despite being a dick to Lila myself, something about the way her face fell when she talked about this guy didn't sit right with me.

"He was happier when I stayed at home. He didn't love when I went out, or tried to meet new friends. I don't want to get into it, but he definitely put a damper on my spirits for a while. So when I finally got out of that relationship, I vowed to always live life intentionally. It's why Charlie and I started our business. It's why I always try to look on the bright side when I can. It's why I try to have fun with my clothes." She shrugged. "Life is too short to put myself in a box and worry about what everyone else is thinking, you know?"

I desperately wanted to ask her for more details, but the sad, far-away look in her eyes made me stop. I didn't want to push her. Here I was, trying to share something about myself, and now she was the one sharing. Except, maybe that was intentional on her part. She was trying to get me to be more comfortable.

I exhaled. Screw it. What did I have to lose?

"I grew up dirt fucking poor," I started. "My parents had me real young, and their parents cut them off. They were always struggling, for as long as I can remember."

Lila waited a moment before responding, like she was scared I might run off or something.

"That's tough," she finally said. "They seemed like wonderful people. You know, from the two seconds I spoke to them."

"They are. And don't get me wrong, we got by okay. They always made sure I had food and what I needed for school. But I didn't always look like this, either." I gestured to myself. "I was a bit of a late bloomer. And you can imagine that being the scrawny, poor kid didn't win me any popularity contests. I only had one friend."

"Oliver," she finished.

"Exactly. We were neighbors growing up. I was always shy, but Oliver just rang the doorbell at our house one day and decided we should be best friends. We were inseparable until my parents lost the house and we had to move."

She sucked in a breath. "I'm so sorry."

"It is what it is. We moved into a motel, which made me the laughing-stock of my middle school. But Oliver didn't give a shit. He stuck by me. Even when the other kids were bullying me, he always had my back."

"What about your parents? They didn't try to intervene?" she asked.

"It was tough." I flinched at a particularly painful memory. "I'll never forget one day I came home in the second grade. A group of kids had pushed me down and taken my sketchbook. . . I was always drawing back then. They ripped the pages out and scattered them all over the playground. I spent the whole period trying to find the papers and collect them. I held it together the rest of the day, but as soon as I got home, I started to cry. I'll never forget the look on my dad's face. He looked so. . . so helpless. Like it killed him that someone could treat me that way. I felt weak. I felt his weakness in me. Like we were attached by it." My chest tightened just thinking about my dad's face that day. "I don't know. Ever since that day, I told myself I wouldn't be weak. It took me a while to build up a thick skin, but I never did let my dad see me cry again."

"You were just a kid," she said sadly.

"A kid who grew up," I continued. When I met her eyes, they were glassy with unshed tears of her own.

"Crying isn't a weakness, Harrison. And kids are assholes. Your dad only looked at you that way because he loves you."

"I guess. But emotion just seemed like a liability to me. People would always be horrible, but I was in control of how I reacted to them. If they couldn't get a rise out of me, then it was like I won." I shrugged. "Unfortunately, it was a small town, and I had to deal with those assholes all through school. I was always a bit of an outcast. Thankfully, Oliver got me through most of it. Anyway, as I got bigger, I stopped having to take as much shit. And the harder I made myself, the less everyone else bugged me."

She gave a slight nod, as if that small glimpse into my past was her key to understanding why I turned out the way I did. The relentless bullying during those formative years had left me with no choice but to build a wall around myself, one that no one could get past.

Lila pulled her legs onto her chair and wrapped her arms around them.

"You see being human as weakness."

"No," I said quickly without even questioning whether she was right.

Her lip curled up as she stared up at me in silence for a few moments. It felt uncomfortable and raw to share this with her. Even after she'd just shared something of herself, I still couldn't shake the strange feeling of being vulnerable.

At that moment we were thankfully interrupted by food being dropped off at our table. Lila wordlessly leaned forward and started to dive in, our hunger pangs from the long hike taking precedence over the heavy conversation.

"You know," she said in between giant bites of Greek salad, "hiding yourself and constantly being on guard seems like more of a weakness than just letting go."

I sighed and scratched the back of my neck, already wishing we could drop this.

"I know you're not wrong," I said. "But I've been like this my entire life. It's not some switch I can turn off."

"Right." She tapped her fork against her chin thoughtfully. "But this is vacation you. And vacation you doesn't have to live by real you's rules."

"I'm still the same person despite the different geography."

"But you can let yourself relax." She held up her index finger and thumb pinched together. "Just a *little* bit."

"I'm trying." I took a large sip of my blue beverage to make my point.

"But don't just try for me. Try for you. I know Oliver isn't here, but I'm on your side too. Relax and try to enjoy this. You'll never be here or see any of these people again."

"I'll see you again," I pointed out.

"And you should know that I am an excellent secret-keeper. If you want to go back to being hard-ass Harrison after this, by all means, go right ahead. But you owe yourself this chance to just have fun."

I wanted to laugh. "I'm not even sure I know how."

"Good thing you're with someone who's made fun her life's mission." She winked at me, and I could feel the corner of my lip tug up at her confidence.

"Oh my God. Is that a smile?" she teased.

Instead of snapping the scowl back to my face, I let my grin grow bigger instead.

"Shut up. Harrison is smiling." Lila quickly whipped out her camera. "You need to take a picture with me right now. I must commemorate this moment."

Shaking my head, I leaned toward her and let her snap the selfie, the colors of the sunset in the background.

"Going to send that one to Ollie too?" I asked.

"Nope." She beamed up at me. "This is just for me."

As we continued to eat and talk, I could feel decades of pressure and tension slowly drain from my body. Because the funny thing about Lila was that, even though I didn't particularly want to, I trusted her. She felt a lot more like home than anything else on this trip. But it was more than that. She was good, through and through.

I had never vocalized how being bullied as a kid had affected me. Not even to Oliver. Because with Oliver, I didn't need to explain myself. He knew how I was, almost as if I were a reflection of his own self. The dark and moody side to his coin.

Lila, however, needed to know. She needed a little piece of

me to understand why I couldn't just have fun. Why I had all these walls in place. And I had finally given her one.

Maybe that was why I had resisted her for so long. Deep down, I'd always known I'd be safe with her. That thought freaked the hell out of me, but like she said, this was all just temporary. And it was past time I took a break from the prison of my own making.

FIFTEEN

Lila

———

THE JOURNEY BACK TO OUR HOTEL WAS A BIT OF A JUMBLE. Maria had instructed us to take the bus, but what she had neglected to mention was that every tourist in the area would be catching a bus out of Oia at exactly the same time.

"This is a nightmare," Harrison had grumbled when we'd finally secured a spot on one of the packed busses.

He had kept me close the entire time, shielding me from the crowd. I couldn't help but feel secure whenever he towered over me. When he wasn't using his intimidation tactics on me, I actually really appreciated them.

Our conversation had flowed more easily at sunset than ever before, but we couldn't keep it going during the ride back. I sat in the last available seat, thanks to Harrison's insistence, while he stood beside me, wedged between the people packed into the aisle. At every bump or sharp turn, my face pressed lightly against his stomach—which, I must add, was rock solid underneath his flimsy T-shirt.

When I finally stepped off the bus, I let the fresh air waft over me. The bus let us out closer to our hotel than the heart

of town, a fact I was very grateful for. I needed a break from
the bustle.

"That was a perfect day," I said, falling into step next to
Harrison.

"It was pretty good," he responded easily.

"Wow! I must be dead or dreaming, because there wasn't
even a hint of sarcasm in that comment." I nudged him with
my elbow, and to my absolute delight, Harrison rewarded me
with a small smile.

"What can I say? Someone has me wanting to turn over a
new leaf."

"You mean it?" I asked, unable to hide my enthusiasm.

"I don't really have much of a choice, do I?" he said, voice
lighter than it had been this entire trip. "She's incredibly
persuasive."

It might not sound like a compliment to the outside
observer, but I could sense the shift in our dynamic. Since the
day I'd met Harrison, I had wanted nothing more than to win
over his grizzly-bear personality. After almost a year, I
assumed I'd never be successful. But this accidental forced-
proximity vacation might just be the ticket to secure my status
as a friend.

I glanced over at him, only to see his bicep bulging underneath his T-shirt, and I whipped my head around to face
forward again.

Now I just had to convince my body that friendship was all
I was looking for.

My eyes kept being drawn toward the giant elephant in
the room—or, I guess I should say, giant *bed* in the room.
Earlier, when we'd dropped our stuff off, we had changed

and left so quickly I'd barely had time to register the situation.

Now, back at the hotel, it was all I could think about. My palms grew damp and warm, so I tried to discreetly wipe them off on my leggings. Harrison didn't seem affected at all as he perched on the edge of the bed and peeled off his shoes. Of course he wasn't affected. Look at the guy. While I went on failed date after failed date, he probably had a lineup of women at his beck and call. Probably badass women covered in tattoos. Compared to them, I probably looked like a kindergarten teacher to him.

"Damn, it feels good to not have to share a room with a bunch of prepubescent males," he said, falling back onto the bed.

"They're nice." I felt the need to defend the guys. They might have been young and a little exuberant, but they were fun. "Isn't that part of the joy of traveling? Meeting people you'd otherwise never have crossed paths with."

"I'll have to take your word for it. You're the one who's good at all this stuff," Harrison said, but his usual gruff tone now carried a hint of affability. He was making an effort to keep his guard down, which seemed to include the closed-off way he typically approached conversations with me.

"I'm not any better at this than you," I pointed out, moving to the dresser pushed up against the wall. "It's not like I ever have any time to travel."

Harrison's shirt had hiked up, and his stomach peeked out from beneath the hem. Just as I feared, his abs were rock hard. He propped his head on his hand and locked eyes with me, and I jerked my gaze away.

I busied myself with sifting through my suitcase, moving clothes to the drawers until I found what I was looking for. A simple black-patterned midi dress with spaghetti straps, a low back, and a flouncy skirt with a slit.

"Little fancy for pajamas." Harrison sat up and eyed the dress with a furrowed brow.

"We're going out, remember? Nigel asked us earlier."

Harrison's signature scowl returned at the mention of that. "That was an empty offer."

"Didn't seem like it to me. Besides, we're only here for a few days. We have to make the most of it, and that includes checking out the night life."

Harrison tipped his head back and groaned, his neck flexing in the process. I had expected resistance, but there was no way he was talking me out of this.

"Lila, please no. Do we have to?"

A little flutter released in my chest at the sound of my name on his lips.

"You don't have to," I insisted, moving toward the bathroom to change.

"If you're going then I do have to, don't I?" he griped.

I turned to smirk at him before closing the door, taking off my shorts and T-shirt, and hopping into the shower for a quick body rinse.

"You're seriously getting ready right now?" Harrison's deep voice from the other side of the door made me shiver.

"I'll just be a few minutes and then you can rinse off," I called, pretending to be oblivious to his displeasure.

He mumbled something inaudible.

After quickly washing up, I slipped into my black dress, fluffed out my hair and applied some minimal makeup.

When I emerged from the bathroom, Harrison was seated in the small chair, a stack of clothes on his lap.

He glanced up at me, cocking an eyebrow.

"If you're wearing that, then I *definitely* have to go."

"Is that your way of saying I look alright?" I smiled and pretended his words hadn't just set fire to my entire body. What had he meant by that, exactly? Did he think I looked good? He had never so much as given me a compliment before, leading me to assume I was so far from his usual type that he barely registered me as a woman. But now, with the way his eyes dragged slowly over me as he stood, I was starting to second guess that.

"If this is how you clean up, you really should have landed a guy by now. They must be idiots," was all he said as he brushed by me and closed the bathroom door. When the sound of the shower came on, I let out a breath and allowed myself to look as flustered as I felt.

Why the hell did my body have to respond to him like that? This whole ordeal would be a lot more convenient if I didn't find every physical thing about him so damn appealing. And was he right? Were all the men I dated idiots? I sure liked to think so, but after all these mediocre experiences, part of me wondered if I might be the problem.

Harrison emerged a few minutes later wearing black jeans and a buttoned up short sleeve black shirt.

"You clean up nice, too," I said. The understatement of the century. He looked perfect. His hair was down, falling in loose waves just above his shoulders. His tattoo sleeves peeked out from his shirt, making me recall the one time I had tried to ask him about them, many months ago.

"*I couldn't even tell you how many tattoos I have, let alone what they all mean,*" he had bit out with a glare. I had never made the mistake of asking again.

He sighed. "Let's just get this over with."

"Not until you turn your attitude around."

"My attitude is fine—"

"Nope." I stood up and pointed a finger at him. "What

did we just talk about, while watching the most beautiful sunset that probably has ever graced this earth?"

Harrison eyed me warily. "I said I'd try harder to enjoy this."

"Exactly. I appreciate you opening up to me, and rest assured that you came to the right person. Because nobody knows fun like me. Just remember that tonight, nobody cares about us. Are we silly tourists? Of course we are. But *no one cares*! The only person who will remember you from tonight is you. Doesn't that make you want to make this worthwhile? We're going to have fun. Say it with me."

"We're going to have fun." Although there was no sarcasm in his voice, the word "fun" falling from Harrison's lips almost made me want to burst into laughter. I felt bad that he was so uncomfortable, but considering he usually wanted to make me crawl inside my own skin, this power shift was a welcome change.

"Now, let's go see if the guys are ready."

"I'm sure that was an empty invitation. They don't want to go out with us."

A knock came on our door and I threw Harrison a knowing smile before walking over and swinging it open. The trio of guys stood there, each with their hair slicked back and wearing a festive shirt.

"Can't believe you ditched us for a private room," Mark said.

"Yeah. Not cool," added Will.

"You lot ready to go?" Nigel asked with a grin.

"They make me feel geriatric," Harrison grimaced as he set down the shot glass Nigel had insisted we take. "If they try to shove any more alcohol down my throat, I'm going to have to start tossing it over my shoulder when they aren't looking."

I laughed, enjoying the slight buzz. "You're an amateur," I leaned in closer to him to whisper. He smelled *good*. "I've only been taking a sip and setting them back on the bar."

He raised an eyebrow. "You trying to keep your wits about you while we all get plastered?" He questioned me, a smile playing on his lips.

"Please, I'm half your size." Feeling brave, I poked his muscle. "You'd already be dragging me home if I tried to keep up."

"One more round," Nigel cheered, this time thankfully returning with beer. He passed us each a bottle and I took it, grateful to have something to hold.

"At least this I can nurse for the next hour," Harrison said in a low voice that only I could hear.

"Don't let Nigel notice," I warned. "He'll challenge you to some sort of chugging contest."

The bar hummed with energy, packed shoulder to shoulder with people. TVs flashed sports overhead while the music pounded from the DJ booth at the front, shaking the air around us. I hadn't been to a place like this in ages; maybe since right after graduating college. While this was nowhere near my typical scene, it was fun to be somewhere so lively. The noisy crowd—dancing, laughing, and talking over the music—was enough to keep me energized and completely in the moment. Especially since I refused to allow myself to get drunk on this trip. No way was I wasting a single moment in Greece stuck in bed with a hangover. I also didn't trust myself with the combination of Harrison and low inhibitions. Not when I was already getting this comfortable with him after just one decent conversation.

Since we'd arrived at the bar, he'd made sure to keep me

close by his side. It did something to me. He didn't take his eyes off me for a second in the busy room, and when the crowd thickened, he hovered a hand near my waist. He didn't touch me, as much as I wanted him to. He simply kept his hand there to keep anyone else from bumping into me. Every so often his knuckles brushed against me and my whole body lit up.

"You all are a blast," Mark said loudly, grabbing Harrison and me around our necks and pulling us in for a sloppy hug.

"I think you're having more fun than everyone else in this bar combined," Harrison said, patting his back and shifting slightly so that he was between Mark and me.

"No, seriously. I'm coming to the U.S. after this and we'll all go out," Nigel slurred, joining his friend and slinging an arm around him. "Where's Will?"

"Ah, he went off that way. Followed some chick."

"We need to find chicks of our own," Nigel said.

"You all are sharing a six-person room," I reminded them with a laugh. "Not exactly the right circumstances for bringing a girl back."

"Depends what you're into," Mark said, wiggling his eyebrows.

Harrison glared at him. "Watch it," he said, tone bordering on harsh.

They both tipped their heads back, cackling.

"You're so sensitive about your girlfriend." Nigel whacked Harrison's shoulder.

"She's not my girlfriend." Harrison rolled his eyes. I'm sure he was just irritated that he had to keep repeating the fact, but hearing it still stung all the same.

"You keep telling yourself that," Mark yelled over the music.

Nigel leaned in past Harrison to give me a squeeze and a

kiss on the cheek. "Lily, if he won't make an honest woman out of you, I will." Nigel winked at me before Harrison shoved him aside.

"Seriously, back off," he bit out. "And for the millionth time her name is Lila."

Nigel just chuckled. "Awfully protective over someone who isn't your girlfriend."

"She's still my responsibility," he said.

"Whatever." Nigel shrugged. "Mark, let's go talk to that table of girls in the back." The two of them disappeared into the thick crowd, leaving me alone with Harrison. Well, alone in a packed bar.

His responsibility. His words reverberated in my mind. Ew. Was that really what he thought of me?

"What's wrong with you?" He asked, meeting my eyes.

I didn't realize I had folded my arms across my chest. In fact, my whole body had stiffened. Frowning up at him, I waited for him to get the hint. But instead of recognition flashing into his eyes, he continued to stare at me blankly.

"What?" he asked again.

I gave an exaggerated sigh before saying, "Nothing," and shouldering past him to find a spot at the edge of the bar. Suddenly, I desperately needed some air. One wall was lined with open windows, and I stopped to inhale the fresh night air.

"Hey, don't storm off like that." Harrison was beside me in a second. So much for getting some space.

"I hardly stormed off," I said.

"I can tell when you're upset."

Our eyes met, and I noticed the concern etched across his face. I wasn't used to seeing him look at me like that.

"I'm not upset," I conceded. "It's just. . ."

"Just what?" He leaned against the wall and ditched the almost-full beer he was holding on the table behind him.

"I don't get you," I admitted.

His mouth parted slightly and he shook his head. "I mean, I'm not exactly an easy person to get. But I opened up to you back there at the—"

"I know," I added quickly, not wanting him to feel that everything he'd shared with me had fallen flat. "I appreciate all that. It's just with me. . . you've been so protective this whole time. You insist on coming along everywhere I go, even though I'm perfectly capable of handling myself and you clearly didn't want to."

"I was never going to let you go alone."

"But I could have, and I would have been fine."

He scowled. "I don't care. It wasn't happening."

I let out a huff of frustration. "Regardless. You act like I'm this burden that you have to keep track of. And then you just referred to me as your 'responsibility.' Like I'm some kid you're stuck babysitting." I was sick of pretending like he hadn't hurt my feelings. The packed crowd and charged atmosphere had me feeling braver than I really was, which is why I said what came next. "And you keep acting like someone mistaking me for your girlfriend is the most offensive thing possible."

"It's not that at all," he said, flustered. He raked a hand through his hair and leaned in closer to me so he wouldn't have to yell as loud over the music. "Is this about Nigel? Because I drove him off?"

"It's not about Nigel, God, he's basically a child." I shuddered at the thought. "It's the fact that you act like the very idea of us together disgusts you. Doesn't exactly make me feel great, Harrison."

My cheeks burned hot.

He held my gaze for a moment, a sigh escaping his lips. "The thought doesn't disgust me. Have you seen yourself?"

A surge of something stirred inside me at that, but I pushed it aside.

"Yes, I have. And I'm clearly the last woman on the planet you would consider dating. But that still doesn't mean you have to act like the idea repulses you. Do I wear too much color for your taste? Does my optimism nauseate you?"

"Stop it." Harrison shocked me by grabbing my upper arms and holding me in place, then he lowered his face so it hovered only a few inches away from mine. Acting purely on instinct, I licked my lips, and I swore I saw something like hunger flash in his eyes. His throat tensed as he gulped and shook his head, breaking himself from the temporary daze.

"You're right, you're not my usual type. But that doesn't mean you aren't incredible in your own right. I'm sorry I've been a dick to you in the past. I know I have, but that's just how I am." He let go of me and locked his fingers behind his head, obviously flustered. "And I didn't mean to act like the idea disgusted me. If anything, I'm just sick of talking to those guys and repeating myself. I'm sorry it came off like that, okay?"

Suddenly, I felt stupid. Very, very stupid.

"Shit," I groaned, tipping my head back. "I never should have brought this up. This has nothing to do with you."

"Seems like it does," he said, the corner of his lip twitched.

"No, no, no." I hid my face with one hand and waved my other between us. "This is all me spiraling and projecting my own insecurities."

I massaged my forehead, wishing the ground would swallow me whole.

"This wouldn't have anything to do with all those dates

you're always going on, would it?" Harrison asked gently. Even through the pounding music, all I could focus on was him.

"Nope. Please forget I said anything. My little outburst was already humiliating enough."

"Come on. You can talk to me."

At that, I removed my hand from my face so I could raise an eyebrow at him.

His eyes glistened and a smirk played on his lips. "What? We're turning over a new leaf, remember?"

"I just don't get it," I said, throwing one of my elbows up on the windowsill and leaning against it. "How do people meet their person? I'm trying so hard, and I'm alone as ever."

"You're asking the wrong person." He shrugged. "I've never even tried before."

"Well, let me tell you, it's certainly not worth the effort. You've been smart to save your time."

He winced at my pessimistic words. "Maybe it's good that you put yourself out there so much."

I bit my lip and studied his earnest expression. This guy standing before me was like a completely different person than the one I got on the plane with a few days ago.

"Lately, I've been wondering if maybe I spent too much time with my ex," I said. "What if I was supposed to meet my soulmate in high school, and I just picked the wrong guy? Or what if it was that lab partner I was a little too flirtatious with in college? Or maybe I was supposed to end up with the guy at the coffee shop who asked for my number, but I turned him down because I had a boyfriend."

A group of dancers got too close to Harrison and he had to lean in closer to me to get space. "I don't think it works like that, Lila."

"I'm starting to think I'll have to settle for some guy who

lives out of a van and will insist on waiting five years before proposing to me," I said bitterly.

Harrison chuckled. I wasn't used to the sound, and it made me feel drunker than any of the alcohol I'd had earlier. "Please do me a favor and don't settle."

We stared at each other for a second. My mouth went dry. "You want to get out of here?" I asked.

"More than anything," he said, his voice thick with relief.

We pushed our way through the crowd until we finally stepped outside. The heart of the town thrummed with activity, bars blasting music, though many tourists had already drifted away for the night. We began our trek down the long, winding pedestrian street back to our hotel.

The silence was almost blaring and after our conversation at the bar, I felt the need to defend myself.

"I know I should be more secure," I started. "You know? Content with everything I've achieved. Knowing I've built a successful business and a good life all on my own. But it still feels empty. I still crave something more, something deeper. I guess you could say I'm still 'desperate for a man,' as you've so eloquently pointed out in the past."

Movement to my right caught my attention, and suddenly a hard chest blocked my path. I looked up in surprise to find Harrison standing in front of me.

"You're not desperate," he said. His eyes were filled with regret.

"It's fine." I waved him off. "I kind of am, actually."

"You're not." His eyes were hard, but not in their usual intimidating way. "I should have never said that. That's one of my gifts, unfortunately—figuring out what will get a rise out of someone and using it to my advantage. I should have never used it against you, though."

"I'm no one to you. I shouldn't be affected by it."

He blew out a sharp breath and looked pained. "Lila, I don't know who you are to me, but you're sure as hell not no one. Not anymore."

Now I knew what people meant when they said they felt faint.

"Oh," was my only response before he nodded gruffly and we resumed our walk.

This day felt like it had stretched into an entire year. How was I supposed to survive the rest of the trip with him looking at me like that? Like I actually meant something to him.

SIXTEEN

Harrison

"Are you sure about this?" Lila eyed me warily as a man came around and tightened her helmet. I resisted the urge to shoulder him out of the way and do it myself.

"Maria did say it was the best way to see the island," I pointed out.

"But every blog in existence talks about how unsafe it is," she whispered.

"Oh, you'll be fine," the man renting us the four-wheeler boomed with a thick Greek accent. "The ones worried about safety are never the ones that crash."

"See?" I said.

"You're sure you know how to drive one of these?" she questioned me for the millionth time.

"I'm sure, Lila."

Somehow, my patience had grown in the little time I'd spent with her. Maybe it was the escape from real life, but today I felt completely at ease. It had taken nearly an hour over breakfast today to persuade Lila that we should rent an

ATV to see the island. I could tell she was interested, despite her reservations, and I wanted her to have this adventure.

Normal Harrison would have rolled his eyes and dropped the topic immediately. But new Harrison wanted to experience this with her. New Harrison recognized that, if he was gentle and confident with his words, he could convince her this was going to be fine. More than fine. This was going to be *fun*.

Just thinking the word felt odd to me. *Fun* was entirely new to my vocabulary, but what could I say? Lila brought out a new side of me. Perhaps this was the exact reason I had kept her at a safe distance before. But after yesterday, she had officially weaseled her way into my mind, where she now resided rent-free. And she likely wouldn't be evicted any time soon. Not after I had spent last night tossing and turning, knowing only a feeble pillow brigade kept me from her warm body. More than once last night, I had thought about how easy it would be just to lean down and capture her lips with mine. They looked so inviting. . .

"Let's see you start it up," the man with the rental company said.

I forced my concentration back on the safety demo we were being given. It was still early in the day, so the roads were relatively empty. I felt confident in my driving skills. I would go the speed limit, and I wouldn't do anything remotely stupid.

A few minutes later, Lila and I hit the road. I quickly discovered an unexpected benefit of this excursion: Lila had to press herself against my back, wrapping her arms tightly around my waist. While the position wouldn't do much to quell any wandering fantasies I was having, I wasn't complaining.

Her chest pressed against my back and I forced myself to give driving my full attention.

"Left or right up here?" I asked at the first light.

Lila had been given another map by the counter guy at the rental company, who had circled various stops we might want to check out.

"Um, I don't remember," she said.

I smirked and turned to look at her, but she was pressed so tightly against me I could only see the top of her helmet.

"Can you check the map? We're stopped, and I promise I won't go until you're hanging on again."

Quickly, and only releasing half of her grip on me, Lila unfolded the map and spun it around.

"Left," she finally said, before crumpling the map between us and resuming her vice-like grip around me.

My lip curled up in amusement as the light turned green and I eased onto the gas.

Lila let out a small yelp and held on even tighter.

Chuckling, I shifted my face slightly so my mouth was closer to her ear, but my eyes were still locked on the road.

"We're only going twenty kilometers an hour. Relax, or you might crush one of my ribs."

"Sorry," she called over the wind, and loosened her arms just enough to let me take a full breath.

The winding roads in Santorini were relatively straightforward and easy to navigate. Lila had picked out the farthest point on the map to try first—a lighthouse located on the southern tip of the island.

Just based off direction, I didn't have much trouble getting us there, but I did have to ask Lila to check the map one additional time. She had glanced at it so hastily before stuffing it away, I wasn't convinced she knew where we were.

We eventually turned onto a road that hugged the edge of the cliff and overlooked the vast sea. Lila gasped behind me.

"Are you seeing this?"

There was a large shoulder on the road just ahead, so I slowed down and came to a stop. We both took off our helmets so we could get an unobstructed view.

"Wow," she breathed. I couldn't help but watch her as she stared out over the water in awe before pulling out her phone to snap a few pictures.

She was wearing tiny jean shorts that showcased her sun-kissed legs, a testament to the time we'd spent outdoors yesterday. A loose white T-shirt billowed around her in the wind, slipping off one shoulder. Her smooth skin was almost too inviting.

"This is even prettier than I imagined." She turned to me and I tore my gaze away, cursing myself for getting caught staring.

"Lighthouse should be just up there," I mumbled.

Five minutes later, we pulled into a small gravel parking lot with only two other cars. A short path led to the front of the Akrotiri Lighthouse. The lighthouse itself was set atop large boulders, facing the sea.

"This is so cool." Lila sounded giddy as she scurried across the rocks, almost slipping in the process.

"Careful," I barked, moving quickly and grabbing her elbow.

"I'm fine." She waved off my concern and positioned herself on a large rock. She plopped down and looked up at the lighthouse before turning back to the sea.

I sank down next to her and did the same.

"Smile." She held up her phone to take a selfie of the two of us with the lighthouse in the background. Shifting a few times, she struggled to get us both in the frame with her short arms.

"Give me that." I held out my hand for the phone before lifting it up and snapping a few pictures.

"You have to smile," she insisted, pinching my side. The small gesture caused my whole body to light up.

"I am smiling," I said, but widened my grin a little to appease her.

"How unreal is this?" she asked. "Would you have ever in a million years thought that you'd be in Greece with me, sitting at an ancient lighthouse?"

"I definitely saw this coming," I said dryly.

She smiled up at me before slapping my leg.

"They say sarcasm is the lowest form of humor, you know."

"Who's they?" I challenged, unable to keep the playfulness out of my voice. Being around Lila had made me feel more relaxed and comfortable than I had in years. And while that freaked me out more than a little bit, it was hard not to savor the unfamiliar feeling.

"The executive board of humor," she said seriously.

Letting out a small laugh, I shook my head. "Whatever you say, Lila."

Her name tasted sweet on my tongue. Almost as though, if I said it enough, I could lay some sort of claim over it.

SEVENTEEN

Lila

"So, you weren't kidding. You do own a swimsuit."

Harrison took the lounge seat next to mine and eyed me with a soft glare, but the twitch in his lips told me that his scowl was anything but sincere. I adjusted my sunglasses, taking immense pleasure in the fact that I was creeping into whatever good graces he possessed. He didn't hate me anymore. I could tell. It almost felt like he liked me. . . but I didn't want to get my hopes up too high.

"Believe it or not, I can relax." He sat back as if to prove his point and scanned the immense black sand beach before us. He put his hands behind his head, causing his rather large biceps to bulge in the process. Harrison shirtless was certainly a sight to see. His sleeves of tattoos stopped at the edge of his pecs, leaving the rest of his chiseled abs and chest bare. Yeah, this wasn't helping my crush in the slightest.

After the lighthouse, we had driven around for a while, just taking in some of the sights. We'd even gone to the very tip-top of a cliff to see an old church that had been touted as having the best view on the island. While it certainly did have a breathtaking view, the fact that it was hundreds of feet above everything else had resulted in me panicking a little tiny bit on the way up. Harrison, ever the complainer, had insisted I'd punctured his spleen by holding on too tight.

After that, we had stopped at a little restaurant for lunch. When we had arrived and spotted the beach stretching out before us, I had insisted we stay for a while. Thankfully, we'd had the foresight to bring our bathing suits.

"You know what, you do look relaxed."

"Aren't you glad you listened to me?" He gestured to the four-wheeler that sat parked behind us.

"I guess you're right about some things," I said easily, shrugging.

I could admit when I was wrong. Driving around the island had been one of the highlights of the trip so far. There was something magical about the breeze in our faces as we climbed hills for views of the sea. This whole day felt like a release.

"Your order." The waiter arrived and set down some type of feta dip with pita and the coffee Harrison had ordered. I winced when I saw it on its own. Shoot. I had ordered an espresso. The pick-me-up of a little caffeine had sounded perfect for midday, but the waiter must not have heard me.

"Thank you," I said but at the same time Harrison asked, "You ordered an espresso, didn't you?"

"This is fine," I quickly said, giving the waiter an apologetic smile.

Harrison furrowed his brow and frowned. "Uh, I think we had an espresso too," he said easily.

"No problem." The waiter smiled. "I'll bring it right out."

Before I even had time to object, he was gone.

"You didn't have to do that," I mumbled.

"Didn't have to do what? Ask him for what you ordered?"

"It was an honest mistake. I hate to cause a scene over something like that." But when the waiter came back seconds later, carrying a small glass cup with the perfect shot of espresso in it, my heart swelled with pleasure and I took a grateful sip.

Harrison lifted a brow and took a sip from his own cup. "Politely asking for what you ordered is hardly causing a scene."

"Maybe I didn't say it loudly enough," I replied weakly.

He snorted. "You definitely did. Why are you being so weird about this?"

My skin bristled in defense. "I'm not being weird. I just don't want to make anyone's life harder."

I could feel his gaze on me but kept mine fixed to the waves in front of us.

"I don't want you to take this the wrong way," he started.

"When has that ever stopped you from saying something before?"

"All I was going to say is that you're too much of a people-pleaser."

"There's nothing wrong with being a people-pleaser." He was right, though. My insatiable drive to be liked inevitably made me the biggest people-pleaser of them all. But what was so bad about that? "I'd rather be a people-pleaser than actively try to scare off everyone who comes into contact with me." I grabbed a pita and started shoveling in the food resting on the small table between us.

Harrison blew out a breath. "Fair enough. But trying too hard to appease others isn't healthy."

"Oh, as opposed to you who would rather die than do somebody a simple favor?"

He groaned and tilted his head back. "Damn, Lila. I

wasn't trying to start a fight about this. I just don't like the idea of you not standing up for yourself."

"I stand up for myself when it matters." I swallowed the bite I was chewing. "Like when a certain someone used to be an asshole to me for no reason. I definitely didn't let him walk all over me. I'm not completely spineless."

"I know that," Harrison said, purposefully keeping his voice gentle. "The only point I was trying to make was that it's okay to say no sometimes, or to ask for what you want. You aren't being difficult, and people will still like you."

"You didn't like me," I pointed out, cringing at how pathetic that sounded. I scooped up another bite of dip. Nothing like stress-eating to calm the nerves.

"I don't like anyone," he said, turning in his chair so that his feet were on the sand and he was facing me. "*Except* you."

I rolled my eyes behind my sunglasses. "Sure, you say that now because we're stuck on this trip together, but—"

"Lila, I've always had to push you away because you're the most likable person I've ever met, okay? You need to stop trying so hard."

I tipped my espresso back, polishing it off with one last gulp before setting it back on the table. I was unsure of what to say next. Part of me wanted to continue to deny that I tried too hard, but I knew he was right. I was slammed at work because I couldn't say no to anyone, and I refused to delegate. Even the whole thing with helping Harrison at his shop—I hadn't had the time for that, but I was so desperate for him to like me that I'd convinced myself I did.

"I promise, I won't try too hard in the future." I saluted in his direction.

Harrison ran his hand along his jaw and assessed me.

"What? I'm serious. I'll try."

"I hope so," was all he said.

Who was he to be giving me advice? Our blossoming friendship had started, like, seventy-two hours ago. I guess he'd had plenty of time to observe me before that, though.

"You're so annoying," I said, in a tone that didn't mask at all the effect he had on me.

Before he could continue the conversation, I pushed myself off the lounge chair and made a beeline for the water just twenty feet in front of us. Tentatively, I stepped in. The water was warm. Not tolerably cool—actually *warm*. And it was so clear, I could see straight to my toes even as I took a few more steps out.

"You can't just get up and leave in the middle of a conversation," Harrison called from the shore.

"What? Sorry. I can't hear you." I let my chin fall into the water to hide my smile as I looked back at Harrison. He stood at the edge of the water with his arms crossed over his chest. The beach was almost completely empty.

"Really mature," he shouted back.

"Come on, get in. We haven't even been in the water yet. That's a total crime." I dipped my head back, submerging myself completely before standing back up and letting the water run off my hair. "This is seriously perfect." I sighed with contentment, letting the water wash over my body like some sort of all-powerful healing potion.

"It looks cold," Harrison replied. He eyed me suspiciously as if I were trying to suppress a shiver and, if he kept an eye on me, I would eventually break.

"It's the Mediterranean just after summer. I promise you, it's warm."

The lines etched in his forehead told me he still didn't believe me completely, but he at least waded a few steps in. Once it was clear I wasn't lying, he walked in farther until he was chest-deep. I did my best to keep my eyes off his tattooed arms and pec muscles and focused on his eyes instead.

"You were right. This is nice," he said, stopping only a foot away from me.

"Told you."

He stood a few steps farther out than me so that we were almost eye-level.

"Why do you care so much about being liked?" he asked, staring at me intently.

Groaning, I dipped my head back again.

"We're still on this topic?" Never would I have guessed that Harrison would be the one to insist on continuing a deep conversation and I would be the one trying to run from it.

He shrugged. "What else have we got to do?"

I knit my brow trying to think of a succinct answer. While I was no stranger to therapy, I didn't usually discuss these types of things with anyone other than Charlie. And Charlie had never really said anything about my tendencies to put others' needs before my own. Sometimes she intervened, if it affected the business or I was wearing myself out too much, but she had never seen it as a character flaw. Not the way Harrison seemed to.

"I don't know," I finally said. "Maybe it's the curse of being an only child?" I knew that wasn't it completely, but it felt like a good place to start.

"Your parents put a lot of pressure on you?" he questioned.

"What? No, not at all." I thought about my parents and how kind and supportive they had been my entire life. "If anything, they showed me how much value could come from just being nice. They're seriously the sweetest people. They call me every week like clockwork and they try to visit me when they can. They're so proud of me and Charlie and our company. They brag about it to pretty much anyone who will listen."

"They sound great," he said. He raised an eyebrow, encouraging me to continue.

Finally, I let it spill out.

"My ex was hard to please." That was the understatement of my lifetime.

"The one you thought you'd be with forever?"

"That's the one and only. What I didn't mention is that our relationship didn't just not work out, he kind of sucked."

Harrison's eyes hardened and his hand stilled in the water. "How so?"

Sighing, I lifted my feet off the ground and floated, feeling comfort in the feeling. I hated talking about him.

"We met when I was only fifteen and we dated all through college. It should be a crime to date that young. I was so naïve and aspirational when it came to romance; I thought a first love was the most magical thing that could exist. My parents had been high school sweethearts. My grandparents too, on both sides. I always thought that was the dream. Probably why I latched onto my ex so hard and never let him go, even though he clearly wasn't right for me. I hate thinking back on all those wasted years when I could have been enjoying myself and instead, I was appeasing him."

Harrison didn't say anything. He just watched me as I gathered my next thought.

"He was just. . . so wrong for me. He hated everything I did. What I wore, my hobbies, how I acted. He thought I was embarrassing." I shuddered thinking back on it. "I know it sounds silly; it wasn't like he was overly cruel or anything. But being so young, and having someone who you think hangs the moon tell you to keep it down if you're laughing too loudly, or pulling you aside during a party to tell you that your jokes aren't funny and people are giving you strange looks. . . those kinds of things just really add up. Eventually, I think I was putting on more of a performance for him than living for myself, if that makes sense."

Harrison winced. "Fuck," he muttered. "I'm sorry."

"It's not your fault."

"No, I'm sorry for every prickish thing I ever said to you," he added quickly. When I looked up, his eyes were burning a hole straight through me.

"You couldn't have known." My hands drifted back and forth, letting the water run through my fingers. "Plus, that's just the way you are."

"It's not the way I should have been with you," he said more forcefully.

We locked eyes for a moment before I tried to shake off his comment.

"Anyway," I continued. "I guess, because he never gave me much affirmation, I sought it out other places. Volunteering to run a fundraiser because a teacher asked, joining a club in college I had no interest in, just because they were low on membership, going above and beyond when someone asked for my help at work. I loved seeing the grateful or relieved look on someone's face and knowing I caused that. Maybe it started as a way to overcompensate, but it's kind of addictive."

"You're perfect the way you are." My eyes widened at Harrison's statement. "I didn't mean you should go changing yourself. I just meant. . ." He looked back to the shore before staring at me again. "I just meant to make sure you're watching out for yourself. Don't let anyone take advantage."

We stood in the water a few seconds, unsure of who should speak next. Finally, I smiled to myself.

"You know, we aren't that different."

He lifted a brow, clearly surprised that was where my train of thought had arrived.

"How so?"

"We both care entirely too much about what people think. You suppress everything to ensure you scare them off, and I do everything they ask—and things they don't ask for—in the hopes of winning them over."

"That doesn't exactly sound like a great combination."

Shrugging, I couldn't help but feel he was wrong. "Maybe we're balancing each other out."

His eyes roamed over my face. "Lila, if anyone could balance me out, it's you."

EIGHTEEN

Harrison

"HEY! HOW'S IT GOING?" OLIVER'S FACE FILLED MY SCREEN as I sat by our hotel pool waiting for Lila to get changed for dinner.

"What the hell are you calling me for? Isn't it the middle of the night there?" I asked.

"Almost five in the morning. Charlie wants to do a sunrise hike."

"Sad I'm missing that," I said, not meaning it at all.

"Lila doesn't have you waking up first thing to do some sort of activity? I find that hard to believe."

"She let me sleep until seven today." The corner of my lip tugged up just thinking about the eventful day we'd shared. We had spent hours wandering the different beaches before we got back to the hotel and collapsed for a nap. The one bed had been a little tricky last night; just knowing she was lying next to me in her little sleep shirt did not do good things for my self-control. But this afternoon we'd been so exhausted that we'd fallen asleep immediately. I had even woken up to her head on my chest before discreetly slipping away so that she wouldn't be embarrassed.

"Harrison, are you smiling?"

My mouth fell into a frown as soon as I noticed the shit-eating grin on my best friend. "What's it to you?"

"I knew it. You're loving it. You like Lila now, don't you? Admit it."

"Why do you always have to be so—"

"Upbeat? Optimistic? Amiable?"

"I was going to say obnoxious."

"It may shock you to know, but being in a good mood is *actually* not synonymous with obnoxious."

"Lila is cool," I finally said. There, that was all he'd get out of me. In reality, that was a giant understatement. I hadn't enjoyed myself with anyone like this in years. In fact, she had made me realize that it had been something that was missing from my life. I was so used to being focused on acting a certain way at all times, I had completely missed out on how good it felt to let loose a little.

"When's the wedding?" Oliver probed.

"What is your obsession with setting us up?" I hissed, glancing up to make sure the door to our shared room was still closed.

Oliver grinned back at me as he closed a door behind him.

"Because maybe I think she'd be good for you."

"How would you know?" I felt defensive, although I didn't know why.

"Are you serious? Dude, I'm your best friend. We're basically family. You don't think I have any clue what kind of girl you might mesh with?"

"She's perky," was all I said.

"Fuck, *I'm* perky."

"Right. And I can't handle another you."

Oliver rolled his eyes. "No, I think you need another me. I've tried for years to get you out of your shell and failed, so might as well give Lila a go. Plus, you know she likes you."

That was news to me. A slight flicker of something resembling hope came to life in my chest before my mind snuffed it out.

"She definitely doesn't," I insisted, although I'd be lying if I said I hadn't noticed how her gaze had lingered on me at least a few times today when we were swimming. Maybe *like* was too strong a word, but there was definitely some sort of mutual attraction brewing.

"I don't know, man. She's always asking about you. Seeing if you're coming to things, or if she comes to the house and you're not there she asks where you are. Seems like she has some level of interest."

"You think?" I tried to add concern to my voice instead of intrigue.

"Not just me. Charlie thinks so, too."

I was sure Lila would be just as thrilled as I was to learn that Oliver and Charlie were discussing our non-existent, improbable relationship behind our backs. But still. . .

"Charlie said that?" If her best friend thought so, then maybe there was some truth to Oliver's ramblings.

"Yep." The smug look on Oliver's face was more than I could take.

"Nothing is going on with us." I felt the need to repeat. "Go on your little sunrise hike and stop bothering me."

"I'd say I wish you were here, but I think you're *exactly* where you're supposed to be." He winked just as I ended the call.

"Fucking Oliver," I breathed, attempting to rub the tension out of my neck. He was full of shit. I knew that. But his words still scratched incessantly at the back of my mind.

Did Lila like me? I mentally went over our entire acquaintanceship. Aside from her constant attempts to befriend me, I really didn't see any substantial evidence that would lead me to believe she could have a crush. Which was good, in theory, because we were absolutely not a compatible pairing, despite whatever shit Oliver was spouting.

"Hey there." Nigel's overly cheery voice sent a shiver down my spine. Dealing with him was the last thing I wanted right now.

"Hey." I nodded in greeting.

"You and Lily going to join us for another night out?" he asked. I didn't like that hopeful look in his eyes. I didn't care how harmless Lila thought these guys were; if she gave them even a suggestion of interest, I guaranteed Nigel would take it and run with it.

"It's Lila," I corrected him. I wasn't sure if she liked the nickname or not, but I certainly didn't appreciate it. "And I don't think so." I stood up, so he would remember that I had nearly five inches on him. Probably overkill, but whatever.

"You sure? Should be a good time."

"Not tonight," I said, praying he would leave before Lila walked out of our room. She had said she was completely wiped after spending all day driving, but I wouldn't put it past her to still insist we go out.

"Hey!" Her cheery voice rang out behind me, and I tipped my head back and groaned.

"Lily." Nigel's smile stretched when he saw her, and I didn't like the way he held his arms out for a hug. I especially didn't care for it once I caught sight of Lila's dress. The soft blue fabric made her skin glow, and her hair popped in contrast. It was strapless and dipped just a little by her cleavage—the same cleavage I'd probably glanced at one too many times when she had been wearing that bikini earlier today.

"Come out with us," Mark—or possibly Will—called from the entrance to the shared room. I still wasn't one hundred percent sure who was who. The other one appeared, and the two of them ambled into the shared courtyard.

Lila looked back at me, and I tried to give her my best 'I'm completely exhausted and also I just don't want to go' look.

The corner of her lip twitched, and she winked at me before turning back to the boys.

"Sorry, we were just going to do dinner and then crash. We've been out basically all day."

"Maria said you rented a four-wheeler. When we asked if we should do that the other day, she said not to." Something like a pout formed on Nigel's lips.

"Oh, well, they can be dangerous," Lila offered while I snorted. These guys did not exactly scream responsibility. I could see why Maria wasn't encouraging them to go flying down the roads on one of those things.

"Ah, no worries. We made other plans for tomorrow. They replaced you with three American girls in our room who are. . ." Nigel looked back at Mark and Will, and they all snickered. I fought the urge to gag. Lila elbowed me in the ribs, a silent reminder to be polite.

"Hey, you should come with tomorrow," Will—or Mark said.

"Yeah, definitely," Nigel clasped his hand around Lila's bare shoulder and I stifled the sudden urge to grab her waist and pull her against me. "We're all headed to Mykonos for a day trip on the ferry. Going to check out some beach clubs. Should be a good time."

I'd rather fly the forty hours to Fiji than join them, but I bit my tongue and forced myself to wait for Lila's response.

She might want to see another island, and I wasn't going to deny her that.

"That does sound fun." She eyed me, trying to read my expression. I kept my face neutral, but judging from the way she smirked, I'm sure she knew the thoughts running through my mind.

"Why don't we let you know in the morning. When are you leaving?" she asked instead.

"We'll probably head out of here around nine."

"Great. Maybe we'll join you."

"Yeah, maybe," I said under my breath.

The trio of guys finally waved their goodbyes, and I was left alone with Lila. Alone with Lila and that stunning-as-hell dress.

"You're not seriously considering going with them, are you?"

Lila laughed. "There it is."

"There what is?"

"I knew you were biting your tongue when they asked us."

She looked me up and down with her green eyes, making it impossible not to feel guilty. I had told myself I would stop holding us back on this trip. If Lila wanted to do something, damnit, I was going to do it. It was only a few days in the grand scheme of life. I was going to make sure she would not have any regrets because of me.

"I'm sorry; we can go if you want. But is it so insane that I don't like those guys?"

"Yes. They're nice."

"Okay fine." I threw my hands up. "Maybe dislike is too strong a sentiment, but at the very least I find them annoying. I'm not dying to spend the day stuck on another island with them. Can't we hang out just the two of us? We can go to Mykonos if you want to, I just don't want to go with them."

Lila flushed for a moment, looking taken aback. But as quickly as her flustered appearance came, it was gone, and a devilish smile was in its place.

"Just the two of us?" she mused.

"You know what I mean."

"That you're obsessed with me and we're best friends now? I accept."

I dragged my hand over the stubble on my chin. "Fine, yes. We're best friends. If that's what it takes to not hang out with those guys tomorrow, you're my favorite fucking person on this entire planet, okay?"

"At least on this island," she said through a laugh.

That was the undeniable truth. The thought of what we'd be after this trip lingered in my mind. While this might only be temporary, my feelings for Lila had shifted in a way that felt permanent. Friendship had always been tough for me, prob- ably always would be, but going back to how things had been between us? That felt impossible now. I *liked* her. Not seeing her every day already felt wrong. I'd gotten used to her cheery greetings, and the way she dragged me along on whatever little adventure she had in mind. I had even started to look forward to it.

Lila led the way to the gate of our hotel, almost running into Maria in the process.

"Good evening," she greeted us with a smile. "How was your day?"

"Amazing." Lila's eyes brightened as she regaled Maria with the story of our day.

Her whole demeanor lit up as she spoke, her energy infec- tious. Something about it stirred an ache deep in my gut—her sincere, candid love for life. Her kindness and her openness to people and experiences. It should be something fostered. Something protected. Not something to be picked apart or critiqued. For the millionth time since we'd set off on this strange journey, I mentally berated myself for ever being an ass to her.

"Where are you going for dinner?" Maria asked us when Lila finished telling her all the places where we'd stopped.

"Just somewhere in town," Lila said. "We were heading out there now."

"Can I make a suggestion?" Maria asked.

"Of course! Please," Lila exclaimed.

"There's a small family place just down the road. It's not in town, but the food is amazing. You have to try it. They're always full, since they don't have many tables, but it's so far out of town the tourists don't usually find it."

"That sounds perfect." Lila smiled up at me.

"Just turn left instead of right at the main road. It'll be at the first fork you come to. You shouldn't miss it."

Lila thanked Maria. I was about to thank her as I walked by, but she winked at me instead and whispered, "Very romantic," under her breath.

MARIA HADN'T BEEN KIDDING. THIS RESTAURANT LOOKED LIKE it was straight out of a painting. It was nestled in an older building, and we found it easily thanks to the lanterns strung on wires out front. The inside was just as atmospheric. Paintings hung along the wall, and small tables lined both sides of the room, lit only by the dim candles on the tables and the low lamps above. Each table had a different patterned tablecloth, and ornate rugs lined the walkways.

Lila sat across from me at the small table, sipping a glass of wine. We'd already inhaled the best meal I could ever remember having, with various meats, and risotto, and a few other sides. While the food had been delicious, the company probably had more to do with it.

"Cheers," she said, holding out her glass to me.

"Cheers," I responded automatically. "Uh, for what?"

"For the perfect end to the perfect day."

Something about her referring to a day spent with me as 'perfect' fed my ego in the best possible way.

"It was pretty perfect," I admitted.

"Oh no, not you getting sentimental on me." Lila tapped her chin and leaned in closer to me. "I never thought I'd see the day."

She looked amazing in this lighting, her cheeks tinged red from the wine and a look of complete contentment about her. Plus, that dress. Fuck.

I couldn't even blame my wandering thoughts on the wine, because I'd only had a few sips. But my inhibitions seemed to need very little convincing to abandon me high and dry.

"Is this trip everything you were hoping it'd be?" I found myself asking, eager for more validation that I actually wasn't the nightmarish travel companion she'd originally thought me to be.

She sighed and looked at the ceiling for a moment before answering. "I don't know that I had many expectations. I was obviously excited to go on a trip with Charlie, but this is so far from what I imagined, I hadn't even had time to process what I thought it would be."

"Definitely different than anything you could have envisioned." Her answer left me deflated. "I'm sorry you didn't make it to Fiji with everyone else."

"Can I make a confession?" she whispered, even though the bustle of the restaurant easily drowned out our conversation from the tables next to ours.

"Tell me."

"If I could go back and make sure we were on the right flight. . . I'm not sure I would."

There it was. My heart raced, pounding harder than if I'd just sprinted around the entire building.

"I wouldn't either," I said, before I could think too deeply about it.

She smiled at that, and a swell of pride filled my chest. I was finally putting smiles on her face instead of ripping them away.

Lila giggled. "Although, I'm sure it would be fun to have Oliver around. If you think I try to fit a lot in a day, he'd take it to the next level."

"He'd have us on some random horseback-riding excursion or jumping out of some plane he found by talking to a local."

She laughed and shook her head, twisting the stem of her wine glass between her fingers.

"I really needed this trip. I'm always moving so fast I forget to enjoy life, sometimes."

"I think I needed this too," I said, hoping she'd know what I meant.

She caught my eye and tipped her head.

"It's funny to think about all the times we've been in the same room, but it took being stuck together halfway across the world to actually get to know each other."

I winced. "Sorry about that."

"No, I get it now. And I'm glad you finally felt safe enough to open up with me."

Her words felt like fire. Instead of responding, I picked up my water glass and took a sip just to have something to do.

"I'm trying to block out the fact that we only have two more days of this trip and then it's back to reality."

I blew out a breath, eternally grateful to her for changing the subject.

"What does a typical day look like for Lila?" I asked.

"Well, first I wake up at five—"

"Five?" I questioned. "Like, every day?"

"Every day. I like to make it to yoga before I come back and have my coffee and breakfast and head into work. I'm usually the first one there, but that's just because I'm a morning person. Then I spend the whole day running around like a chicken with its head cut off, trying to do a million things before leaving for the day."

"Then what?" I pressed.

"Then. . ." she thought about it. "Honestly, not much lately. I used to spend so much time with Charlie, running networking events or building the business after working our day job, that once we transitioned into running ConnectHer full-time, I wasn't sure what my life actually was. And now she has Nathan, and this whole life, and I'm so happy for her. We still see each other, of course, but it's different, you know? She used to be, like, my only family out in Denver, but now she has this whole other family of her own."

"You still fit into it."

"I know that. It's just different. Maybe it's pathetic that I'm so desperate to meet someone, but I just want that."

"What?"

"*That!* That feeling of total comforting bliss that I've found my partner. My chosen family. The one who I can drag to the farmers' market, or some concert I've been wanting to see. Who wants to cook dinner with me, or go get takeout and watch reruns of our favorite show, the one that we still watch together even though we could quote it in our sleep."

For a minute, I thought about what I'd do if Oliver met a

girl and decided to settle down. I'd have to move out. I wouldn't see him as much. I realized I kind of got her point.

"You can do all of that yourself," I said gently, urging her to see that the life she'd built for herself was already complete.

"I know," she whispered. "I'm proud of myself—and of my life. I know I don't need anyone else, but I want them. You probably think it's stupid."

"I don't," I said quickly. And I meant it. Despite the fact that a few days ago, I likely would have called all that stupid and then some. But after getting to know Lila, I didn't think that at all.

"But this trip has been good for me. It's given me a lot of clarity." Her eyes lit up with determination.

"Clarity on. . ."

"It's been a good reminder that I'm going to be fine no matter what happens. With Charlie getting married, I've been so stressed about falling behind. But it's all in my head. I realize that now. Whatever is meant for me will happen when it happens. I can't keep trying to force it."

"Does that mean you're calling it quits on the dating apps?" For reasons I didn't want to examine, a surge of hope jolted through me at the mere thought.

She tilted her head back, letting out a playful groan that danced in the air between us. "For now, at least."

"Good," I found myself saying too quickly. Heat shimmered in the air between us before she cleared her throat and looked around.

"Enough about me," she said, her voice sounding forced as it rose an octave. "Did you ever figure out your website?"

NINETEEN

Harrison

THE WALK BACK FELT BRIEF, YET EVERY STEP SEEMED CHARGED with something unspoken. As we crossed the street, I couldn't resist the urge to press my hand gently against the small of her back, savoring the subtle connection. When I unlocked the hotel room door, we stepped inside and the atmosphere shifted. Despite the lightheartedness of our stroll, an unfamiliar tension hung between us, palpable and electric. I glanced at her, wondering if she felt it too.

"That was nice," she said, dropping her bag to the table on her side of the perfectly made bed.

I nodded slowly as I watched her reach awkwardly behind her, trying to grasp at her zipper.

I tensed as I watched her struggle before she finally let out an exasperated sigh.

"Shit," she mumbled, before turning to look at me uncertainly. "Would you mind?"

I flexed and unflexed my hands as I walked over to her.

Play it cool. You are not on literal fire right now at just the thought of touching this woman.

My fingers closed around the zipper, my knuckles brushing the silky skin of her back in the process. Her whole body shuddered, and goosebumps prickled her perfect skin.

Slowly, I pulled the zipper down. When I reached her lower back, I knew I should stop. Instead, I hesitated. When she didn't pull away, I continued, drawing the zipper all the way down. Her dress came open and I could just see the top of her lacy underwear.

"Fuck," I breathed, unable to help myself. I traced a finger up her spine, savoring the feeling of her skin.

"What are you doing?" she whispered, still not stepping away from me.

"Nothing smart," I muttered. My hand dipped toward the curve of her waist and I gripped her lightly, spinning her toward me.

She came willingly and stared up at me, her eyes reflecting the same lust that had to be in my own.

"Tell me this is a bad idea," I breathed, reaching up and softly running my finger along her bare collarbone.

She licked her lips. "Is it such a bad idea?" She released the hand that had been clutching the top of her dress to her chest. The blue fabric dropped away, revealing a flimsy, black lace strapless bra.

I let out a sharp exhale, and the finger that traced her collarbone migrated down to trace the top of each of her perfect breasts.

She whimpered at my simple touch and that was enough to set me off completely. Without a second thought, I moved my other hand to the nape of her neck and tipped her head back before kissing her. Her lips were soft, and she tasted just as sweet as I imagined. I pressed against her and I couldn't resist moving one hand to her back, letting it fall until it hovered over her ass. I squeezed it gently. The way she bit down on my lip in response had me grinning against her mouth.

"I've always wanted to do that," I said, before binding my lips back to hers and taking the opportunity to slip my tongue inside her mouth. If you asked me yesterday about kissing Lila, I would have convinced everyone, even myself, that I had never thought about it. But doing it now felt like I was living out a very real, very suppressed fantasy. Her soft frame fit perfectly against mine, and every touch felt like something I had wanted to do forever.

To my absolute delight, she backed us both up until she was against the wall. That just got me fired up even more, and I hitched her leg up against my hip. I almost lost my mind when she started grinding against me.

She grabbed my shirt collar, my shoulders, the back of my head; anything to bring us even closer together. She panted as she tangled her fingers in my hair.

"Shit, I want you so bad," I said.

"Then take me," she said, already trying to unfasten my belt. "I've thought about this so many times."

She likes you, you know?

Lila's admission and Oliver's words from earlier hit me like a ton of bricks. I froze, but didn't back away as Lila continued to kiss me, moving her lips to my neck.

"Hold on," I breathed, trying to regain control.

"What? Why?" she questioned before sucking on my earlobe and almost causing me to lose all cohesive thought.

"Just hold on a minute," I said, more forcefully this time. I grabbed her shoulders and pushed myself away so I could look her in the eyes.

She searched my face, looking for answers.

"What's wrong?" she asked.

"It's just. . . I just. . . " I let out a frustrated sigh. "I don't want you to get the wrong idea."

Her eyebrows shot up. "The wrong idea? What, like you don't want to have sex with me right now? Because, sorry to tell you, if that's not the idea you were going for, you were very much giving all the wrong signals."

"No, it's not that. Trust me, I do very much want to pin you up against this wall and feel your body writhe underneath me."

She shuddered at the thought, then shook her head. "Then what is it? Why did you stop?"

"I don't want anything more."

Her expression dimmed, and I realized I was about to dig my own grave, but I couldn't stop. Every fiber of my being screamed that I would regret this, but the words spilled out anyway.

"Oliver mentioned. . . he said something about you liking me, or something? I don't know, he's probably full of shit. You know Oliver. But yeah. He said you might have a crush on me, and I don't want—" I held up my hands and gestured between the two of us. "I don't want to lead you on right now."

The desire had been completely extinguished from her eyes. Now her cheeks were flushed for a different reason.

"He *said* that?"

"Yeah," I breathed. She shrugged away from me, and I wasn't prepared for just how fucking empty I'd feel at her absence.

"So, just to be clear, you were hoping for a quick vacation fuck, and then we'd never speak of it again?" she questioned, striding to the other side of the room and ripping open the dresser drawer before grabbing a T-shirt and throwing it on.

"That's not— no—"

"You're right, maybe I did have the wrong idea. Because I thought spending hours opening up to each other might actually mean something to you."

"I never said I wanted a relationship," I replied, hating the immense distance that was rapidly forming between us. I searched for something to say that would make this alright, but I came up empty.

"I didn't either," she said with exasperation, pacing the room. "I mean, okay, well, technically I did. But I never said— nor implied—that I wanted one with *you*."

"I just—"

She held up a finger from across the room.

"And just because I want a relationship doesn't mean I'm some desperate person who expects every guy she sleeps with to propose."

"I don't want to hurt you." My words were weak and I felt sick with remorse. This was all wrong, but I didn't know how to make it right.

She cradled her forehead and shook her head. "No, you were right to stop. This was stupid. I mean, where could this possibly lead?"

I could think of a *lot* of good places that what we were doing might lead to, but I thought better of saying anything and snapped my mouth closed.

"This is the trip getting to us. We're in a romantic setting and we had a nice dinner. It tricked us into thinking we wanted to have sex with each other."

"Did it? Because I—"

"Nope, stop talking." She waved a hand at me. "Do me a favor. Let's never speak of this again, okay? Okay."

With that she stormed past me and went straight for the

bathroom, leaving me standing there feeling like a massive idiot. Especially since I didn't even truly believe what I'd said.

Maybe I wasn't worried that Lila would get the wrong idea.

Maybe the ideas already swimming through my own damned mind were the things starting to scare the shit out of me.

TWENTY

Lila

———

"How am I supposed to face him?" I hissed, holding my phone close to my face and pacing across the hotel patio. Meanwhile Charlie gawked at me from the other end of the line.

"I can't believe you two actually almost hooked up."

"We were literally one move away from hitting the bed." I groaned just thinking about the events of last night. After I had finally come out of the bathroom, my tail between my legs, Harrison was already in bed either pretending to sleep or actually conked out. Either way, I was grateful I didn't have to face him. After securing a pillow barrier between us, I lay awake on my side of the bed for hours, replaying every second of the humiliating experience before exhaustion finally took over.

"Oliver called it," she said, shaking her head in disbelief.

"Oliver? I'm going to kill him," I spat. "Put him on the phone. Do you know what that little troll did?"

Charlie opened her mouth to guess, but I continued before she had the chance.

"He told Harrison that I had a *crush* on him. I mean, what the hell? I know they're best friends, but I thought he had some sort of allegiance toward me."

Charlie winced.

"What?" I demanded, taking in her guilt-ridden face.

"I told Oliver I thought you might like Harrison," she admitted.

My lips parted as I stared at my backstabbing best friend. "How could you?"

"I'm sorry. It wasn't like this whole thing to betray you or something." She said, waving her hands and pacing on her end as well. "I just said I noticed you always looked at him. I don't know, Lila. You're my best friend. I know what you're like when you find a guy attractive. I thought it was harmless to tell Oliver. I didn't think he would actually say something to Harrison."

"They're best friends!" I whisper-shouted. "And room-mates. Also, Oliver can't keep anything to himself. Of course he was going to tell Harrison."

"Sorry," she said weakly.

Sighing deeply, I massaged my forehead with my free hand. "It's not your fault," I muttered. "You weren't completely off the mark."

"I know," Charlie said sadly, trying to give me an encouraging smile.

There was no use obsessing over what had happened last night. What was done was done. And it wasn't like Harrison hadn't *wanted* me. I could take a little solace in that fact. I wasn't sure what the hell I was going to say to him, mind you, but we only had two days left on this trip. Unfortunately, if the past two days were any indication, these next two would feel more like two weeks.

"Anyway." I finally sighed and slumped into one of the

deck chairs. "Enough about me and my predicament. Tell me about Fiji."

Charlie gave me all the details for the next twenty minutes before graciously wishing me good luck and ending the call.

I set my phone on the table next to me and stared out at the sea lapping against the shoreline. My brain urged me to go get an espresso, but my body was still too wired just thinking about last night.

Would Harrison pretend like it didn't happen? Would he want to talk about it? Both options sounded equally unappealing. If he never mentioned it again, then I would know for sure that I had absolutely zero effect on him. But at the same time, bringing it up—just to be essentially rejected again—also sounded awful.

And the worst part was that my top-secret crush, the one I had never told anyone about, was somehow public knowledge. Or at least public lore. Which wasn't even fair, because it's not like I could control it. Trust me, if I had the power, I would certainly not be crushing on a guy like Harrison. Despite how far we'd come on this trip, there was no way he could ever be the kind of guy that I needed.

He definitely didn't remind me of my ex; that would be a cruel and unfair comparison. But his harsh attitude didn't exactly mesh with the way I wanted to live my life.

In his defense, mind you, he'd opened up a lot in the last two days. Yesterday, he had been down to try anything and hadn't shied away from visibly enjoying himself. But that had just been one day.

A small part of my mind reminded me how much I'd enjoyed seeing him like that, knowing it was my influence at play. I didn't just like it—I'd loved it. It filled me with a strange sense of satisfaction.

Ugh; I was *so* confused.

"Lily," Nigel called from behind me.

I turned in my seat to find him approaching me with Mark, Will, and three girls.

"Morning," I said, forcing a cheery voice.

"These are the new roommates," he gestured to the girls. They were all cute, and while probably younger than me, they at least looked like they had a few years on the guys.

"Hi," the dark-haired one said. "Nigel said you were American, too."

"We are," I said.

"We?" she arched a brow.

"Oh, me and the guy I'm traveling with—Harrison. He still hasn't woken up yet."

"We're about to grab breakfast and then catch the ferry to Mykonos. You have to come," Nigel said.

"That does sound like fun," I admitted.

It was obvious that Harrison wasn't dying to go anywhere with these guys, but after yesterday, *I* wasn't dying to be alone with him. Biting my lip, I stared at the door to our room. Should I wake him up? Go without him? My gut told me he would be pissed if I went with the second option. And although everyone seemed normal enough, I probably shouldn't wander off alone with a group I barely knew. Still. . . the chance to get away from him for the day and avoid dealing with my embarrassment was *very* tempting.

"I'll go," I said, still not sure what to do about Harrison.

Just then, the door to our room opened. Harrison stepped out, wearing a simple white T-shirt and black shorts. Something flickered across his face when he saw me standing there, but vanished when he noticed the rest of the group.

"Morning, handsome," Nigel called. "You ready to go to Mykonos?"

"I CAN'T BELIEVE YOU WERE GOING TO GO WITHOUT ME. DO you know how stupid that would have been?" Harrison said in a low, irritated voice as we took our seats on the ferry. The rest of the group from our hotel was already seated a few rows ahead of us.

"I wasn't going to go without you."

"Really?" He leaned in, eyebrows raised, and nerves swirled in my stomach. "Then why were you all standing around ready to go when I walked out?"

"I was going to get you," I insisted, although internally I had been debating *not* doing just that.

His gaze hardened. "You're lying."

"What does it matter?" I asked as the ferry started to move. "We're both here now."

"It matters because I need to be sure you're not going to run off on me just because things got a little complicated last night."

My pulse quickened and I looked away. The ferry swayed back and forth as it moved through the water with surprising speed.

"Hey." Harrison's voice was much softer this time, which just made it that much more impossible to meet his eyes. "We don't have to talk about it if you don't want to. Just know that I really don't want anything to change between us. I'm. . . I'm having fun with you. Just like you wanted. We're only halfway through this trip and I really don't want that to stop now."

"I don't want it to stop either." The butterflies in my stomach were getting a lot more aggressive.

After a minute, he let out an exasperated sigh. "You can't even look at me." His voice was a mix of disappointment and frustration.

"Yes, I can," I insisted, briefly meeting his eyes before proving his point and ducking my head again. I lifted my tiny crossbody bag onto my lap, eager to pull my phone out for a distraction. But as soon as I felt the weight, I realized it was too light.

"Shit," I said, rummaging through the contents. It was useless. I knew without even looking that my phone wasn't in there. Images flashed in my mind of me setting it down on one of the small tables by the pool. I had been so flustered when the group approached me, and then when Harrison came outside, I had completely forgotten to grab it. Now I could only hope that Maria would find it and get it back to me later.

"What?" Harrison demanded.

"I forgot my phone." I groaned and leaned my head back, feeling queasy.

"You don't have your phone." I could hear the edge in his voice. Even though my eyes were sealed shut, I was sure that if I opened them I'd find him glaring down at me with a disapproving look.

"That's so irresponsible," he berated. "We're in another country. What if something happened to you?"

I opened my mouth to defend myself, but before I could answer, my stomach churned violently. I covered my mouth with both hands and bolted out of my seat, sprinting for the bathroom I had passed on the way in.

Thankfully, I made it to a toilet stall just in time to lose the little breakfast I had consumed. The relief I felt was instant, but I knew another wave of nausea wouldn't be far behind.

Squatting there, desperately trying to keep my butt from touching the tiled floor, I pressed my cold hands to my hot face. Just when I was starting to feel better, the ferry rocked forcefully and bile crept up my throat again. This time, hardly anything came up when I leaned over the toilet.

"Ugh, disgusting," I muttered, flushing the contents away.

"Lila!" A deep voice called from the entrance.

Tilting my head back, I let out a long groan. I didn't want anyone to see me like this, let alone Harrison. Hopefully the fact that this was a women's bathroom would be enough to keep him from barging into the stall.

"Fine!" was all I could manage to call back. Complete sentences were too much for me right now.

After another few minutes, Harrison called again. "Come here!"

Assessing my body, I realized that while still feeling like my stomach was on a roller coaster, I didn't feel the need to throw up again. I stood slowly, bracing my hands on my knees on the way up. Exiting the stall, I winced at the sight of myself in the mirror. My skin had turned a shade of ghostly white. I turned on the sink and splashed some water on my face, before cupping my hand and lifting some into my mouth. My breath tasted like death, but there was little I could do about that.

Thankfully, one bright spot about getting a bout of motion sickness meant I no longer cared how I appeared to Harrison. I was too weak.

He stood in the doorway with a small plastic bag, eyebrows pinched together.

"You alright?"

"Great," I said, walking right past him to get back to my seat as quickly as possible.

He kept pace with me, reaching out and grabbing my elbow to steady me as the boat rocked. Finally, I stumbled into my seat and pulled my legs up so that I could cradle my chin on my knees.

Harrison sat down next to me and rummaged through the

bag on his lap. He brought out a small pill bottle and opened it before shaking a couple out.

"Here," he said, handing me the pills and an electrolyte drink.

"What's this?" I took them from him.

"For motion sickness. I got them at the snack counter."

"How'd you know?" I asked, knocking them back and taking a few cautious sips of the drink.

"You were completely green. It was obvious." He opened another bag and thrust a few crackers in my direction. "Eat these."

I blanched at the thought. "No way."

"They'll help," he insisted.

"Yeah, help me puke again."

He tilted his head and gave me an irritated look. "You shouldn't take those pills on an empty stomach. You need something."

I sighed heavily before taking a cracker and slowly nibbling at the edge.

"You're a bossy caretaker."

"I have mints for you too, when you're feeling up to it."

"Thank you," I mumbled, feeling grateful that for a minute, what had happened between us last night could be completely forgotten. I knew the weirdness would resurface as soon as the ferry docked and my mind cleared, but for now, this moment felt nice. Despite the nausea, and the fact that I probably looked a bit pathetic.

"Now, keep eating that and rest your head on my shoulder."

"I'm fine—"

"Do it," he insisted.

"Bossy," I said again weakly, but I complied. And I had to admit, the steadiness of his strong shoulder did feel nice. Plus, he smelled really good. Which didn't feel fair when I felt as gross as I did. I closed my eyes and brought the cracker to my lip, continuing to eat it in tiny bites.

"Why did you agree to come on this if you get seasick?" Harrison asked, after I had a few moments to collect myself.

"I don't, normally," I whispered. Charlie and I had gone on a boat trip just this past summer with ConnectHer, and I'd been completely fine. It was probably the nerves twisting my stomach as a result of last night, but I didn't want to admit that to Harrison. "It's probably because we're inside," I offered.

His eyes narrowed as he looked around the large ferry. "We can try to stand up top on the way back. How are you feeling now?" he asked, shifting so that his shoulder was a little lower and I could nestle even further into the crook of his neck.

"Better," I said, still keeping my eyes sealed shut. "It's the cracker."

He let out a small chuckle.

We sat in silence after that, until eventually, I dozed off.

TWENTY-ONE

Lila

"Mykonos!" Nigel, Mark, and Will called out in strange attempts at a Greek accent for the fifth time since we'd arrived on the new island. The girls from our hotel—whose names I'd found out were Baily, Paige, and Kate—shared an unimpressed look with me.

We had shared two taxis when we'd arrived at the Old Port a couple hours ago. And when someone had suggested a girls' and boys' taxi, I had probably accepted all too eagerly. Harrison hadn't been happy about it, but I had scrambled into the back of the cab faster than he could object.

Despite sharing a sweet moment on the ferry, memories of last night still invaded my mind, like an unwelcome visitor.

Any time I'd managed to get myself to meet Harrison's eyes, all I could see were visions of my humiliation. But this day trip had been a karmic gift of massive proportions. I didn't know what I'd done to deserve this distraction, but I was immensely thankful for it.

The trio of girls were actually great. They were all in their senior year of college and studying abroad in Paris. They had decided to come to Greece on a whim during an extended weekend break. Even though they were only maybe five years younger than me, I felt like their mom. Or, at the very least, their cool older aunt.

"So, you two aren't a couple?" Paige, the one with short dark hair, asked.

"Nope," I responded, glancing back at a miserable-looking Harrison.

House music bumped through the DJ's speakers, and I could barely hear anything even though we stood on the edge of the crowd.

"Mind if I have a go?" Bailey, the most outgoing of the three, asked, tipping her sunglasses down and eyeing Harrison hungrily. I shoved aside the little spark of jealousy that ignited within me.

"He's not much for flirting," I said, which wasn't even a lie. Even if nothing had happened between Harrison and me, and even if I'd never had a crush, I would have bet money that Harrison wouldn't be interested in any of these girls. They were sweet, but they were young and just wanted to have a good time. I couldn't see Harrison lasting for more than two minutes in a conversation with any of them.

"Shame he's so stiff," Bailey continued. "He could really use someone to loosen him up."

"Trust me, I've been trying." I glanced at Harrison again, who looked incredibly out of place. He sat in a lounger and slowly sipped a beer, looking like he wished he were anywhere but here. We made eye contact briefly before I tore my gaze away.

My heart went out to him a little. If last night hadn't happened, I would have asked him an hour ago if he wanted to ditch this party and go back to the town to explore. That was really all I wanted to do. But being stranded alone with him now. . . I just wasn't ready for that. Perhaps I was being immature, but shame and discomfort still gnawed at my gut, and I couldn't quite shake it.

We were at a beach party specifically designed for tourists to get drunk and dance as DJs hyped us all up. Nigel, Mark, and Will were obviously in their element, and hadn't left the dance floor. The girls and I were having fun, but after dancing for a few songs we had already taken a break at the edge of the crowd.

"You should try harder." Kate, the most introverted of the three, looked between me and Harrison. "He looks so sad."

Bailey snorted. "Sad? More like scary."

Paige nodded in agreement. "You couldn't pay me to approach him."

Kate shrugged. "I don't know. His eyes look sad to me."

My heart sank at that, because she was probably right. There was a lot more to Harrison than the tough exterior he presented. He'd finally let me scrape away at it and now I was over here, desperate to get some space. The guilt started to seep in. I should never have let that kiss happen. When he'd unzipped my dress, I should have stepped away. I should never have leaned into his touch. I should have—

"Lily, open up." Nigel appeared in front of me, attempting to pour a shot of something toward my closed, unready mouth. I dodged it, letting the clear liquor flow to the ground instead.

"Alright, buddy," I said, lightly tapping Nigel's chest. "I think you need some water."

I went to hand him the almost-full glass in my right hand, but as he reached to grab it, his sloppy movement knocked it clean out of my hand. It went sailing toward me and drenched my right side in the process.

"Shit. I'm so sorry," he said, grabbing my arm.

"You okay?" I hadn't even noticed him approach, but Harrison was suddenly at my side.

"Fine," I grumbled, but forced a smile. "I was hot anyway."

"You're all wet." Nigel giggled before Harrison pushed him away from me. It wasn't aggressive, but it was firm.

"Give her some space," he said, his voice casual yet somehow still threatening.

Nigel held up his hands. "Okay, I won't touch your girl."

Harrison turned back to me as I was assessing the damage. It wasn't lost on me that he hadn't corrected Nigel's words this time.

"Shit." I held up my tiny cloth bag that was now completely soaked. Since I didn't have my phone, it didn't really matter that the bottom of the bag was now drenched. One silver lining, I supposed.

"Are you okay?" Harrison asked again.

"Fine." I tried to keep my tone casual, but the water was the least of my worries. What unsettled me more was the way his gaze lingered on me, heavy and unyielding. I needed to get away from it. From him.

"Let me get some more waters," I said.

The dance floor was packed, a sea of bodies moving in sync, but I navigated my way carefully along the edge, dodging the pull of the more enthusiastic dancers as I headed toward the bar.

His presence loomed behind me. I knew he was there without turning to look.

"Can we get out of here?" Harrison asked under his breath, following me to the bar.

"Um, maybe in a bit." My answer was noncommittal. I wouldn't mind leaving, but nerves ate at my stomach at the thought of the two of us alone.

The long tiki bar hugged the back of a building that practically spilled onto the sand, acting as the line between indoors and out. Inside, the space was mostly concrete, and although there was a second dance floor, it wasn't nearly as crowded. I edged my way to the bar and waited for the bartender to catch my eye.

"Can I just talk to you for a second?" Harrison grasped my forearm. The light touch of his fingers sent an electric wave of energy through me. It was almost as if he felt it too, because he yanked his hand away.

"Here?" I yelled over the pulsing music.

"Ideally anywhere *but* here. But since that's where we are. . ."

"What's up?" I asked, furrowing my brow. He wasn't really going to bring up last night, was he? Not here.

"Last night was—"

I held up a hand, unable to stifle a groan. "Not now, Harrison."

"We need to talk about it," he forced out through gritted teeth. I couldn't tell if his pained expression was from remorse or because of how uncomfortable this conversation was about to be.

"Tell you what," I said, resigned. "Why don't we just enjoy the rest of our time here, and maybe talk about it when we're back at the hotel."

"But—"

"But what?" I snapped. His eyes hardened a bit at my curt response.

"Okay," he said.

My heart twisted a little when he turned to leave, and it took restraint not to reach out and grab his arm. He looked like a wounded puppy. Or a wounded wolf, maybe.

I pinched the bridge of my nose and sighed. My short

replies were entirely due to my embarrassment, and that wasn't fair to Harrison. We were both adults. We had both wanted things. He hadn't done anything wrong by being clear and saying he had no interest in a relationship with me. He'd explained it himself—he just didn't want to hurt me.

While I waited for the bartender, I peeked over my shoulder. Harrison had returned to the edge of the crowd, but I could still make out his tall frame. He kept his eyes on me and didn't turn away when I met his stare. I offered him a weak smile.

The bartender finally looked my way and poured four glasses of water when I asked for them. I would have gotten more, but feared I would accidentally dump them on myself. If my dress got any wetter, I might as well just jump straight into the ocean.

As I made my way back to the group, I decided it was time to stop making things awkward with Harrison. It wasn't fair when we'd made so much progress. Our friendship—or the start of a friendship, at least—meant something to me. I wouldn't ruin it over a silly kiss. Even if that silly kiss and the way his big hands had brushed gently over my skin were absolutely all I could think about.

"Here you go." I forced Nigel, Will, and Mark to each take a glass from my outstretched hands. Thankfully, they didn't fight me on it and knocked back their waters.

"We want to go check out town," Bailey said, her eyes flickering between the boisterous boys and me.

"But the party is here," Will argued.

"Yeah, we're just getting started," Mark agreed.

"Then it might be time to split up," offered Kate.

"No way." Nigel pouted and slung an arm around each of the girls' shoulders. "We have to stick together."

Kate and Bailey looked at each other, clearly stifling an eye roll.

"I'm ready to go," I offered.

"Thank fucking God," Harrison muttered, hovering at my side.

Mark and Will groaned in protest, but Nigel snapped his fingers. "I've got it. There are bars in town. We can do a little bar crawl while we explore."

Paige and Bailey opened their mouths as if to protest, but then shrugged as if thinking better of it. Sometimes, just agreeing with the drunk party animal was the path of least resistance. While I doubted any of us wanted to go to another bar, we could easily sneak off and do our own thing once we got back into the narrow, winding streets of Old Town Mykonos.

"Let's go," Paige and Bailey said in unison.

We made our way through the party, back inside, and to the front of the building. There was a U-shaped driveway in front where we could wait for a cab to take us back into town. We called for two and waited.

When the first cab arrived, the girls piled into the back seat. I moved to join them in the passenger seat.

"Wait," Harrison said, grabbing my arm. "Let's ride together."

I looked at the cab, then back to him. "We can't all fit," I pointed out.

He looked like he wanted to argue, but I could promise him that there was no way in hell Bailey, Paige, and Kate were going to allow themselves to get split up.

"It's fine. It's, like, a twenty-minute ride and we'll be together again." I tried to reassure him.

We'd all agreed on a meeting spot at the edge of town, the same place where we'd gotten picked up.

"Twenty minutes," he repeated. His protectiveness warmed my heart. No matter how strange things were between us right now, he was always looking out for me.

"I'll see you soon." I took a chance and winked at him to break the unnecessary tension. The corner of his lip quirked up, and he let me fold into the passenger seat. Once I was secure, he lightly shut the door behind me.

The ride was quiet for me. While the three girls gossiped in the back, I tuned them out and stared out the window. This island was so different than Santorini, yet still unmistakably Greece. Air from the open window beat against my face. It was almost too strong, but I welcomed it. It felt stimulating after the morning I'd had.

I cursed myself again for letting last night get into my head. We were only here for another day and a half. While I'd tried to let go this morning and just have fun, I had been extremely self-conscious the entire time and it was affecting me.

Not anymore. Harrison and I were finally on good terms after all this time, and I wasn't about to let last night get in the way of that. I was being stupid for allowing his rejection—if you could even call it that—to burrow into my insecurities. Maybe I'd always had a little crush on Harrison, but that hadn't been based on anything other than the physical. Now, I knew him a lot better. He'd become a friend. I couldn't ruin that for some fantasy.

Deep in my bones, though, I knew my crush was only getting stronger the more I got to know him.

I sighed and shook my head, attempting to shake the thought out of my mind. As soon as we both got back into town, I was turning over a new leaf. I'd smile at Harrison like I meant it, tell him last night was nothing to worry about, and enjoy the rest of our time here. Then, when we went home, hopefully a fragment of our friendship would remain. It would be beyond strange to go back to the way things were, after all this.

The girls and I got out of the taxi once we arrived on the outskirts of town, right where a main street ended and the narrow pedestrian streets began. We stretched and yawned, the hours spent in the sun making us all a little groggy.

"I need an espresso, stat," Bailey said.

"Same," I agreed.

"Once the guys get here, I'm thinking we just drop them off at whatever bar they want to go to and do our own thing," Bailey continued. "I'm dying to check out all the shops."

We waited on the curb for them.

And waited.

And waited.

Kate pulled out her phone to check the time again. "Could they really be twenty minutes behind us? I saw their taxi pull up right after ours."

A knot twisted in my chest. I reached for my phone, but panicked when my fingers only brushed the thin cloth of my bag.

"Shit," I exclaimed. My heart was full-on racing now.

"What?" Page asked.

"My phone. I forgot it back at the hotel."

Bailey patted my shoulder reassuringly. "I'm sure it's fine. They probably just got sidetracked by another beach party, or something."

"Harrison would not let that happen," I insisted. Worry churned in my gut.

"Maybe their taxi got lost," Kate suggested.

"Maybe," I said, not convinced.

"You can use my phone to call Harrison," Page offered.

I frowned and shook my head. "I don't know his number."

212 · TRIP SWITCH

Hell, I didn't even know Charlie's number by heart. Not having access to my phone made me realize how absurd that was. I needed to memorize a few phone numbers in the future. "Do one of you have any of the other guys' numbers?" I asked hopefully.

They all looked at me with sympathetic eyes and shook their heads.

Shit.

"I'm sure they'll be here any minute." Page leaned into the road, looking for signs of the car.

After twenty more minutes, though, the girls started to get restless. They didn't have the same anxiety I did that something was wrong. But, at the same time, it hadn't been nearly long enough to go into complete panic mode.

"Come on, Lila. Come to the shops with us. We'll still be nearby. They'll find us once they eventually show up," Bailey said.

"Yeah, and we can come back to this spot in an hour or two just to see if they're here."

I gave them a tight-lipped smile, trying to control the thoughts racing through my brain. Could they have gotten into a car accident? Been abducted? The idea that someone would abduct four fully grown men seemed unlikely, but I really couldn't think of another reason why they weren't right behind us. Harrison wouldn't have abandoned us willingly, that was for sure.

"Maybe their car broke down." Paige snapped her fingers, as if that were a genius revelation.

"I guess," I said.

"Or maybe the guys did drag Harrison somewhere else, and he's trying to corral them, or get his own taxi. You saw them. They're a bit of a handful right now." Bailey folded her arms and shook her head.

"Please come with us," Kate said. "We don't want to leave you here without a phone."

I desperately searched the road, hoping that this was the moment I would finally see the signs of the boys' taxi arriving. But there was nothing.

"Okay," I finally said, my tone defeated. I followed them into town, telling myself all the while that Harrison had just gotten caught up with something silly. He'd be here soon, and he'd find me. I was sure of it.

TWENTY-TWO

Harrison

"ARE YOU FUCKING SERIOUS?" I BARKED, UNABLE TO KEEP THE rage out of my voice.

"Lighten up," Nigel said, clapping my back, too drunk to care about the pure fury radiating off me. I shrugged my shoulder violently and he staggered backward.

"It's just one more stop," Mark slurred.

"Thirty minutes away! You couldn't have picked something closer to town?" I raked my hand through my hair, insanely frustrated with myself that I hadn't noticed we'd been driving in the opposite direction this entire time. I had been heavily distracted by a certain redhead. One who I was sure I'd messed everything up with.

"This beach is supposed to be legendary for parties," Nigel argued, pointing at the beach club in front of us.

Music blared out of speakers and guests lounged in chairs sipping cocktails, but overall, at least from what I could tell, it was a pretty tame environment.

Groaning, I pinched my eyes.

"Seems deader than I thought," Will said.

"Maybe because it's two in the afternoon." I gestured at the sky.

"The other place had a party." Nigel pouted.

"Because the girls *specifically* looked up which beaches had a DJ during the day." My voice was thick with frustration. These guys were a freaking mess. Of course, they'd expected to just stumble around and find another party. They couldn't come up with a successful plan to save their lives.

"Could you find us another party?" Mark asked me.

"What about the bar crawl? The one we're supposed to be on *in town*?" I asked, glaring at the three of them.

"That's a good idea," Nigel slurred. "Let's go."

"Jesus Chri—" They were impossible. They couldn't keep to task for more than five seconds. "Well, now we're on the other side of the island, genius," I added.

"I just want to party." Mark started jumping up and down as a club beat came on over the speakers.

"It's our birthday," Will whined.

"I need to call Lila." I tuned out their incessant chatter.

I pulled up her contact info and I waited for her to pick up. But instead of her voice on the other end of the line, an older woman with a Greek accent answered.

"Hello," Maria said. "I think you left your phone outside."

My heart dropped.

"*Shit*," I cursed, pulling the phone away from my ear for a second before bringing it back. I had completely forgotten Lila had lost her phone. Talk about the worst fucking timing I could think of. "That's Lila's phone," I said, my mind already racing with the need to find her.

"I'll hang on to it for her," Maria said.

I thanked her and ended the call.

Now, not only could I not reach Lila, but she was also by

herself, on an island we weren't even staying on, without a phone.

"Shit. Shit. Shit." I started to pace. This was all my fault. I should have insisted that Lila and I get our own taxi. I should have remembered that she didn't have a phone. I had been too hung up on thoughts of last night, and I hadn't even thought about it. I should never have been that careless with her.

We didn't even know these people, not really. Even if I turned around now, I'd still be over an hour late meeting her. Would she wait around? Would she wander off without a phone? The thought terrified me.

A high pitched scream came from behind me, and I spun around. Nigel was on the ground, clutching his nose, while blood spurted from underneath his hand.

"What the hell?" I demanded, stalking over to them.

"He tripped," Mark said.

"How bad is it?" Tears were in Nigel's panicked eyes.

"Move your hand so I can see," I ordered.

He took his shaky hand away from his face. His nose was swelling up and there was a large gash underneath it. I was no expert, but it looked like it needed stitches.

"Did you brace the fall with your face?" I asked.

"He didn't brace it at all." Will chuckled, but Nigel's sobs made him snap his mouth closed.

"It's bad. I know it is. Oh my God."

I fought the urge to roll my eyes at his dramatics. He was acting as if he'd lost a limb rather than just scraped his face on the pavement.

"What do we do?" Mark asked, looking to me with panic in his eyes.

"Shit." I blew out a breath. These guys were a liability that, somehow, I had become in charge of.

"One sec." I walked toward the entrance to the beach bar.
"Where are you going?" Nigel demanded. "We need you."
"I'll be right back," I said. "Keep applying pressure to that cut."

Even though I had this mess to deal with, the only concern I had at the moment was for Lila. The sooner I dealt with this situation, the sooner I could find her. And I needed to find her as fast as possible.

Once inside, I tracked down one of the managers who turned out to be incredibly helpful. He called us a taxi and told me where the nearest clinic was. He also gave me a few towels to help with the bleeding.

"Here." I threw one of the towels at Nigel once I was back outside. Instead of calming down, he had ramped up to hysterical.

"Will I need stitches?" he asked.

"Probably. Hold the towel on your face," I instructed.

"Oh God, I hate needles."

"It's not so bad. I had to get my hand stitched up last year," Will said.

"My face will never be the same." Nigel moaned in agony.

"Good thing it wasn't pretty in the first place." Mark chuckled to himself.

After what felt like an agonizingly long time, the taxi finally pulled into the parking lot.

The driver took one look at us and shook his head.

"No. Not in my car."

"Please." I wasn't above begging at this point. "Just to the clinic down the road. And see—" I held up a couple of clean towels and opened the back door. "He'll sit on these."

The driver still looked angry, but gave a curt nod.

"Get in."

"WHERE ARE YOU GOING?" NIGEL GRIPPED THE WINDOW TO the front seat of the cab.

"Back into town." We'd arrived at the clinic to drop off the boys. When I'd stayed in the car and instructed the driver to keep going, Nigel, Mark, and Will all protested.

"We need you," Will insisted.

"No. You don't. And I need to find Lila." I glared at them all. If they didn't back off this taxi and let me go in the next ten seconds, my patience would be completely gone. It had already been almost two hours since I'd last seen her. My throat tightened just thinking about it.

"What do we do?" Mark asked.

"Turn your asses around and walk through the door!" I exclaimed, pointing behind them at the clinic.

"Can you come with u—"

"No. You're three grown-ass men. Figure it out."

"But—"

"Go!" I said, narrowing my eyes and daring them to challenge me again.

"He's right. We got this." Mark patted Nigel's back. "We'll get you fixed up in no time."

"Great," I mumbled, my body sagging with relief when they finally backed away.

"See you later," Will said waving, still not looking completely sober.

I gave them what could only be called a sarcastic wave as the driver pulled away from the clinic and they disappeared behind the doors.

He let out a gruff sigh and we both exchanged a look of respite.

"To town?" he confirmed.

"Yes. As fast as possible."

The drive stretched on for what felt like hours. I sat in the passenger seat, foot tapping aggressively against the floor. What could Lila have possibly thought? There was no way in hell she'd think I'd just ditch her. The idea was too preposterous. I just hoped she'd stuck with the girls. Logically, I knew she would be alright; it was unlikely that anything had happened to her. But I would continue to spiral until I saw her face again.

She wouldn't have tried to go back to Santorini on her own, would she? Surely, she would have waited for me longer than a few hours.

Part of me wondered if this all had to do with my piss-poor excuse for communication last night. Would she even have wanted to tag along on this trip if I hadn't messed everything up yesterday?

As soon as the words had come out of my mouth—about being worried that she had a crush on me—I'd regretted them. They'd tasted bitter when I said them, and even now, almost a full day later, the aftertaste remained. It wasn't right. It wasn't how I felt.

I didn't know what it felt like to want someone like that, not just for their body, but for everything else they were as well. The closest I'd ever come to a relationship was sleeping with the same girl for a few months. Inevitably, it would end when she wanted me to open up more and I refused to oblige.

Lila had gotten in, though. Despite me resisting at every opportunity, she had nestled her way right into all the important parts of me. I hadn't known how to handle it. I hadn't been planning on making a move last night, but it just happened. And it happened before I'd had the chance to sort through these new feelings.

What I said hadn't been completely wrong. I didn't want

to hurt her. That was the last thing I could cope with. I still wasn't entirely sure what I did want, but it was unfair to her not to let her know the full truth. Which was that I felt a lot for her. Probably a hell of a lot more than she felt for me. That scared the shit out of me, but she deserved to know everything.

I doubted I could ever be good enough for her. That hurt to think about, but I couldn't see a world where I could offer her even a fraction of what she'd already given to me. But I was selfish, and I was going to tell her what I felt, and deal with the rest of it later. I didn't know how to do any of this, but I also couldn't let her go.

I'd intended to tell her all this and lay myself bare the second I saw her this morning. She'd had other plans, which apparently involved avoiding me like the plague. I didn't blame her, but I was also done letting her tiptoe around the subject. She was going to hear what I had to say, whether she liked it or not.

Now I just had to find her.

My foot bounced against the floorboard as the edge of Old Town came into view. I'd instructed the driver to drop me off at the same place we'd all originally planned to meet. I jumped out of the car and scanned the immediate surroundings. My stomach sank when I saw no signs of Lila or the others.

I cursed myself for the hundredth time for ever allowing us to be separated in the first place.

My only move was to head into the maze-like pedestrian streets. I'd have to wander down them and hope to find her. I didn't want to think about what I would do if I didn't. While there was always the possibility she could have headed back to Santorini when I failed to show, I couldn't even fathom the idea of leaving this island without being sure of where she was.

I set off jogging down the cobbled streets. I kept my pace quick, but still slow enough that I could jerk my head in every direction to make sure I didn't miss her. Thankfully, my brain was already wired to hyperfocus on Lila, so any faces that weren't hers all seemed to blur together.

After fifteen minutes of searching, I stopped in the middle of a particularly crowded intersection to stand on a step, attempting to examine every passerby. My heart raced for reasons that had nothing to do with my sprint around the town.

Then, my heart nearly stopped altogether. Fifty feet away, disappearing around a corner, was a flash of red hair on top of a sundress. My chest exploded with relief as I hopped down from the step and tore off after her.

TWENTY-THREE

Lila

THE PACKED STREETS HAD CLEARED OUT A BIT SINCE WE'D first arrived in town, as hordes of tourists shuffled back to the port to rejoin their cruise ship.

Bailey, Paige, and Kate had gone a little while ago to catch their ferry. They hadn't wanted to leave me, but had prebooked earlier tickets back to Santorini for a dinner reservation they'd made for tonight. I had thought about going with them; at least that way I could try to track down my phone back at the hotel. But in the end, I couldn't stomach leaving without knowing where the hell Harrison was. And if you get separated from someone and can't communicate, the best spot to wait for them is the spot in which you last planned to meet, right? I wasn't sure, but the logic made sense to me.

My worry had grown immensely in the past few hours, but I wouldn't allow myself to turn into a blubbering mess. I refused to collapse into full-on panic until I was back at our hotel in Santorini and he wasn't there. But I wouldn't even allow myself to think of the possibility.

My eyes started to blur as I looked in yet another shop

window. I had been dying to shop when we'd arrived this morning, but now nothing could ease my wandering mind.

If I just had my stupid phone, none of this would be happening.

"Lila!"

My heart sprang into my throat and I almost cried at the sight of Harrison running toward me. I took a few steps toward him, and he dodged a few passing tourists before colliding with me. He wrapped his arms around me and tugged me tightly to his chest. The hug might have taken me by surprise if I wasn't so relieved to see him. I nestled into his T-shirt and breathed him in. When he rested his chin on my head, all of my tension and fear melted away.

"Are you alright?" he asked, not loosening his grip on me.

"Are you kidding?" I wanted to laugh. "Are *you* alright? What happened? I've been freaking out thinking about you lying in a ditch somewhere."

He brushed his hand along the back of my hair.

"It's a long story." He sighed and pulled back. His eyes searched mine, and my stomach dipped as if I were in some sort of free fall. The look in his eyes felt new.

Before I could question him further, he reached into his pocket and pulled out his phone. "Can you do me a favor and just hold onto this until you have yours back?"

I smiled. "I don't need—"

"Please," he begged. "For my own sanity. Then at least I have a way of reaching you."

I took it from his hands and smiled. "Okay. If it'll make you feel better."

"It will," he said, not breaking eye contact.

He ran a hand along his jaw and looked me up and down, as if searching to make sure every hair on my head was in the correct spot.

"So? What happened?" I asked.

His eyes narrowed. "Nigel and his asshat friends happened."

I raised an eyebrow, waiting for him to continue. Instead, he reached up and tucked a lock of my hair behind my ear. My breath caught in my throat. He was acting strange, almost nervous.

"Those idiots dragged us halfway across the island. I'll tell you everything, but first, can we finally talk about last night?"

My lips parted in surprise.

"Last night? What? You want to talk about last night after we've just been separated for hours by some mysterious event you haven't shared the details of?"

"Lila," he said, sternly yet gently. "All I've wanted to do is talk about last night since the moment it happened."

"But—" I started to protest, but snapped my mouth shut when I saw his look of fierce determination.

"Lila," he said my name again slowly, with care.

"Harrison," I said, my knees feeling like they could buckle at any moment.

He reached up and traced his fingertips lightly along my chin. I took a shaky breath. He pulled his hand away and raked it through his hair, squeezing his eyes shut.

"Fuck, I'm bad at this." He let out a breath as I held mine, waiting for him to continue.

While I mentally prepared myself for rejection, his intense resolve told me something else was happening here.

"I lied last night. Or maybe lied isn't the right word. I think I thought what I was saying was the truth, but it wasn't."

My eyebrows pinched together.

"I'm so confused."

He let out a frustrated laugh. "Shit, sorry. I suck at this."

Harrison lifted his hand like he was going to touch my face again, but stuffed it in his pocket instead.

"Maybe. . . Maybe I'm not worried about you wanting more. Maybe I'm worried that I do," he said.

My heart slammed against my chest.

"This is hard," he muttered, which made me let out a nervous laugh.

"Look, I've never let anyone in like this. I don't know what to do, or where this could go. But what I am certain of is that I don't want it to stop." He stared at me intently.

"Then why did you stop it last night?" I questioned.

"Because I'm scared," he whispered. "I know that's so fucking lame, but there it is. You're a hell of a lot more to me than some vacation fling, and that fact alone is terrifying. I don't even know what letting someone in like that looks like. And I wasn't lying when I said I didn't want to hurt you. That scares me too, because there's no possible way I'm the right guy for you." He paused and searched my face. "But I don't really care. Because if there's even a shred of you that wants this—wants me—then I'll happily take whatever you'll give."

A smile spread across my face. My nerves were still present, but the twisting feeling now felt more like butterflies than nausea. This was everything I'd always hoped he'd say, and had never in a million years expected to hear.

"Are you going to say anything, or just leave me hanging?" he asked, an unmistakable note of concern in his voice.

"I got to you." I grinned and poked his chest. I nearly gasped when he captured my hand with his own and crushed me against him.

"You got me," he breathed.

He dipped his head and kissed me, slow and firm. One hand came up to cradle my face while the other gripped my side, holding me close.

After a moment, he broke away. A rare smile crept onto his lips. I beamed, knowing I'd put it there.

"Today sucked," he said, which made us both break into a laugh.

"Well, it isn't over yet," I pointed out.

"True," he said, tangling my hair in his fingers. Never in my wildest dreams did I imagine I'd ever describe a look from Harrison as adoring, but that's exactly what it was.

"Want to go shopping with me?" I asked, batting my eyes innocently up at him.

He pressed his lips to mine again immediately, spreading heat through my entire body.

"Lead the way," he said. I took a chance and threaded my fingers through his. He let me, and even squeezed my hand.

As we weaved between the whitewashed buildings, I savored the way his hand felt in mine. I didn't care that we hadn't really decided anything, or that we only had one more day. Soon we'd have to face reality—and our friends. I didn't know what this meant or what we were, but this moment felt too right to worry about any of it.

"So," I said as I stopped at the nearest gift shop. "What happened to the rest of the guys?"

Exhaustion tightened his features.

"I dropped them off at an emergency clinic, like, twenty minutes from here."

I turned to him, raising a brow.

"Okay, now you're going to need to tell me the whole story."

TWENTY-FOUR

Lila

"DID I EVER TELL YOU THAT YOU LOOKED GOOD IN THAT bathing suit?" I sent a splash of water in Harrison's direction. Instead of retaliating like I expected him to, he took a quick step forward and grabbed me around the waist before I had time to protest. I screeched with laughter as he thrust us both down, threatening to dunk my head underwater, but stopping just when he reached my neck.

He kissed my nose and smiled. "Not half as good as you look in that bikini, I'm sure."

Sunset had already enveloped the island when we finally got off the ferry back in Santorini. When I had suggested we go for a little evening swim, I had fully expected Harrison to offer some sort of resistance. But there was none. In fact, it was getting harder to remember what Harrison had been like when he was challenging my every suggestion.

He cradled me in his arms so that I was floating in the pool. I traced one of the larger tattoos on his arm. A dragon, circling a flame.

"You know, I asked you about your tattoos once. You were pretty snarky about it," I said.

He winced. "Sorry about that. You can ask me anything you want now."

I smirked up at him. "Trying to make it up to me or something?"

He leaned down to kiss the top of my head. "Always."

I pressed my cheek against his chest. Despite the absolutely surreal feeling of being together like this, I couldn't deny that I felt more content than I had in a long time.

"Do they all have meaning?" I asked, tracing another one, this one of water lapping against a cliff.

"Some," he said, craning his neck to look down at the one under my hand. "That one I got for my dad. I have a few for my mom—her favorite bird and her favorite flower. Both of their names are on my other arm."

"They must really mean a lot to you."

"They do. They've sacrificed a lot for me. I just wish they'd let me do more for them."

"Stubborn?" I asked.

"Proud," he said.

I continued tracing the dark lines. "Are any of these for a girl?"

"No," he said. I could hear the smile in his voice. "I do have one for Oliver, though."

I dipped my head back and laughed at that. "No way. Which one?"

"It's a wolf on my back. We were supposed to get matching ones, but he chickened out after I got mine."

I snorted. "That sounds like Oliver. At least you were already covered in tattoos, or that could have been bad."

"That was only, like, my third one. But I didn't mind. I

knew I'd always be able to give him shit for it." He chuckled at the memory.

"That makes it all worth it, then," I said.

"Do you have any tattoos?"

A blush crept onto my cheeks, a residual effect of still being slightly self-conscious around him. "I've always kind of wanted one, but I'm a little nervous."

"I could give it to you," he offered. Suddenly, the whole idea felt pretty intimate.

When I didn't answer, he trailed one finger along the many earrings in my right ear.

"You clearly aren't afraid of needles, with all these piercings."

"That was more of an eff-you to my ex than anything else," I explained, tipping my head to get a better angle of Harrison's face. "He thought more than one earring in each lobe was trashy. So, naturally, as soon as I dumped him, I went straight to a piercer. I also contemplated dying my hair blonde, but I'm glad I didn't go through with it."

His jaw clenched at my explanation. "He sounds like a piece of work."

"You have no idea," I said.

Harrison surprised me by dropping his head to place a soft kiss on my forehead.

"So, last day tomorrow," I said, wariness coating my voice.

He sighed and dropped my legs so that I stood next to him in the pool.

"Don't kill me, but I'm kind of excited to get back." The dagger he'd just inserted into my heart twisted a little.

"Oh?" I tried to sound as nonchalant as possible.

"Yeah. I don't typically spend this much time away from the shop. And I feel like—" his eyes searched mine before they moved to the evening sky that spread out in front of us. "I feel like I have a lot of new ideas after this trip."

"Like getting a working website," I teased, letting any anxiety I felt about his comment float away.

"Definitely." He smirked down at me. "Although, I might still need your help with that."

"Say the word and I'm there," I said easily. The water cradled me as I floated, my fingers slicing through its warmth. I moved my hands in gentle arcs around my body, feeling the light, comforting pressure against my skin.

I tipped back my head and sighed. "I guess I'm excited to get back, too. Hopefully the office didn't implode without both Charlie and me there." I stopped drifting and placed my hands on the edge of the pool.

"I'm sure it's fine," Harrison said, moving to stand next to me, his leg brushing mine. He kept occupying my space in the best possible way. "Maybe now you'll feel better taking more time off in the future."

"Maybe," I agreed, hoping he was right.

Eventually, we toweled off and headed back to our room. The ominous one bed now sent a thrill of excitement through me instead of solely nerves.

Would he make a move? Would I have to?

My body was on literal fire just looking at him, damp and shirtless. It took everything in me not to reach out and run my hands along his abs, up to his pecs, and along his tattoos.

He must feel it too.

"I almost forgot," he said, breaking me from my trance.

"Hmm?" I asked, not fully capable of forming a coherent thought at the moment.

"I got this for you," he said, picking up the jeans that he'd discarded on the bed and pulling out a small box.

Joy surged up inside me as I took it from his hands.

"It's nothing," he said, rubbing the back of his wet hair. "I just saw one while we were shopping today, and it made me think of you."

I opened the box to find a dainty evil eye necklace nestled inside, a swirl of blue and clear crystals on a short silver chain much like the one I had admired our first day here. My eyes started to blur.

"I thought you said it was stupid."

He shook his head and took the necklace from my hands. He placed one hand on my waist and gently spun me around so that he could fasten the chain around my neck.

"I was the only one being stupid." His breath on my neck made me shiver.

"I'm glad you finally see it my way." I turned in his arms and smiled up at him.

"I'm starting to see a lot of things your way," he murmured.

"Thank you for this." I reached up to touch the necklace and Harrison dropped his head to place a soft kiss on my forehead. When he pulled away, there was heat in his eyes, and he tightened his grip around my waist.

I tipped my head, giving him full access to my mouth. His taste was addictive, like I could never get enough of him. His tongue gently touched my lips, and I opened my mouth to let him in.

The kiss was soft but insistent, and he held me tighter, his fingers digging into my sides. My own hands were wrapped around his back, and it felt so natural to touch him like this. To kiss him. This Harrison was so different from the one I thought I knew. Getting to know him like this, without all his walls in place, had just made my attraction to him flourish into something real.

Something that I couldn't deny.

Harrison took his time, kissing me slowly and thoroughly, like we had all the time in the world.

"You're not going to panic and stop again, are you?" I asked against his lips. "Because if you're still worried that I have a crush on you, spoiler alert: I definitely do."

I could feel his smile. "I think I have the bigger crush. Like I told you earlier, I'll take anything you're willing to give. I'm yours, Lila."

My insides coiled tightly at his words as my mouth continued to explore his. My heart pounded and desire surged through me. Even though it was far too soon, and I'd never admit it out loud, I was already falling for him. A fall I was powerless to stop.

I ran my hand along the smooth skin of his back. When he moved his hand up to trace the underside of my breast, I let out a small moan.

For all the dating I'd done recently, I wasn't a fan of casual hookups. It had been a while since someone had touched me like this, and I didn't think I'd ever anticipated a touch that much.

He backed up a few steps and I let him lead me to the bed. When the back of his legs hit the edge of the mattress, he sat and pulled me into his lap.

I straddled him, my arms resting on his shoulders and my fingers knotting in his thick hair. He moved his hands up my sides, his thumbs brushing against the sides of my breasts. Only the thin fabric of my bikini top kept me from feeling his touch directly on my skin, and I shivered with anticipation.

He kissed his way across my jaw, to my neck. Heat built in my stomach as I rocked gently in his lap.

"This is so much better than I imagined," he murmured into my neck.

"So, you admit you've imagined this," I breathed.

"Maybe a few times," he said, chuckling.

I tugged his hair and pulled his mouth back to mine. My nipples hardened as they rubbed against the flimsy fabric of my top, and I arched my back to increase the friction against his bare chest.

His hand still traced the side of my breast and I moaned into his mouth, silently urging him to move his hand further.

He must have sensed my thoughts, because a second later he pushed the thin fabric aside, exposing my nipples. I let out a sigh of satisfaction.

He ran his thumb over one nipple, making it harden even more, then did the same with the other, until both my breasts were tight with arousal.

"These are perfect," he murmured.

I leaned back to watch his face. "They're okay."

"More than okay."

His eyes met mine as he squeezed the soft flesh of my breast. He was staring at me like I was the only person in the world, and right then, I believed it.

The air left my lungs as I watched his head move forward and his mouth close over one nipple. When his tongue flicked the tight bud, it sent a pulse shooting straight to my center.

His mouth was warm and insistent as he sucked and teased, massaging my other breast with his free hand. I arched into him, melting underneath his touch.

My hips rocked against his erection, the thin fabric of his shorts leaving little to the imagination.

"Harrison," I whispered. "You make me feel. . ."

He pulled away, his eyes locked on mine. "How do I make you feel?"

I rocked my hips against him and smiled.

"A lot," I admitted.

His hands slid to my hips, pulling me tighter against him. "Like what?"

"You make me nervous," I whispered.

"Don't feel nervous," he said, before taking my other nipple in his mouth.

"You make me happy," I whispered.

He released my nipple, his mouth moving back to my lips.

"Me too," he said, softly.

I was overwhelmed by both the tenderness of his touch and the sincerity of his words.

"And, currently, you're making me feel wet," I said, my voice low and throaty.

A slow grin spread across his face. "I should really do something about that."

He picked me up and turned, laying me on the bed, then stripped off his swim trunks, leaving himself completely naked.

I stared at him and licked my lips. When he moved toward me I fell back, allowing him to hover over me.

"I can't believe this is real," I whispered.

He let out a soft chuckle. "Neither can I."

With two fingers, he traced my stomach until stopping right at the top of my tiny bikini bottoms.

"Sure you don't want me to stop?" he asked gruffly.

"I didn't even want you to stop yesterday," I breathed, arching my hips ever so slightly so his fingertips collided with the elastic of the pesky fabric that separated us. Then he moved his hand between us and gently slid my bikini bottoms down my thighs.

"I want to taste you," he said, staring me in the eyes.

A pulse throbbed between my legs at his words. "I'm not going to object to that."

He smiled. "Good."

He gripped my thighs and spread them wide open. His warm breath on my sensitive skin sent shivers through me. It wasn't just his touch that was driving me up the wall, it was the fact that it was Harrison. This person whom I had admired from afar, but never dreamed I would actually get to touch. Now, here we were—me spread out before him, at my most vulnerable, and him on his knees ready for worship.

When his tongue finally came into contact with my skin, I nearly shot off the bed. I moaned when he brought his fingers up to brush my most sensitive spot, and almost lost it right there. He used his tongue and fingers to work me until I was panting and writhing on the bed.

When I thought it couldn't get any better, he moved his fingers from my clit and slid them inside. He worked his tongue in time with his thrusts, and I felt myself climbing toward the edge.

"Yes, right there," I whimpered.

He pulled his fingers out and used his whole mouth, his tongue circling and his lips sucking.

I cried out as my orgasm shook through me. I shuddered under his touch and his grip tightened, his tongue continuing its assault until the last wave passed over me.

He looked up at me, a smug smile on his face. "Was that better than the fantasy?"

"I never said I fantasized about you," I insisted, although my shaky voice held barely any resolve.

He climbed up the bed and pressed a soft kiss to my temple before pressing his lips against mine. I could still taste myself on his mouth, my stomach immediately clenching with renewed desire.

"Well, that was better than any fantasy for me," he said.

"You're welcome," I joked, smiling against his mouth.

I deepened the kiss, sliding my tongue into his mouth and

tangling my fingers in his hair. My nipples pressed against his bare chest which amplified my desire.

Twisting our bodies, Harrison rolled me on top of him in a tangle of limbs. I pressed myself to his length and nearly cried out just from the friction.

"Lila," he groaned, gripping my hips as I started to rock into him. "We don't have to do everything in one night."

I smiled and rocked my hips again, feeling his dick tense with arousal. "I thought you were done stopping me?"

His lip curved up. "Good point. I'm all yours."

I moved my hips again, and a surge of satisfaction washed through me as he let out another groan.

"Fuck, I want you so bad."

His raw words had my insides cartwheeling with joy. I hadn't felt this good—this comfortable with a man—since. . . since maybe ever. My ex had never treated me like this, like I was something precious he was lucky to have. And any hookups I'd had since then had felt almost clinical. This was something else entirely.

Harrison kissed me fiercely and I dissolved into him, ready to have him fully.

"Take me," I said against his lips.

My body buzzed as he flipped us over again and pushed me into the mattress.

"If you insist," he growled.

When he positioned himself over me, his expression changed, and the raw emotion behind his eyes nearly took my breath away.

He brushed his thumb over my cheek. "Are you sure about this?"

I smiled. "Yes."

He reached into the nightstand and produced a condom. I eyed it.

"Did you really bring those on what you thought was a friends' trip?" I demanded, a laugh escaping me.

He didn't look the slightest bit sheepish as he tore the wrapper off and slid the condom on. "No."

My brows pinched. "Then when—"

"I got them today. While we were shopping," he said, shifting so that he was back over me. "I wasn't expecting anything, but. . ."

"You're so obsessed with me," I teased, lightly pinching his sides. But when I felt the tip of him at my entrance, I gasped.

"Yep," he said, then sealed his lips to mine.

With his mouth on mine, his tongue teasing me, he slid slowly inside. I stretched for him in the most intoxicating way.

I moaned, wrapping my legs around his waist, hardly able to process how good he felt. How good everything about this moment felt.

He began to thrust, slowly at first. I tilted my hips up, savoring everything. I didn't feel vulnerable, lying naked beneath him; I felt wanted, and alive, and aching for more. The connection between us felt unreal and I couldn't get enough.

"More," I said.

He grinned, his teeth glowing in the soft light. "So eager."

My smile was cut off by a moan that escaped me when he picked up the pace. He thrust harder and I tightened my legs around him, my nails digging into his shoulder blades as I met him thrust for thrust. The pleasure was overwhelming, and I couldn't contain the moans and gasps that escaped my lips.

"Yes, just like that," I got out, my words barely a whisper.

Harrison groaned with desire.

I was on fire, and the only thing that could put it out was him.

"Harder," I begged.

He grunted, speeding up, his movements more desperate. "Fuck," he growled.

The sound of his pleasure tipped me over the edge and a second orgasm tore through me. I pulsed around him, and the feeling of his thrusts, coupled with his ragged breathing as he approached his own release, intensified mine.

He stiffened and then shuddered. He cried out my name, and thrust once more.

As he collapsed on top of me, my body still trembling from the aftershocks, I realized that there was no going back. We hadn't even begun to discuss what the hell this was, but it certainly wasn't casual. At least not for me.

The irony didn't escape me. This was exactly what Harrison had been worried about last night—sleeping together, and me immediately catching feelings. He had barely pulled out of me and already my emotions were too overwhelming to process.

I didn't say anything as he gazed into my eyes and cradled the back of my head carefully with his hand. Maybe we hadn't said everything that needed to be said yet, but his look told me he was feeling this too.

Maybe it still scared him, but I just hoped he'd face it this time.

TWENTY-FIVE

Harrison

"WE DON'T HAVE TO GO IF YOU DON'T THINK YOU CAN stomach it," I insisted.

"For the last time, I want to go. The ferry was just bad for me because we were inside."

"You're sure?" I eyed her up and down, not wanting her to brave this activity just because I had come up with it. Or rather, Maria had.

After Lila and I had spent that incredible night together, I'd barely been able to sleep. I was too focused on how perfectly she fit, wrapped in my arms as she drifted off. I woke up earlier than her for the first time and went in search of Maria. Lila had spent the whole trip dragging me around, and I wanted to plan something for her for a change. She deserved it for putting up with my grouchy ass this whole time.

Maria had suggested a boat to the volcano, where we could get out and walk around. It sounded perfect, but I was wary of taking Lila on another boat after she'd gotten sick the last time. I'd made a list of alternatives, but when I'd

240 • TRIP SWITCH

presented the volcano option to Lila, she had gotten so excited and insisted she would be fine.

"Look," she said, patting her bag. "I've got my motion sickness medicine and some crackers. I'll be fine."

"Okay," I relented, leaning down and kissing her on the top of the head without even thinking about it. When I pulled away, she looked a bit taken aback.

Shit.

Was I not supposed to do that? Were we not there yet? Affection came easy with Lila, easier than it had ever come in my entire life. I had no idea what the hell I was doing, but I hoped she'd be patient while I figured it out. I'd likely be a bumbling fool, but I needed to make her realize that I'd do anything for her.

Making plans for today was just the start. I had to show her that I was worth her time, even though I knew I probably wasn't.

"Eh, it's our hero!" A loud voice exclaimed.

"Oh no." I groaned, dropping my head back.

Nigel, Mark, and Will joined us at the hotel entrance, all carrying large backpacks.

Lila gasped when she saw the huge bruise under Nigel's eyes, his swollen nose, and the large gash that had since been stitched up.

"Looks worse than it is," Nigel said, his voice a hell of a lot more casual than yesterday, when he'd practically been weeping.

"You'll have a sick scar after this, mate." Mark grinned.

"The girls will love it," Will added.

"Thanks for your help getting us to the clinic. Even if you did ditch us." Nigel clapped me on the shoulder.

"Glad it all worked out," I said, my voice flat. I narrowed

my eyes at him, hoping they would get the hint that we wouldn't be having some long, drawn-out goodbye.

"Anyway, we're on our way out of here. Lovely meeting the two of you." Nigel said as he adjusted his backpack straps.

"It was great meeting you, too," Lila said, her voice just as warm as it always was. Why did she have to be so nice all the freaking time?

"Bye, Lily." Nigel smiled and held open his arms.

"Oh, uh, bye." Lila awkwardly gave him a short hug. I had to forcibly restrain myself from not stepping between the two of them.

"Harrison." Nigel turned toward me and I glared at him.

"Bye," I said, folding my arms across my chest.

"Perhaps we should exchange numbers or something?" Nigel asked holding up his phone and shaking it in an invitation.

I shrugged. "Nah, I'm good."

Lila coughed to disguise a laugh. She cleared her throat and then took his phone.

"Do you have social media?" He nodded as she typed something before handing his phone back. "Here's my account. Why don't we follow each other? I'd love to keep up with your future travels."

"Perfect." Nigel grinned. He, Mark, and Will waved their goodbyes, but this time when Nigel tried to give Lila another hug, I slung an arm around her shoulder. Fuck it. She could call me overprotective all she wanted; I wasn't giving this guy any more opportunities to touch her.

"Good going," I said when they'd finally retreated. "He's definitely going to stalk all of your pictures."

She snorted. "I followed him from the ConnectHer account. He's just going to see a lot of pictures from networking events."

My lip tugged up. "Nice."

We strolled into town, keeping a hurried pace so we'd arrive at the port in time for our boat tour. The weather was perfect for our final day in Greece. The sun bathed everything in warmth, while a cool, fresh breeze kept the air perfectly balanced. The water appeared calm too, thankfully.

"At the bottom of all these steps?" Lila asked through a smile.

"Yep." I said, looking down the hundreds of steps built into the cliffside.

"Can you handle it? I know hiking isn't your thing," she teased, starting the trek down.

"I'll be fine. Plus, there's a gondola to take us back up later." I pointed above us to the carts rising up the side of the cliff on a thick wire.

"Thank God for that. I couldn't handle your incessant whining if we had to walk up this."

I bit back a chuckle, savoring how good it felt that she was comfortable teasing me now. I no longer made her nervous. At least not in the ways I used to.

After nearly fifteen minutes of walking down the steps, we boarded a small open-air boat. It had a few rows of seats, two that lined the sides, and one that came down the middle. I let Lila choose our spot. No surprise, she picked front-and-center where we'd have the best view of everything.

Lila stood to record a video of the boat, rotating to capture everything. The middle-aged man sitting next to us glowered up at her.

"Can you sit down?" he asked, scowling.

"Oh—" Lila flushed, but I shot up to stand by her side.

"She'll sit when she's finished recording." I glared at the rude man, daring him to speak to Lila like that again. As soon as he took in my expression and my size, he paled. His wife elbowed him and offered me an apologetic smile.

"Sorry," he muttered.

Lila chuckled before finishing her video, and only then did we both take our seats.

"What?" I demanded.

"Nothing. It's just—" She bit back a smile. "That would have been you, a few days ago."

I winced. "Well, I'm lucky I found someone to set me straight."

A perky tour operator walked to the front of the boat and greeted us over her microphone. She gave us some safety instructions and then we were on our way.

I held my breath as soon as the boat started moving. But even as we started rocking slowly, Lila appeared fine. Not a trace of green dotted her rosy cheeks. She nestled into my side and my chest swelled with some unfamiliar feeling. Pride? Possessiveness? Whatever it was it felt good.

When the boat pulled into the small dock at the volcano, I stood up first, holding out my hand to help steady her.

"This is perfect for our last day." Lila beamed at me, letting me help her up.

The volcano seemed more like an island to me.

A trail wound its way from the boat all the way up the side of the volcano, through a landscape that was rugged, almost otherworldly. The tour guide led the way for our small group. As we hiked up the trail, she pointed out the different layers of volcanic rock we could see underneath our feet.

Lila slipped her hand in mine, listening intently to the guide. I found it hard to focus on anything other than the way her thumb occasionally brushed across my knuckles, or the coolness of her silver ring pressed into my palm.

"Wow, not since 1950," Lila said, looking up at me expectantly.

I blinked a few times. "What?"

She rolled her eyes, a smile playing on her lips. "Since the last eruption. Are you even paying attention?"

"Of course," I said, my eyes studying her face.

"Not to me. To the tour." Lila laughed.

The tour guide could have been spouting out the secret to eternal life and I still don't think it could have pulled my attention away from the girl at my side. The one I couldn't believe I was lucky enough to be here with.

The tour continued and I tried my best to pay attention to all of the rapid-fire factoids the perky guide shouted at us. Mostly just so I'd be prepared in case Lila quizzed me again. But even as I attempted to listen, my brain just couldn't compute. Instead, it was stuck on one very singular track.

"You look cute when you're interested," I whispered. I snaked my arm around her waist while the guide told us all about the volcano's biggest eruption, the one that had formed the caldera thousands of years ago.

"Pay attention." Her stern voice held little weight when she smiled like that. I brushed her hair from her shoulder and traced her bare skin lightly.

"I can't help it, you're very distracting."

Lila shook her head against my chest. I was already convinced that I'd never get sick of holding her.

The guide finished her spiel and instructed us to feel free to explore, but to be back at the boat in thirty minutes or it would take off without us. That got some polite chuckles from the group.

"Take a picture of me," Lila said, scrambling up onto a rock on the path. She spread her arms out wide and smiled.

I took out my phone and snapped a few.

"Come here." She gestured for me to join her, and I did so without argument.

"Isn't life better when you aren't resisting me at every turn?"

"Yes," I said, staring into her eyes.

Her cheeks turned an adorable shade of pink before she smiled and snatched my phone. She held it out in front of me and snapped a few selfies of the two of us. Our rocky surroundings drifted off into the blue water and our faces were front and center.

She tickled my side without warning.

"Hey!" I exclaimed, unable to hold back a laugh.

"Perfect." She showed me the picture she'd just taken. Her smile was big, staring into the camera. I was facing her, caught mid-laugh.

"Is this the happiest picture of you in existence?" she asked.

"My mom might have some baby photos of me smiling. I'm sure she'd love to show you."

Lila's eyes widened almost imperceptibly.

Had I said the wrong thing? Was it too soon to talk about our parents? I meant the comment in the friendliest of ways. Plus, technically, she had already met my parents. But whatever had flashed across her face was gone now, as she returned to examining the picture.

"Should we send this one to Oliver?" she asked.

"I think we better hold off on that."

I took my phone back from her and slipped it into my pocket. The last thing I wanted to deal with was a million questions from Oliver when Lila and I hadn't even talked things through yet.

Speaking of which, should I bring that up? What would I even say? Was this a relationship? Was it way too soon for that? I was completely out of my element here, and I didn't want to mess anything up with Lila again by not handling whatever this was in the best possible way.

"Oh. Okay." She interrupted my spiraling thoughts and gave me a weird look before nodding her head toward the trail. "We'd better follow the group back. I don't want to get left behind."

We walked back, strolling in a comfortable silence, her hand loosely threaded in mine. At least the silence was comfortable for me. Shit, should I be talking? I glanced down at her, but she seemed perfectly content, gazing out at the horizon and using my arm to steady her feet since she wasn't watching where she stepped.

We boarded the boat again and Lila snuggled in as the boat cruised along the calm waters. Whatever was going on between us felt heavy. Heavy in the best possible way, like the weight of my emotions was blanketing me, offering me comfort and security. I could drown in this feeling and be better off for it.

I could only hope that Lila felt the same way. This transformation I'd undertaken was all her doing, and it still didn't make me half the man she deserved. But I'd show her what I could offer and just pray that it could be enough. Maybe I didn't have a fancy job or a lot of friends. Maybe I was tech illiterate and had a hard time loosening up. But I was loyal. I would do anything for the small inner circle I let into my life. The circle I now realized she was at the center of.

The realization quickened my pulse.

It was way too soon to be having thoughts like these. This was exactly why I had kept my walls up all these years. Yet somehow, she'd gotten in. She had created a crack that hadn't been there at the start and slipped right through with ease.

And just as my walls were an impenetrable force field to break, they were also just as hard to escape.

I was hers in whatever way she'd have me. I just prayed she'd be patient with me as I navigated it with my piss-poor communication skills.

We'd be on our way home tomorrow. We'd figure it all out then.

No sense in freaking her out now.

TWENTY-SIX

Lila

I WAS COMPLETELY FREAKING OUT.

In my desperate, misguided attempt to be the cool, chill girl for once in my life, I'd managed to let the entire last day of the trip slip through my fingers without mentioning the status of our relationship once.

Now Harrison snoozed peacefully beside me, hugging me tightly to his chest. Our bags were packed and ready by the door. In less than twelve hours, we'd be at the airport on our way home. After a blissful final day in paradise, I should be sleeping just as soundly as the man curled around me. Instead, my mind raced with possibilities and questions.

I needed to get up. I needed to pace.

Suddenly, I couldn't breathe.

Carefully, I peeled Harrison's arm away from my waist. I moved at a snail's pace so as not to shift the mattress too much. I got to my feet, turning to check that Harrison was still asleep. To my relief, he was still out cold, his cheek smushed against the pillow. One stubborn lock of his hair had sprung free from his small bun and lay across his face.

He looked freaking adorable.

I tiptoed toward the door, and turned the latch slowly. I eased the door open and stepped out into the cool night air. Now outside, I could finally breathe, and I could feel how damp my body was. My T-shirt stuck to my clammy chest. I pinched the top of it and waved it to fan it out and get some air flow.

I slumped into the small wicker chair on our patio and breathed a sigh of relief. My head felt clearer than it had all night. To say that today had been amazing would be an understatement. And the fact that Harrison had planned it, all down to our dinner reservation, had absolutely melted my heart. He wasn't the same man I'd arrived here with.

That both excited and terrified me. This bond that we'd built—the one I'd felt was so strong—how would it hold up once we were off the island? Once we were outside of our vacation bubble?

What did Harrison want? How would he act? I knew what I wanted. I wanted to nurture what we'd started, tend it carefully and watch what it could become.

I knew it was too soon, but I wanted to be his girlfriend.

Despite our differences, we felt right. I got him out of his comfort zone and he grounded me. Maybe he was rough around the edges, but he was a good person. I saw it in the way he'd been protective of me from the very start. I saw it in the way he spoke of his parents. I had even seen it before this trip, with his unwavering loyalty to Oliver.

I'd be lucky to have him in my life. I had intended to tell him all that today, but the moment never felt right. Then by the time the evening rolled around, I'd convinced myself it could wait.

But then the doubt crept in. What if my feelings were one-sided? What if returning to the real world would be like stepping into an ice-cold shower? Would this all fade away into a 'what were we thinking?' situation? Was this destined to just become a strange story for our friend group? The great lore of Harrison and Lila's trip switch fling?

I cradled my head in my hands and groaned.

"Everything alright, dear?"

I nearly jumped out of my skin. I probably would have screamed had it not been for the calm, comforting tone of the voice.

Maria stood before me, wearing blue pajamas and carrying a large laundry basket. I clutched a hand to my chest and swallowed my heart, which had jumped into my throat.

"Sorry, you scared me." I sat up in the chair. "I'm fine, just couldn't sleep."

She smiled. "That makes two of us."

"I just figured I'd get some air," I said, meeting her warm gaze.

"Your boyfriend doesn't have the same problem?"

"He's not. . ." I stopped my sentence. While it still wasn't the truth, denying it felt wrong, too.

Maria chuckled and shifted her basket. "Not so sure anymore, eh?"

My face likely said it all. I could feel it growing hot.

"I knew it. I could sense something between you two." She tapped the side of her head. "I'm glad I got you out of that shared room."

My eyebrows pulled together. "What? But you said—"

She laughed harder. "I have another shared dorm room that I could have put more guests in."

Her laugh made my lip tug upward. "That one bed almost got us into a lot of trouble, you know."

She waved a hand. "I took my chances. I saw the way that

he looked at you. This island is meant for young love. I couldn't let you waste it."

"Well, love is a very strong word." I bit my lip. "We don't. . . we didn't." I groaned and cradled my face again. "The truth is, I have no idea what we are or what's going to happen." Blurting this out to Maria made me feel better, even if she was virtually a stranger.

The skin around her eyes crinkled as she studied me.

"You know, when I met my husband, I knew he was the one. You kids make things so complicated. You take time for granted."

Sadness gripped me as she stared off into the night sky.

"I'm sorry," I said. "Here I am rambling about my problems. They're so silly." We sat in silence for a minute.

"He used to snore. It kept me up at night. Now that he's gone, the funny thing is, I still can't sleep. So I've given up trying." She gestured to the laundry basket. "The only difference now is it's so quiet."

I sniffled. I could barely imagine being in love, let alone losing it. Her grief must be overwhelming.

"I'm sorry." I whispered.

"Don't be." She shrugged. "I'm okay. Life happens, and I'm grateful for the time I had with him."

"You're lucky to have loved someone so much."

She snorted. "Luck had nothing to do with it. It took work, and communication, and mutual respect. You could have it too, you know." Her head tilted in the direction of my room, where Harrison still slept soundly.

"We'll see." I said, not knowing what else I could offer her.

She gave an exaggerated eye roll.

"There is no 'we'll see,' there is only 'I'll try.'" she said, walking away. "Good night, and safe travels tomorrow."

"LILA, THAT'S ROBBERY." HARRISON LOOKED APPALLED AS I set a book on the counter and waited for the cashier to ring me up.

I sipped my overpriced coffee, savoring the life returning to me.

"It's my ritual," I insisted, swiping my card.

He cocked an eyebrow and picked up my selection to examine it.

"*The Body Downstairs*. A romance on the way here and a murder mystery on the way home. Should I be worried?"

"Not if you hand it over and stop questioning my purchases." I took the book from his hands.

After barely getting any sleep last night, I didn't have any capacity to stress about where Harrison and I stood as we made the journey home. I was far too exhausted. I had passed out on his shoulder almost immediately for the entire flight from Santorini to Munich. Now, just one long haul flight from Munich to Denver, and we'd be home. It felt natural to be here with Harrison this time, completely different from how it had felt running into him at the Denver airport before this whole debacle had even started.

It was fine that we hadn't talked anything through. It wasn't like we were being separated, not really. We shared friends, we had each other's numbers. We only lived ten minutes away from each other, for crying out loud. Everything would work out just fine. My stress last night had been for nothing.

When we boarded our flight, Harrison took my luggage and put it in the overhead bin. He looked good in his gray sweats and black T-shirt, and it felt freeing to no longer have to pretend that I was immune to his good looks. I started to climb into my seat, but bumped into Harrison who had started to do the same.

"Oh, sorry," he said, jumping back.

"It's fine." I smiled. "Do you want the window?"

"No, no. I don't know what I was thinking." He shook his head. "Go for it."

My eyebrows pulled together, but I stepped into the window seat. While he hadn't been cold or distant yesterday or this morning, there was something different about Harrison now; something I could only describe as awkwardness.

He slid into the aisle seat. The flight attendant came by and we both asked for coffee. It would be a struggle to stay up this whole flight, plus wait until a decent time to go to sleep once we arrived back in Denver, but it was the only way to avoid jet lag. Harrison glanced over at me before looking back at his personal TV screen. He looked at me again and opened his mouth before shaking his head and turning away.

"What?" I asked, keeping my voice light.

A small pit formed in my stomach. Not panic, exactly, but it still didn't feel great.

"Nothing," he said, forcing the smallest of smiles. "Are you just going to read, or. . ."

"Probably," I said. "Or maybe we could watch a movie? Press play at the same time, and—"

"Nah, I'm good." He looked pained by the suggestion.

"Oh, okay." My smile faltered. Why was this so weird?

Harrison opened his sketchbook and started drawing. When it became clear he wasn't trying to engage in any additional conversation, I placed my noise-cancelling headphones over my ears and pressed play on some random movie.

Two hours into the flight, and none of the movies I tried did anything to distract me.

254 • TRIP SWITCH

Harrison had been bent over his sketchbook the entire time, not so much as looking up even when I glanced over.

I wiped my clammy hands against my sweats. The air in the cabin tasted especially stale. Every moment of progression toward our end destination made me feel heavier, as the weight of all the unsaid words finally caught up with me.

Had I been naïve to think we had anything real? It wasn't like I was the first person in the world to be temporarily blinded by a vacation romance. I had been convinced it was more than that, but with every passing second, the person sitting next to me felt more and more like a stranger. It was absolutely not what I wanted, but I felt powerless to stop it.

When the meal service came by and we were served our food, he finally glanced my way. I shot him a smile. He smiled back, but barely, and it looked uncomfortable and forced.

We ate our overly salty trays of food in silence. I almost wished we were back in coach so at least our elbows would occasionally bump into each other while we cut up our lunch.

I should say something, but what? It would just be weird now.

So we sat in silence for the remainder of the eight-hour flight.

I NEVER THOUGHT I'D BE SO HAPPY TO SEE THE DENVER airport once we landed and deplaned. The silence had been suffocating. Harrison's brows were drawn together and his gaze was locked ahead.

"It's good to be back," I said in what might be the most pathetic attempt at conversation in the history of humanity.

He looked at me as if surprised to hear my voice. "Oh, yeah."

We breezed through customs, and before I knew it, we were back in the main terminal. Down that escalator right in front of us was the TSA line where we had first run into each other, before this whole thing started.

Suddenly it felt like no time had passed, like we were in some weird *Twilight Zone* episode and the trip had never actually happened. The only evidence that it had was my pounding heart and Harrison's expression of concern. He no longer scowled at me. Now he just looked lost. I wanted to hug him, but he felt miles away.

"Are you taking the train?" he asked at the same time I said, "I parked in the garage."

I laughed uncomfortably as he scratched the back of his neck.

"You drove?" he asked.

"Yeah. Do you want a ride?" I offered. I wasn't sure whether I wanted him to say yes or if I wanted a little space to breathe.

"Don't worry about it." He shook his head and hitched his finger in the direction of the train platform. "The train goes right by my place. I don't want you to go out of your way."

I felt a stab of disappointment. I guess even with the awkwardness, deep down I wasn't ready to walk away from him.

I forced myself to smile and swallowed down any weird energy.

"I guess this is it, then." I meant it as a joke, but as soon as the words were out of my mouth I became terrified that they held a grain of truth.

His face contorted into an odd expression, as if he desperately wanted to say something but couldn't get it out. He was standing next to me, so he reached around my shoulders and pulled me in for a side hug.

A side hug.

"I'll call you," he said.

"Uh huh," I choked out.

I gave him a little wave before scurrying away as fast as my legs would carry me.

There was traffic, so my ride home gave me the perfect opportunity to hyper-fixate on every beat of the strange interaction Harrison and I had just shared.

What did it mean? Did he not want to make this work? Make *what* work? We'd never actually talked about anything. But he said I was more than a vacation fling. That had to mean something. Unless the weird vibes I could sense radiating out of every pore in his body were actually regret.

My thoughts swirled all the way home, throughout my shower, and continued while I cozied up under a blanket in front of my TV.

My finger hovered over his contact in my phone a dozen times. I couldn't bring myself to text him. Now that I was back in my living room, the magic between us felt even more like a lucid fever dream.

So instead of Harrison, I messaged someone else. Charlie was back from Fiji and would lovingly help me dissect the situation like only a best friend could.

TWENTY-SEVEN

Harrison

"FINALLY. I ALMOST FORGOT WHAT YOU LOOKED LIKE."
Oliver slammed the refrigerator door closed and placed a
hand over his heart as I stepped into the house.

I rolled my eyes before taking off my shoes and heading
straight for the couch. Oliver strode out of the kitchen and
hovered over me.

"Tell me all about Greece. How was the town? What did
you do? How was the company?" He smirked down at me.

"How was Fiji?" I asked instead of attempting to answer
any of his probing questions.

"Oh, you know, pretty good. Up until the last day when I
convinced Nathan to go parasailing with me."

"What's wrong with that?"

"Nothing, in theory. But it was an especially windy day
and we may have lost a teensy bit of control up there. We
were fine, but Charlie wasn't thrilled. I think I'm banned from
dragging Nathan on any more death-defying stunts—at least
until after the wedding."

"At least then she'll inherit everything," I said.

Oliver snickered. "Still so cynical. But don't think I'm letting you evade my questions. How was your trip?"

"It was good," I told him in the understatement of the century.

"*Good*," he repeated. "That's it?"

"Yep." I hardly wanted to confide in Oliver when I was still stressing about how painfully awkward the entire fucking trip home had been.

I had convinced myself I needed to make some sort of declaration or grand gesture, but when it came down to it, I had no clue what the hell I was doing. Each silent moment kept building on the last until all of a sudden there had been this insurmountable wall of uneasiness between us. I had created it, yet I still didn't know how to tear it down.

"Spill," Oliver insisted.

I got up and brushed by my best friend. "I need a shower," I said, eager to delay this conversation for at least a little while longer.

But Oliver was nothing if not persistent. I had just stepped into the shower and dipped my head beneath the spray when I heard the door to the bathroom open.

"A little privacy, please," I barked out.

"It's my house," he said.

I tore the curtain away to glare at him, but he was just sitting on the closed lid of the toilet without a care in the world.

"What happened between you and Lila?" he asked. "Was it weird traveling with her?" He asked the questions like he already knew everything.

I rinsed the shampoo out of my hair and sighed. "Did Charlie say something?"

"Nope. But your tone just told me everything I need to know."

"Damnit, Oliver. We haven't figured out anything yet. The last thing I want to do is share all the details with you."

"No, that's exactly what you should do, so I can make sure you don't mess anything up."

"I probably already did," I mumbled. I rinsed off and reached out of the shower to pluck a clean towel from the rack.

"How so?" Oliver questioned.

I tied the towel around my waist, opened the curtain, and walked right by him into my room, slightly slamming the door to ensure he got the message that he was not welcome.

"Harrison, did you guys hook up? Are you together? I knew it." His voice came through muffled from the other side of the door.

I opened the top drawer of my dresser and grabbed a clean T-shirt, excited to be reunited with clothes that I hadn't had in my suitcase the past five days.

"Come on, tell me," he said, his voice getting louder.

It was clear Oliver wasn't going to let this go, and I supposed maybe I could use his advice.

I threw open my door and shouldered him out of the way before trudging back into the living room and crashing on the couch.

"Something happened. Okay. You happy?" I waved a hand as he strode into the living room and folded his arms across his chest.

"Of course I'm happy. I've been trying to get you two together from day one. Now tell me everything."

I groaned and dragged my hands over my face before relaying a basic synopsis of Lila and my time together in Greece. Skipping over some of the more intimate moments, of course. He might be my best friend, but he didn't deserve *those* kinds of details.

"You were right. Lila is incredible, but I probably messed it all up."

"How could you possibly have messed it all up in such a short amount of time? I know you're capable, but that's fast even for you."

I launched a pillow at his face but he caught it with ease, irritating me further.

"The flight home was so weird. I kept psyching myself up to say something, but I couldn't figure out what. I just sat there like an idiot."

"So you just kissed her goodbye and left?"

"No." I grimaced.

"You didn't kiss her goodbye?" He looked appalled.

"I side-hugged her."

"A *side hug*. Why didn't you just tattoo 'I just want to be friends' across your forehead."

"Because I don't."

Oliver whistled and shook his head. "That's what she thinks, guaranteed."

"No, she doesn't," I insisted, although I wasn't sure what I thought she thought. I couldn't tell whether the flight home had been weird because I was making it weird or because she was second guessing everything. Maybe I wasn't as appealing under the harsh fluorescent lights of reality. Maybe she regretted it all.

My chest tightened at the possibility.

"Dude, I can see you spiraling. It's written all over your face."

"I'm not spiraling," I lied.

"You're forgetting that I know you better than anyone," Oliver pointed out.

"Fine. Maybe I am spiraling." I pinched the bridge of my

nose, forcing the pounding in my head to recede. "I don't know what to say to her."

Oliver snorted. "You say how you feel, dumbass."

"I don't want to freak her out."

"You're probably already freaking her out."

He had a point there.

"Look, you've never had a relationship before."

"I was with that one girl that we met when we first moved out here, for, like, six months. What was her name, again? Natalie? Natasha?" I tried to remember, but all I could see was a blur of a face with blonde hair.

Oliver dipped his chin and shook his head. "Like I said, you've never had a real relationship before. You've always had one foot out the door."

I opened my mouth to argue, but I knew it was the truth. I never allowed myself to be fully invested, because if I was never fully invested, I'd never give someone the opportunity to hurt me. With Lila it was different. Even after such a short time together, she still held all the power. It'd kill me if she didn't want this anymore—or didn't want to try. Which is probably why I'd acted like such an uptight mess the entire way home.

Oliver perched in the chair next to the couch.

"There's a reason I've been pushing you and Lila together. I knew she'd be good for you, and I thought you'd be good for her, too."

"We're nothing alike," I said, feeling defeated—like I'd already ruined everything beyond repair just by being tongue-tied.

"The two of *us* are nothing alike," Oliver continued, gesturing from his chest to me. "But you're still my best friend. And I want to see you happy, man. I want you to find someone who brings out the joy in you. I've seen it in small doses over the past twenty years, and I want to see it more. You don't need to be a hard ass all the time. You're allowed to enjoy your life."

"I know," I conceded. But I only knew that because Lila had made me realize it. She'd had more of an effect on me in the past few days than anyone else had on me my entire life. She was special. And I couldn't just let that slip through my fingers without giving it my all. Maybe I'd come off frazzled, and maybe I'd say the wrong thing, but I had to try.

"I'm not good enough for her," I said, but I was already up off the couch and searching the crowded coat hook for my jacket.

"You should probably let her be the judge of that," Oliver said before I closed the front door behind me.

TWENTY-EIGHT

Lila

"THE WIND HAD PICKED UP SO MUCH, AND THEY WERE GETTING whipped around." Charlie shook her head. "I thought I was about to lose Nathan before I even had a chance to marry him."

I chuckled and pulled my fleecy blanket up around my chin. "I can't believe I missed all of this."

Charlie tilted her head back and groaned. "Me either. I seriously missed you so much."

I had texted Charlie as soon as I'd gotten home, desperate to talk about Harrison's weird energy. Twenty minutes later, she turned up at my house in an oversized sweatshirt with a bag of snacks. We'd been resting, watching cheesy movies, and chatting ever since. God, I loved her.

"I'm glad Greece was amazing, but Fiji would have been a hundred times better if you were there," she said, causing me to light up a little. Sitting there with her, gorging on potato chips and cookies, made me realize without a doubt that Charlie was the sister I never had. No matter how our lives changed, she would always be an important piece of mine.

"I messed up," she said.

"How?"

"I checked my work email."

I laughed. "That was a mistake. I almost did, but I'm forcing myself to wait until tomorrow."

Even with my obsessive need to know everything, no one had called our personal phones, which meant there had been no emergencies while we were gone. I was sure the whole office had continued operating just fine.

"I shouldn't have. Everything is fine, of course. I just can't help myself sometimes. I even responded to a few."

I opened my mouth in mock horror. "Oh, Charlie. You didn't."

She laughed and snatched the popcorn out of my hands.

"I can't believe I took this time off and I'm also going to be off for three weeks for our wedding and honeymoon. *Three weeks*. I haven't been away that long since we started ConnectHer."

"And you did such a great job building it that the place will run smoothly in your absence," I pointed out. "I'll make sure of it."

Charlie frowned. "But I seriously don't want you over-working yourself."

"I won't."

"You should really consider hiring someone to be head of brand and take over some of your workload. I know you always say you're fine, but we have the budget for it, and with me being gone for almost a month it could be perfect timing." She looked at me, hopeful as ever.

Instinctively I was about to tell her 'no,' but stopped myself. Why shouldn't I get some help? Freeing up my mind for other things would be liberating. Harrison's words about putting others' needs before my own rattled around in my mind.

"Okay," I said.

Charlie's eyebrows sprang up. "Okay? *Okay?*"

I laughed at her obvious shock. "I can write up the job posting this week and send it over to our recruiter."

Charlie got up and took a step toward me before placing a warm hand on my forehead.

"Hey." I smiled and swatted her away.

"Sorry, I was just checking for a fever." She plopped back down and clapped excitedly. "This is going to be great for you. I don't know why you changed your mind but I'm glad you finally did."

"Me too." I had thought relinquishing control would make me feel frazzled, but instead I felt calmer than I had in years. Just the idea of lightening some of my workload and having more time for myself made me want to cry.

"Greece really changed you," Charlie said.

I sighed. "Yep."

She cringed at my crestfallen expression. "He'll call, Lila. You have no reason to think he won't."

I'd already filled her in on all the major details, including the very awkward and unfortunate flight home.

"He *side-hugged* me." My head fell back onto the couch cushion and I threw my blanket over my head. I was ready to wallow, but Charlie kept insisting the situation wasn't that dire.

"Maybe he was nervous," she said

"Maybe." I'd considered the possibility, but how likely was it when we had already slept together? Already curled up next to each other? Already shared things we'd never shared with others?

Being with him these last couple of days had been so comfortable and natural. Maybe he was nervous now, but that's exactly what the delusional, optimistic side of me would convince myself of.

I didn't want to give up hope, but I also didn't want to look stupid.

"I can't even picture Harrison being lovey-dovey with anyone." Charlie squinted her eyes and stared off into the distance, as if struggling to imagine it.

"Especially me, right?" I mumbled, sinking deeper into my couch cocoon.

Charlie shook her head. "Not at all. I was going to say if anyone was going to bring him out of his shell, it'd be you."

"I brought him out. I just don't know if he wants to stay out."

Sadness hit me at the thought. I'd become ridiculously attached to Harrison in our short time together. Call me delusional, but I could picture it, you know? Us walking around Denver together. Taking him to my favorite restaurant. I was already excited about dragging him to one of those Christmas markets. The whole idea of us made life seem extra new and exciting, like I was in a new city I hadn't explored yet, despite having already seen every inch of this place.

I just really wanted it to work.

Tears brewed hot behind my eyelids and I blinked them away.

Charlie scooted over on the couch and slung an arm around my shoulders. "Don't get yourself worked up. Talk to him first. Today could just have been an off-day. You don't know that he doesn't want this too."

My chest deflated, but I wiped my eyes and nodded.

"Here." She snatched my phone off my lap and tapped the screen a few times before waving it in front of my face. It was a picture of some random dude posing in front of a gym mirror. A dating profile. The first thing in his bio read, *Not looking for anything serious.*

"Do I need to remind you how grim the dating scene is out there?" she asked, swiping away from the first guy. The next one had his profile picture set to one of him at a club with his arms slung around two beautiful women. Charlie crinkled her nose. "See? It's awful out there. You can't give up that easily."

"I'm not giving up," I insisted, taking my phone back and setting it on my cluttered coffee table. "And even if Harrison decides he doesn't want to pursue this, I'm done with those apps."

Charlie's eyes widened. "Seriously?"

"Seriously. If I can't find someone while I'm focusing on myself, then it isn't meant to be." Plus, if Harrison truly didn't want me, I'd definitely have to give myself time to get over it. Was it sad that it would likely take me way longer to grieve our nonexistent relationship than the amount of time we were actually together?

Her eyes softened. "Good. I'm glad you finally realized what a catch you are. You were settling for all those mediocre dates, and it was a waste of your time."

"Yep." I stared straight ahead, trying not to let the whole Harrison situation consume my every thought.

Charlie patted my knee encouragingly. "He'll call. Don't assume the worst."

A loud knock came at the door. Charlie and I looked at each other and stayed seated, instinctively waiting for whoever it was to go away. But after a minute, another knock sounded instead.

"Who is it?" Charlie hissed.

"I don't know. I didn't order anything. Did you?"

"No. It's probably someone trying to sell you something."

Charlie leaned toward me on the couch to peer out the front window that overlooked the porch. We both screamed when a hulking figure entered the frame and looked inside.

Harrison jerked back, looking alarmed, before tilting his head in the direction of the front door, brows drawn together.

"Oh my God, he's actually here," Charlie whispered, springing up. "I told you not to worry." She glanced at the window and then back at me again. "I'm not going to lie, it is so weird to see him here."

I jumped off the couch. "What if he's just here to let me down gently?" I asked, but that negative thought did little to dispel the fluttering sensation in my stomach.

Charlie smacked my shoulder.

"Ouch, that was kind of hard." I glared at her and rubbed the afflicted area.

"Stop being such a pessimist and see what he wants." She grabbed her bag off the coffee table and searched for her shoes.

I rushed to the doorway, hesitating for a moment to check myself in the mirror hung above my coat hook. The bags underneath my eyes were puffy, but not in an overly noticeable way. My hair stuck up in multiple directions. I smoothed it down the best I could before throwing open the door.

Harrison made my tiny front porch seem even smaller. His hair was still damp from a shower, and he wore his signature beat-up bomber jacket over a T-shirt. Maybe it was just the warmer clothes, but he looked different than he had the past few days. He reminded me more of the guy who had always been so cold and short with me. I told myself that this was the same guy I had spent days cozied up with, but was the trip really enough to change everything?

Charlie brushed by me into the small entryway. "I was just leaving."

Harrison stepped aside so she could join him on the porch. "Hey," he said, looking from her to me and back to her. "Uh, thanks, by the way. For sending us to Greece. I know it was an accident, but—"

"Oh, it was my pleasure, really." She winked at me. I narrowed my eyes at her.

"I'll see you two later." She stepped off the porch. As soon as Harrison directed his gaze toward me, Charlie started frantically pointing at his back and mouthing, "Tell him how you feel."

I waved her off. Harrison turned in confusion, and Charlie whipped around and strolled to her car parked on the street. "Bye," she said again.

"Sorry if I interrupted something," he said, returning his attention to me, his gaze searching my face.

"We were just watching bad movies," I said. I wanted to kick myself for not coming up with a better opening line, but I was still a little shell-shocked to have him in my space. This made it all so real.

"I hope this is all right. Me just showing up here," he added quickly.

I shook my head, trying to regain my senses. "Of course, sorry. I'm just a little out of it."

"Me too." He looked pained, which just set my nerves off even more.

"So," I said, but he started to say something at the same time. His lip curled up and he ducked his head.

"Sorry. you go ahead," I said.

"Can I come in?" he asked, his hands stuffed deep into his pockets.

"Of course." I scrambled out of the doorway to let him inside. I'd been so caught off guard by seeing him here, I'd lost all semblance of composure or manners. He stepped inside and looked around before taking off his boots. If seeing him on my porch felt strange, nothing could have prepared me for seeing him inside my house.

He looked incredibly out of place, his dark clothes and hair a stark contrast to my brightly colored space. A twinge of self-consciousness hit me. What if he didn't like it?

"This place is so you," he said, looking past me to my cramped vintage kitchen. He didn't say it like it was a bad thing. He almost said it fondly.

"I mean, did you expect anything else?" I smiled to try to ease my concerns.

"Not at all." Harrison closed the door behind him and we were sealed in. I had to face him, but I wasn't sure I was ready.

"Did you want the tour?" I joked, shifting from foot to foot. "It won't take long."

Now he looked caught off guard. "Uh, sure."

"Some would call it tight, but I would say cozy," I said, walking backward and gesturing to my kitchen. "This is the kitchen where I whip up the best cupcakes you could ever imagine. Now that you're actually nice to me, maybe I'll make some for you." I laughed nervously and immediately regretted saying that. "Then the back bedroom is my office and the first door down the hall is my bedroom." I paused before touching the door to my bedroom. I wasn't quite ready to open that can of worms yet. Instead, I redirected him to the living room. "And here is the main gathering space."

"Where did you find this couch?" he eyed the pink patterned antique.

"An estate sale." I patted the cushion. "I knew it was coming home with me the minute I saw it."

"It is very you." A ghost of a smile came across his lips.

My phone vibrated on the coffee table, causing us both to

lean down to look. When I saw that it was a notification from that stupid dating app, my face paled and I snatched my phone to hide it. I shot a nervous glance at Harrison, hoping he'd missed it, but judging from the death glare I was now receiving I didn't think I'd been that lucky.

"Are you seriously on a dating app right now? We've only been back a few hours." He threw his head back before dragging a hand across his face.

"No, it's not like that." I waved my hands in a panic. "Charlie downloaded it for me."

"Why?" He looked mad, but I knew him well enough now to realize the harsh lines of his features were just masking his hurt. I felt terrible.

"To remind me how bad it is out there," I said, feeling embarrassed although I wasn't sure why. "I was. . . I didn't know. . . I guess I'm confused." I blew out a sharp breath to try and collect my thoughts. I let my eyes drift to the floor because looking at him right now was just causing my brain to turn into jelly.

"Lila, we need to talk." He had taken on a serious tone which made my pulse quicken.

"I didn't know where we stood after today," I continued, desperate to make him understand. My voice was shaky, but I was definitely panicking a little. "I'll delete the dating app right now. Regardless of how anything turned out, I was already planning on it. Charlie was just trying to encourage me not to. . ." Not to what? Give up? Give up on what? I couldn't finish my sentence, because everything just sounded too pathetic and needy.

Harrison seemed to finally notice my nerves, because his dark eyes widened a little. "Hey," he said gently, taking a step forward to grab onto my arms. "I don't care about that, okay?

I mean, I do, but only in the sense that I really, really don't want you thinking about anyone else."

"You don't?" Everything inside me was coiled tightly.

"Of course not." Harrison hunched over so that he could look me more directly in the eyes. "I'm sorry about today, and for being so awkward. I hated leaving you like that."

His words were like a needle being poked into the balloon of my tension. My panic started to trickle away, but I was still tentative.

"You did?" I asked.

"It was awful." His eyes searched mine. "I never should have let you second-guess anything, but I was barely holding it together."

"Because you weren't sure you wanted this for real." I squeaked out.

"No." He snorted and looked at me incredulously. "Because I was *so* sure I wanted this, and I didn't know what to do. Or say. I didn't want to come on too strong and freak you out, so I sat there in silence like an idiot. I made things weird today and I'm so sorry for that."

I squeezed my eyes shut for a moment.

"You have no idea how relieved I am to hear you say that."

I studied his face, realizing that despite nothing changing, I was beginning to recognize him again. This was the same Harrison I'd spent so many hours getting to know. He'd never left. I'd just lost sight of him for a second.

He rubbed his hands up and down my arms. "So, you want this too? No regrets?"

"Yes." I wanted to laugh. "I was so worried the whole way home. I thought you might have changed your mind."

He pulled me into his chest and I wrapped my arms

around him, breathing him in. He tangled his fingers in my hair and sighed deeply.

"I'm so fucking stupid. Please don't hold today against me."

"It's not all your fault. I wanted to say more to you, but I was scared."

He pulled away to study my face. "Scared?"

"That you didn't want me anymore now that the vacation glow had worn off," I said.

He moved his hand to the back of my neck and tugged my face toward his. His lips met mine in a sweet, passionate kiss. Fireworks of excitement went off inside me as I relished how good he tasted. When he pulled away, he had a stern but gentle look on his face.

"I told you already. You've got me. That wasn't some vacation spell I was under. That was all you. I'm yours for as long as you'll have me."

"I know, but—"

He shook his head. "No buts. I meant it with my whole chest." He tucked a loose piece of hair behind my ear. "I know this is new, and I know I'm bad at this, but please know I'm going to try. This—you are really important to me."

My heart squeezed. "You're important to me, too," I said, standing on my tiptoes to kiss him again. He wrapped his arms around my shoulders and held me close.

"Does this mean you'll delete those dating apps now?" he pleaded into my hair.

I laughed and dared to hope for the first time that I would never need to use those apps again.

"Definitely."

TWENTY-NINE

Harrison

"I'M HITTING THE ROAD, BOSS." SHANE DRUMMED HIS HANDS on my chair. "Wanna grab a drink or anything?"

"Nah, not this time. I'm staying late tonight. I have a special client."

Since getting back from Greece three weeks ago, I had started to make more of an effort with Shane. We'd been working side by side for years, and he'd invited me to hang out on a number of occasions. I used to turn him down with ease every time. Now, I'd realized that I hadn't really been 'keeping a tight inner circle' like I'd told myself all this time. Instead, I had been pushing anyone and everyone away. It wasn't healthy. Besides, I liked Shane.

"Look at us, two fully booked Saturdays in a row. Must be the new website." He winked at me.

"Must be," I said.

The old, clunky site had finally had its much-needed facelift, thanks to Lila. I had tried to tell her that I'd figure it out myself, that I didn't want her putting too much on her plate again, but she wouldn't hear of it. Almost as soon as we got back, she'd insisted I bring my laptop to her house so she could overhaul the site. She'd said that even back before the trip, when she was still pissed at me, the website had been keeping her up at night.

The bell above the door chimed and I couldn't keep the grin off my face watching Lila walk into my shop. She had on jeans and a cream sweater with multi color threads woven through it that made it look like a Funfetti cake. It was hard to imagine there had ever been a time where her brightly colored clothes irritated me. Now I found them endearing as hell.

"Hey," she said, tugging at her sleeves and looking absolutely fucking adorable.

"Hey." I got up and walked over in a few strides to scoop her into my arms.

"Well, well, well, if it isn't our savior." Shane smiled at her as he shouldered on his coat.

"Please," she said, blushing. "Your work is what brings people in. I just made it easier to access."

I squeezed her shoulders. "Don't be modest."

She rolled her eyes. "Okay fine. I saved you."

My grin widened as I dipped down to plant a kiss on her lips. Damn, it felt good to do that. Despite both of our busy schedules, Lila and I had managed to spend nearly every free minute together the past few weeks. Much to Oliver's dismay. He had even tried—successfully—to crash our dates on several occasions. But even though it ate into his time with either of us, no one was more thrilled we were together than he was.

"Getting a tattoo today?" Shane asked.

"My first." She shot me a nervous smile, and my chest puffed out with pride that she trusted me enough to ask me to do this.

"It's gonna look great." Shane walked toward the door,

smacking my shoulder on his way out. "Your boyfriend is the best in the business."

"Oh, we're not—I mean he's not—I mean. . ." Lila's cheeks grew even redder as she stumbled over her words.

My eyebrows drew together. "We're not what?"

"I mean, we just haven't talked about it." She twisted a piece of her hair in her hands.

Shane chuckled and threw me a wave goodbye. "I think that's my cue to leave."

The door shut behind him, allowing me to focus all of my attention on the woman in front of me, the one with whom I was completely enamored in every way.

"Sorry, I didn't mean to bring that up in front of him." She groaned and held her forehead.

"You have nothing to be sorry for."

I froze, watching her gather herself. It was moments like these where I wished I was better at all this. For my sake, sure, but mostly for hers. I hated the thought that I confused her in any way. Especially when to me, my feelings for her couldn't be clearer.

She sighed. "I don't want you to feel any pressure. Labels are pointless. I'm so happy with how things are going."

I paused, not fully understanding what she meant. "Labels are pointless," I repeated. Did she not think of me as her boyfriend? Because I had referred to her as my girlfriend numerous times, to my parents and to my coworkers. Was that not right? I had just assumed. . .

"Right. I'm just happy with you. With us." She grabbed my hand and squeezed it. "We can worry about all the other stuff later."

"Shit. This is embarrassing." I blew out a breath and scratched the back of my head. "I definitely thought you were my girlfriend."

Her eyes widened. "You did?"

"Yep." I watched her carefully, but it only took a second for a smile to creep across her lips.

She tossed her head back and laughed. "Why didn't you say anything? I've been wondering when you were going to ask me for, like, two weeks."

"Why didn't *you* say anything?" I asked, appalled that I had been so dense. I hadn't even realized these sorts of things required a conversation.

She laughed harder. "I didn't want to scare you off. I knew we were exclusive. That was enough for me."

"Look at me," I said sternly, tipping her chin up to meet my gaze. "Nothing you could do would scare me off, alright?"

She nodded, and I dipped my head down to steal a quick kiss.

"If forcibly sharing a room together in a foreign country and getting dragged to every touristy destination known to man didn't scare me off, nothing will."

She smirked and shook her head. "You loved it."

"You're right," I said. "Now, Lila. I know I'm already the worst boyfriend in the world, but I'm hoping you'll be able to look past this oversight."

She bit her lip and waited for me to continue.

"Will you be my girlfriend?"

"Yes." She tightened her hold around me. "And, FYI, you are far from the worst boyfriend in the world."

My heart genuinely felt like it might explode from happiness.

An hour later, Lila sat in my chair, her forearm laid out on the armrest, palm facing up toward the ceiling. With one hand, I gently pulled her skin taut, with the other I carefully used my tattoo gun to trace over the simple black design I'd drawn for her.

Tattooing had never felt intimate like this before. I guess nothing I had done before had felt intimate, not like it did with Lila. I couldn't believe that for all these years, I had no idea what I was missing.

When I was finished, I wiped off the excess ink and had her stand so she could look at it in the mirror. Her smile widened as she took it in from every angle.

"It's perfect," she said, looking up at me like I'd hung the stars. I could be with her forever and still never feel worthy of that look.

I admired the new piece, a simple black line drawing of a chrysanthemum. It was my new favorite piece, given the arm that it was attached to. When I'd asked Lila why she wanted that flower, she'd said it was her mother's favorite. Growing up, she'd always told Lila they were the best because not only were they beautiful, but they lasted longer than most other flowers after they'd been cut. It was something that had always stuck with her, and now chrysanthemums were her favorite too. She liked their resiliency.

It fit her perfectly.

Part of me wondered if she'd be upset if I got the same tattoo, somewhere small on my own arm.

For her.

THIRTY

Lila

―――――

"YOU LOOK PERFECT." I DABBED MY EYES WITH A TISSUE.

"You really do," Skylar added, hooking her arm through mine and leaning her head against my shoulder.

"Stop that right now," Charlie scolded the two of us. "I can absolutely not cry off this makeup. I have to walk down that aisle in one minute and I'm already a ball of nerves." She straightened her white lace bodice and examined herself in the mirror.

Skylar and I shared a glassy-eyed glance before sniffling at the same time.

"That's it." Charlie snapped and pointed toward the door. "You two get out of here right now before I lose it."

"We'll see you on the other side." I squeezed my best friend's hand. Her gaze locked with mine and her face scrunched up a little before she shook her head and smiled.

"Love you," she whispered.

"Love you, too."

Skylar and I walked outside the bridal suite, which was really just the primary bedroom of the log cabin Charlie and

Nathan had rented for the occasion. The guest list consisted of only their closest family and friends. Small and elegant, which suited Charlie and Nathan perfectly.

"This is beautiful," Skylar whispered, and I nodded in agreement.

I had become quite close with Skylar in the month leading up to the wedding. After I had cleared all of the unnecessary weirdness from my mind about falling behind or losing my best friend, I'd realized Skylar and I were actually pretty similar. We had bonded at Charlie's dress fitting, cooing and crying over all the same dresses.

Our friendship had been really cemented the night we all went out for a secondary pseudo-bachelorette party. I had insisted, since I hadn't actually gotten to partake in the real festivities in Fiji. Skylar and I drank entirely too much tequila at the karaoke bar we'd dragged Charlie to, and started belting our hearts out. Oliver even crashed the party later in the night, and we'd done a terrible rendition of *Girls Just Want to Have Fun*.

Harrison had arrived to pick up Oliver and me after Skylar and Charlie had gone home. He'd had a disapproving look on his face, but the subtle crinkle of amusement in his eye was so obvious to me now. He'd berated us for drinking too much, but could barely keep from laughing when Oliver cranked up the radio and we sang along—badly—to some old country song.

That was just what life had been like lately. Filled with messy, happy moments that I couldn't get enough of.

Now, Skylar and I walked into the great room of the cabin, where chairs had been set up on both sides of a massive fireplace and faced a wall of expansive windows that overlooked the mountains. After we'd arrived last night, a light blanket of snow had dusted our surroundings, making the outside look like a thousand diamonds glittering in the late afternoon sun.

Nathan stood at the end of the aisle. He looked stoic, as per usual, but I could see the gleam of excitement in his eyes. Harrison and Oliver were already seated in the front row. I caught my boyfriend's eye and winked. He winked back and my smile grew bigger as I walked down the short aisle and stopped by my seat at the front on Charlie's side.

Then it was time. Everyone stood as Charlie approached the aisle, her parents beaming with pride behind me. No one was surprised when she'd insisted on walking herself down the aisle. That was just the kind of person that she was—fiercely strong and independent.

The tears I had been holding on to now flowed freely as Charlie locked eyes with Nathan and wiped her own tears from her cheeks. I glanced at him to see his normally harsh gaze completely soften, like he only had eyes for her.

Their vows were short and simple, but their love and determination shone through each word. I kept stealing glances at Harrison, only to find his eyes already on me each time.

After the ceremony, we moved into the oversized dining room that had been set with a beautiful tablescape full of candles and greenery. Because the wedding was such an inti-mate one, there was just one long table in the center of the room for us all to gather around.

I took my seat next to Harrison and leaned into him. He kissed my forehead and laid his arm around the back of my chair.

"Have I mentioned you look beautiful?" he asked, eyeing my forest-green tea length dress.

"Only about a dozen times," I teased.

"You two are going to make my heart melt." Oliver sat across from us, chin cradled in his hand as he openly stared.

Harrison snorted. "Has anyone ever told you you're over-bearing?"

"Is it even possible to be overbearing with friends?" he asked, picking up his glass of champagne and swigging the contents.

Harrison and I both looked at each other and laughed before saying, "Yes."

"Oh, whatever." Oliver rolled his eyes good naturedly. "You two are together for five minutes, and all of a sudden you don't need me anymore." But despite his words, I could feel his happiness for his best friend emanating from him.

Oliver pulled out his phone to check it before glancing back at the snowboard leaning on the wall behind him.

For most of the year, when he wasn't teaching rock climbing or snowboarding lessons, Oliver worked at a sporting goods store. The three of us had driven up together, and I'd given him a weird look when I'd caught him putting a brand-new snowboard into the trunk of the car.

"I can't believe you brought that to your brother's wedding," Harrison said, eyeing the brightly colored thing.

"It's limited edition and it's beautiful," he argued. "Besides, my friend Giles lives over here and this was way easier than trying to ship the thing to him."

"Whatever," Harrison muttered.

"He's out front," Oliver said, setting his phone down. "I'll be right back."

"You better be back before your toast or Charlie will kill you," I said, laughing.

Oliver saluted us and grabbed the board. It was comical, him dressed in his navy-blue suit for the wedding and carrying the snowboard under his arm.

"He truly is one of a kind," I said as we watched him sneak out the front door.

"Truly," Harrison said.

———

HARRISON HELD ME AROUND THE WAIST AS I REACHED UP TO wrap my hands around his neck. I'd kicked off my heels hours ago, so I had to dance on the balls of my feet to reach. Soft music drifted out from the speakers as a few couples moved across the dance floor, swaying to the music. Charlie and Nathan were in the center of it all, her head resting on his chest. Today had been magical, and I couldn't be happier for my best friend.

"I'm glad I ended up with a plus one after all," I said into Harrison's chest.

He snorted and pulled back to look at me. "Hopefully you're happy about more than just that."

I pursed my lips and pretended to think about it for a minute. "Nope. That's it, really. We can go back to how things used to be between the two of us once this is over."

A smile tugged at his lips as he gripped my waist tighter. "I'm glad you're telling me now."

"I didn't want to wait any longer and risk you getting your heart broken."

He pinched my side and I let out a burst of laughter.

"I think we both know it's way too late for that."

After a few more seconds Harrison said, "Speaking of after this. . . I was going to ask you what your plans are for Christmas."

"Oh?" I asked, a warm feeling washing over me.

"Yeah. I didn't know if you were planning to visit your family or not, but I was hoping you'd come home with me.

My parents are dying to meet you. We could always try to squeeze both in."

"Both," I whispered, my heart already swelling.

He looked nervous. "I haven't really figured out the details yet, but yeah. We could fly to one and then fly to the other on Christmas Eve, or the day after. I'm not really sure, but I can be flexible. I just don't want to be without you."

I gazed up at him and couldn't hold it in any longer. "I love you," I said.

His eyes softened and he gave me a lingering kiss before pulling away. "I love you too," he said against my mouth.

I'd been feeling it for a while, and it felt so beyond right to share it with him now.

All those years I had spent with the wrong guy, thinking I had to force my love story to look a certain way, and then all that time after that, spent stressing and worrying about finding someone. All of it had been for nothing. I could never have predicted that this person in front of me was the one I needed, yet he was perfect all the same.

His loyalty. That kind heart buried underneath a rough exterior. The way I knew I could ask him for anything, and he'd drop whatever he was doing to help me.

I had always thought I needed to find my other half to feel complete. It turned out that I'd actually needed my complete opposite, someone whose jagged edges matched up with all of my uneven ones. Maybe we didn't line up perfectly, but any part that I was missing, his pieces overlapped.

Harrison had shown me what it was like to have a rock in my life; someone I could lean on for support who would never break, or be crushed underneath my weight.

And most important of all, I knew I could never be too much for him.

Epilogue: Harrison

THREE MONTHS LATER

"You've lived here for how many years, and you never acquired a single piece of your own furniture?" Lila asked, gently folding and placing the last of my T-shirts into a large suitcase she'd brought over.

I shrugged and looked around my almost-bare room. "I mean, the bed is mine, but we don't exactly need a second one at your place."

"What about this dresser?" she asked.

"Oliver got that from the side of the road."

"That lamp." She pointed at the large gold monstrosity that stood next to my bed. I think Oliver had pulled it out of a dumpster our first year here.

I scrunched my nose. "Do you *want* that to be mine?"

She huffed. "No, but I just can't believe that moving you into my place only involves a few boxes and a couple of suitcases. I've been pacing around my house all week, moving furniture and figuring out how to make space for your things."

"Hey." I pulled her up from her crouch and crushed her

into a hug. "I love your stuff, okay? You don't need to make space for me. I already feel at home there."

She let out a huff. "But it's so pink and colorful and you're so—" she gestured to my black sweatshirt. "So not."

A grin crept across my lips. "Maybe I'm not on the outside, but inside, it's all pink thanks to you." I patted my chest.

"Harrison, be serious." She pushed off me and folded her arms. "I don't want you to have any regrets about this. I know it's soon."

I hesitated for a moment, trying to assess if she was truly stressed about my stuff, or if it was us moving in together that was causing her concern. Technically, she had been the one to ask me to move in, but I had already been thinking about it. The fact that she owned her place and I lived at Oliver's complicated things, though; I couldn't simply ask to move in to her house, and I also didn't want to suggest we move in together somewhere else. She loved that house. It was her pride and joy.

So, when she'd finally asked me, I had gratefully agreed immediately. I didn't care if it was soon. I didn't have a relationship handbook, or any prior experience to go off of, but it felt right. I liked having her nearby. I hated the nights we spent apart, the ones where I had to text her a simple *Goodnight, I love you*, instead of being able to hold her as I fell asleep.

"Are you having any doubts?" I asked, praying the answer was no.

"What? No way," she said, and relief washed over me. "I just want you to be comfortable. This is a big step."

I held her face in my hands, forcing her to take a breath and meet my eyes. "You're the only person I'm comfortable with, okay? Don't worry about me. The fact that you're letting me into your space is already beyond my wildest dreams."

She bit her lip and let out a small laugh.

"Seriously," I continued. "I don't know how I tricked you into this, but I'm just trying to get in your house as soon as possible before you change your mind."

"Never," she whispered.

"Love you," I said.

"Love you too," she replied.

"Excuse me." Oliver appeared in the doorway, arms folded across his chest. "Not that I'm eavesdropping, or anything, but did you just say you're only comfortable around *Lila*? Because as your best friend for over twenty years, I'm taking that as a personal insult."

I waved him off. "You know you don't count."

"Ouch." Oliver clutched his heart. "The end of an era, and this is all I have to show for it? A dismissive wave from my best friend in the entire world?"

I rolled my eyes but smiled. "Come here."

Oliver stepped around my boxes and held out his hand. I clasped it and went in for a hug, smacking him on the back.

"Thanks for everything, man," I said, knowing he knew I was talking about a hell of a lot more than just a rented room.

"Love you, man," he said.

"Wait. Stay there. I need to get my camera." Lila pretended like she was searching for it, but Oliver grabbed her and pulled her into a group hug.

"I'm so fucking happy for you two, I could be sick."

"We're going to miss you, Ollie," she said. I could see her blinking back tears.

"Hey, no sad faces," he said. "Who knows how long I'll be gone? Might even be back for the summer."

"Speaking of that, what do you want me to do with this furniture?" I asked, gesturing to the remaining pieces in my room, all of which belonged to him.

"Leave it," he said. "I'll be crashing at a friend's furnished apartment, so I don't need anything, and I already told the people renting this place that it came partially furnished."

"I can't believe you're leaving," Lila said, hugging him again.

I couldn't believe it either. I could never have imagined a situation where Oliver was leaving and I wasn't going with him. We'd barely been apart since we met. But while he was still my family, he was no longer the most important person in my life. That honor belonged to the beautiful woman in front of me, the one whom I would follow anywhere.

Oliver helped us get the rest of my stuff to the van we'd rented, and we piled it in. I shut the door, and Lila went around to the passenger side.

"I'll see you around, man," I said to Oliver.

"Don't be a stranger," he said. The moment was harder than either of us realized it was going to be. "I'm serious. Bring Lila and come visit. Key Ridge is only a few hours away."

"We'll be there," I told him, before saying my final good-byes and climbing into the driver's seat.

To my horror, Lila was in tears next to me.

"Babe, what is it?"

"I'm just going to miss him. And watching you two say goodbye?" she choked on a sob. "I couldn't take it."

I smiled and leaned over the center console to kiss her damp cheek. "You're adorable, you know that?"

"Shut up," she said through a smile before clicking her seatbelt into place.

As I made the short drive to her home—*our* home—I let the heavy feeling of contentment settle in. I hadn't even realized how stagnant my life had been until Lila came bursting into it. Now, I couldn't be more excited about this next chapter.

"So," Lila said. "You made me your girlfriend, told me you love me, now you're moving in. For being new at all this, I'd say you're killing this whole relationship thing."

I shot her a half-smile. "Oh yeah? What's next for us, then?"

She tapped her chin and stared out the window. "Another trip, perhaps?"

"I don't know about that." I shook my head and laughed. "It would be hard to top our first."

The End

Thank You for reading Trip Switch! As an indie author, I appreciate your support so much. If you enjoyed it, please take a few moments to leave a review!

*Haven't read Charlie and Nathan's story yet? **Love Linked** is available to read now!*

Keep reading for a sneak peek of…

A small town, snowboarding romance. Available to read now!

Key Ridge

"Seriously, Garrett, wake up! You're going to be late." I threw a pillow at my boyfriend's head and tried to coax him out of our bed for the third time that morning.

"What time is it?" he groaned.

"Seven fifty-five."

Even though we had been together for eight years and lived together for two, his inability to get moving in the morning still irritated me. He always slept through his alarm, so it was up to me to ensure he got up in time for work every day.

I was a morning person through and through and couldn't relate to his zombie-like demeanor. Waking up early to work out, read, or go for a walk was the highlight of my day.

Garrett finally spilled out of bed and went straight for the tiny bathroom the two of us shared. Once I heard the shower start, I breathed a sigh of relief and returned to the living room to savor one more cup of coffee. Settling into our sectional couch, I resumed working on my crossword puzzle.

A warm breeze hit me square in the face through the

window I had left open. Now that it was almost October, the intense and humid heat had at last settled down in Florida. It was a luxury to go outside again and *enjoy* the weather without sweating through whatever shirt I was wearing.

"Hey, Mattie." A damp and shirtless Garrett poked his head out of our bedroom doorframe. "We've got dinner with the crew tonight. You'll probably have to head there straight from work."

My mind worked quickly, scanning through all my upcoming social commitments.

"Tonight? I don't remember you telling me that."

"It's kind of last minute. We're celebrating." Garrett looked at his feet sheepishly and rubbed his short brown hair with a towel. "Will and Lauren got engaged last night."

"What?" I exclaimed, springing up from the couch. Will was Garrett's best friend from the college we had both attended. "But-but they've been together for like five minutes."

"It's been a year, babe. Lauren was really riding on him to propose."

"I didn't know riding someone to propose was an effective strategy." I crossed my arms and glared at him.

"Don't even go there. You know how swamped I am with work. Once I make partner, I'll be able to think about marriage."

My chest tightened in that familiar way it always did whenever marriage came up. The subject of our relationship status was an ever-looming issue between the two of us.

I could recite Garrett's excuses by heart at this point. First, it was "But we're too young." Next, it was "We don't have enough money for a wedding." Now, he had moved on to the "Once I make partner" narrative.

"It's getting old watching friends who've been together a

fraction of the time we have beat us down the aisle," I muttered.

He walked over to me and cupped my chin in his hand, attempting to get me to look at him. I relented and stared back into his blue eyes.

"I love you," he said and planted a kiss on my forehead. "I promise when I do propose, it will be the grandest gesture you ever saw. It will put everyone else's to shame."

"It's not just about the proposal. I want to get married to *you*. I want to start our life together."

"We already have a life together," he responded, turning away from me, and heading back to the bedroom to change.

It was pointless to argue with him anymore about this. I knew I was fighting a losing battle. I should have been more insistent earlier on in our relationship. Once a guy knew he could get away with not asking you after four years or six years, he certainly wasn't going to suddenly have a change of heart after eight.

I walked into our bedroom and shoved past Garrett to get into our cramped bathroom and closed the door. Gripping the side of the countertop, I took a deep breath and scrutinized myself in the mirror.

My long, wavy hair was thick and constantly trying to double in size with the Florida humidity. I fingered a blonde highlight that I had recently added to my light brown hair. I thought it popped against my tan skin, but Garrett had said it made me look high maintenance. My blue eyes were almost as light as Garrett's. When we met in college, I remembered thinking that our future children would look adorable with the blue eyes they were sure to inherit from us. Somehow the thought of children felt further away now at twenty-nine than it did back then at twenty-one.

A soft knock echoed through the tiled room. Sighing, I

opened the door to face my boyfriend, or some would say, roommate. He met my gaze with pleading eyes.

"Please, let's not fight, okay." He grabbed my hand and pulled me into his chest. "I love you."

"Who's fighting? Not me." I gave him a weak smile, knowing the argument wasn't worth it. It never was.

"You're the best." He gestured for me to exit the room first and smacked my ass when I passed him. "We need to get going. How many times do I have to tell you we're going to be late?"

***

"I could use some help with the housekeeping team. They don't respect me and it's causing issues. I have to double-check every room they turn over to make sure they've done a good enough job."

I nodded sympathetically at a property manager I had worked with for years as she rattled on about the latest issues she was facing at one of our resort properties.

"Have you tried setting up a meeting with the owner of the company?" I asked her.

"He keeps giving me the run-around. It's useless. Our old company was so much better."

"Well, we have a contract in place with these new cleaners, so we need to make it work. Their rates were much better, and we're going to close out the year with huge savings. It looks great for our department."

She bit her lip and looked unsure.

"Trust me. It just takes time to build these relationships. You're doing a great job. Keep up the amazing work."

I gave her my brightest smile and continued to reassure her. By the time our meeting was over, I hoped some of my optimism had rubbed off on her. I was known for my sunny disposition and positive attitude at Brook's Boutique Property Management Firm.

I swiveled around in my plush chair and surveyed the view outside my window. Our firm occupied the twenty-fifth floor of a high-rise. When I got my own office last year, I thought I would never get used to the fantastic view. Sometimes I had to pinch myself to make sure I wasn't dreaming. I had gotten a job here right out of college in operations and had risen through the ranks to Director of Property Management.

Despite my best efforts, my mind wandered back to my conversation with Garrett this morning. If only my personal life was on the same trajectory my professional life was on.

There was a knock at my door before it cracked open, revealing a tall redheaded woman looking disheveled.

"Hey girl, how was your weekend?" she asked, sitting opposite my pearly white desk. Sharon from the finance department was the only person I might consider a friend instead of just a coworker.

"Just the usual. Garrett and I went out to dinner, and I hit up the farmer's market on Sunday. What about you?"

"I went to this cute little pop-up bar on Friday and met the coolest guy. Very starving-artist vibes, but he was so hot. Anyway, we ended up going out on Saturday, and you won't believe where he took me." Sharon rambled on about her adventurous weekend.

I felt a pang of jealousy. She was constantly trying new things and meeting new people. It made me feel like such a dull square. I had lived in Florida my entire life, and the only people I hung out with were my friends from college. I thrived on routine, and my idea of an adventure was trying the new sushi place that had just opened up on our block. I was twenty-nine going on fifty.

Actually, my parents were in their fifties and were more

adventurous than I was. They had just gone on a two-week Alaskan cruise and snowshoed on a glacier. I hadn't even *seen* snow in real life before.

"Do you want to grab drinks after work?"

Sharon's question ripped me from my thoughts.

"Can't. Garrett and I have dinner plans." I chewed my lip before continuing. "His friend Will and his girlfriend Lauren just got engaged."

Sharon sat up straight at the news. "Excuse me. They met, like, fifteen seconds ago."

"I know."

"And didn't you tell me Will was a bit of a player?"

"Yep."

"What the hell."

"Trust me. I feel the same way."

"What did Garrett say about it."

"He said Lauren really wanted to get engaged." I wrinkled my nose as if there was a putrid stench in the air.

She scoffed. "And what about his devoted girlfriend of almost a decade? What she wants doesn't matter?"

"It's fine, really. We're just waiting until we're at a more secure point in our lives." My closed-lip smile felt tight.

Sharon rolled her eyes but didn't press the subject further. I knew that she knew what I was saying was bullshit, but she was kind enough not to point it out. I had cried one too many times over a bottle of wine with Sharon for her to fall for the same excuses I rattled off to everyone else.

"Are you ready for the new client pitch this afternoon?" she asked, graciously changing the subject.

"I was just about to go through the deck again. Did you see pictures of this property? It's gorgeous. It looks straight out of a movie. Almost makes me want to move out to the mountains."

She snorted. "Right, and give up your beach days? Not likely."

"Snow just seems so romantic, though."

I sighed and stared at the pictures of the property I had pulled up. It was located next to a ski resort in Colorado. The Key Ridge Ski Lodge. We managed resorts across the state of Florida and had recently opened our portfolio to other states. The prospective client's town was growing in popularity, but they were having trouble scaling. The property was large, and a huge potential money grab for the winter months. I had to nail this pitch.

"I can picture Mike in a Speedo better than I can picture you in snow."

"You're only saying that because he *did* wear a speedo at last year's holiday party."

We both doubled over, cackling, until a knock at the door interrupted our outburst.

"Mattie." My boss, Mike, stepped into my office. "Are you ready for the Colorado pitch? The clients just arrived from the airport. I know we scheduled the meeting for this afternoon, but they're earlier than expected, and I don't want to keep them waiting."

Just then, a gray-haired woman, maybe in her early sixties, and a thirty-something guy walked past my office. The guy was lean and muscular with dirty blond scraggly hair and stubble. He looked rugged and athletic. Although attractive, the scowl he was wearing and the hard set of his jaw were a turnoff for me. Mysteriously moody was not my type, but he was undeniably good-looking, nonetheless.

Sharon gasped. "Was that Giles Stone?"

"Who?" I asked at the same time Mike nodded.

"His family owns the property. He came with his aunt to hear the pitch." Mike made a move to follow them before turning back to me. "I'm going to go with them to the conference room. Meet us there in five."

With that, he rushed out of the room before I could object.

"Who is Giles Stone?" I asked again.

"He's a professional snowboarder," Sharon whispered despite the subject of our conversation being nowhere within hearing range. "Or he was. I think he retired, but he was in the last two Winter Olympics. How have you never heard of him?"

"Oh right, *that* Giles Stone. I'm such a huge fan of snowboarding. I *totally* forgot I have his poster hanging in my room."

Sharon rolled her eyes at my sarcasm. "I'm not a winter sports fan either, but he's gorgeous. There's something extra attractive about a guy that does winter sports."

She came around to my side of the desk and pulled my keyboard toward her. She opened a search engine and typed his name in. Pictures of him filled my screen. They mainly consisted of him in winter clothes contorting his body into crazy positions high up in the air.

I stared at her. "Um, what's attractive about winter sports? You can't even see him underneath all those layers. I can't believe you even recognized him."

She clicked on a picture of him shirtless on the cover of a sports magazine to enlarge it.

"You were saying?" she asked.

"He's okay there, I guess."

"You should read up on him so you're prepared."

"By 'read up' do you mean stare at half-naked pictures? I only have five minutes." I closed the window she had opened. "I need to review this deck one more time. I'm sure snowboarding, or his career, is not going to come up in our presentation."

"If you say so." She walked back around toward my office door. "Hey, if it comes up organically, mind slipping him my number in case he's looking for something to do while he's in town?"

I laughed and tossed a balled-up piece of notebook paper at her.

"Out."

Sitting across from Giles Stone was different than looking at his pictures online. Sharon was right. He *was* gorgeous. And intense. From the moment I entered the room, his deep brown eyes hadn't stopped searing a hole right into me.

His aunt, Bev, seemed nice enough, but she had a slight edge to her. My hand was still throbbing from her firm handshake. All I could do to hide my nerves was plant a massive grin on my face and pretend I was completely at ease.

"Hello, I'm Mattie," I greeted them cheerily. "How was your flight."

"It was fine. We appreciate you flying us out for this," answered Bev.

Giles just grunted in response.

I extended my hand to Giles, and he eyed it like I had an infectious disease. After a few heartbeats, he engulfed my hand in his and gave it a quick shake before dropping it. I noticed him flexing the hand that had touched me.

"So," I turned to Giles. "Colorado, huh? I've always wanted to visit. Must be a beautiful place to live."

"It is," he replied flatly.

His short remark and hard stare had me on edge. This was not the typical demeanor of potential clients.

"What do you think of Florida? It must be pretty different, huh?" I cleared my throat nervously.

He narrowed his eyes. "Obviously."

Bev nudged his arm before turning back to me with a smile. "It's lovely here. Always nice to be in a tropical climate, even if it is just for a quick trip."

Mike cleared his throat. "Well, Mattie is our director of Property Management. She's put together a great presentation for you. I think you'll find it all very informative."

"Thanks, Mike. I'll just get us started, then." I plugged in my computer and my slide deck appeared on the screen in front of us. "Feel free to stop me at any time with questions, but for now, let's just dive right in."

The first few slides outlined our basic structure. We would place a property manager on-site at their resort to handle all the daily operations. They would manage the housekeepers, order supplies, and go above and beyond to keep guests happy.

"And because your property hasn't been updated in a while, our team will make improvements as we see fit to make the space appealing to guests and ensure we capture as many new customers as possible."

Giles mumbled something under his breath. His presence made me uneasy.

"I'm sorry, what was that?" I asked, my voice dripping with politeness.

"I don't think you, or your team, has the first idea what would make us appealing to our customers," he spat. "Our customers *like* our vintage charm. None of them want to stay in a place with the same aesthetic as a sterile doctor's office." He gestured to the conference room we were sitting in.

My lip twitched as I tried to maintain my smile.

"Of course, sir. I didn't mean that the lodge didn't already possess a certain charm. And we would certainly work to create a feel that would appeal to your customer-"

"Please, spare me." He waved his hand as if to dismiss me. "You're so full of shit."

"Excuse me?" I choked out.

"What would a couple of suits that live in Florida know about running a ski lodge? Do you even ski?" He crossed his arms.

"Well, no," I sputtered. "But I know a lot about hotels and prop-"

"That's what I thought. I've heard enough."

He stood from his chair and circled around the table toward the exit.

"Giles, please sit down. You're being rude." Bev shot me an apologetic glance as she tried to talk down her nephew.

"No, I'm done here. I'll be outside."

With that, he stormed out, leaving me flabbergasted. While I didn't always nail every presentation, this was undoubtedly the first time I had lost someone's interest within the first five minutes.

At least Mike looked just as shocked as I felt. A sure sign that it wasn't my pitch that was the problem. Just that the person I was pitching to was an asshole.

"I'm sorry about him," Bev said, rising from her chair. "It's not you. He's got other things going on."

"It's not a problem," I responded through gritted teeth. It most certainly was a problem. I had spent days on this pitch, and he never intended to listen to it—the nerve of that jerk to waste my time.

"Look, despite that scene he just caused, I'm the decision-maker, and I'm drowning."

My ears perked up at her desperate tone. Was there still a shot of landing this?

"We would be happy to take some of that burden off you," I chimed in. "Trust me. This is exactly the type of work our firm was made for. We'll step in and organize all your processes. When we're done, I promise we'll have your lodge running like a well-oiled machine."

I slid a packet of papers toward her.

"Maybe you and your nephew would like to review our numbers and mission privately to see if we'd be a good fit. I've outlined the details here."

She nodded.

"I appreciate a prepared woman." She winked at me.

Mike was sitting so far forward in his seat that I thought he might fall out of it. I could tell he was eager to intervene, but he knew I had a way of reading people. Bev seemed like the type of person that valued her privacy and didn't like to make a production of things. The raw numbers and no bullshit information were precisely what she needed to make a decision.

She took my packet and paused in the doorframe. "I'll review this on our flight home and get back to you. Again, I'm sorry for the outburst and I hope we can move past this if we do decide to go forward."

"Of course," Mike and I said in unison. I'm not sure which of our smiles was bigger.

As soon as Bev was out of earshot, Mike raised his hand, and I gleefully high-fived it.

"What a save. I thought we were screwed when he walked out of here like that. Good job having that write-up prepared."

"We're not in the clear yet." I reminded him. While I was

an eternal optimist, I did try to keep a realistic perspective on things.

"When she sees those estimated returns and reduced working hours, it'll be a no-brainer."

"Fingers crossed," I replied. "Let's just hope if we do land this account, there will be minimal interaction with that pro snowboarder asshat."

Read Key Ridge now! Available on Amazon and Kindle

About the Author

Allison Speka aims to bring a refreshing blend of passion and authenticity to her writing. A self-proclaimed romance aficionado, Allison has been lost in the pages of love stories since she discovered the genre. She met her partner in Chicago before they both picked up and moved to Colorado seven years ago.

Also by Allison Speka

Love Linked: A grumpy millionaire boss, forbidden workplace romance.

Comfort Zoned: A romance about finding yourself and stepping outside of your comfort zone.

Settle Up: A friends to lovers, aspiring rockstar romance.

The Reality Of It All: Set on a reality dating show with a twist... every contestant has been tricked into being there.